The Misunderstandings of

CHARITY BROWN

Books by Elizabeth Laird published
by Macmillan Children's Books

Welcome to Nowhere
Secret Friends
Song of the Dolphin Boy
Dindy and the Elephant
The Fastest Boy in the World
The Prince Who Walked with Lions
Lost Riders
Crusade
Oranges in No Man's Land
A Little Piece of Ground
The Garbage King
Jake's Tower
Red Sky in the Morning
Kiss the Dust

The Misunderstandings

of

CHARITY BROWN

Elizabeth Laird

MACMILLAN CHILDREN'S BOOKS

Published 2022 by Macmillan Children's Books
an imprint of Pan Macmillan
The Smithson, 6 Briset Street, London EC1M 5NR
EU representative: Macmillan Publishers Ireland Ltd, 1st Floor,
The Liffey Trust Centre, 117–126 Sheriff Street Upper
Dublin 1, D01 YC43
Associated companies throughout the world
www.panmacmillan.com

ISBN 978-1-5290-7563-2

1 3 5 7 9 8 6 4 2

A CIP catalogue record for this book is available from the British Library.

Printed and bound by CPI Group (UK) Ltd, Croydon CR0 4YY

For Jane Fior

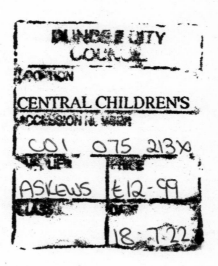

CHAPTER ONE

It was terribly cold in our house in Old Manor Road. On the days when there was ice on the insides of the windows, my father would carry buckets of coal up from the cellar and light a fire in the room I shared with my middle sister, Hope. But on that last winter in our old home I was too weak to notice most of the time.

I'd fallen ill just after Christmas. At first, they thought I had flu, but when they realized I actually had polio, there was a dreadful panic. The doctor sent for an ambulance, and I was packed off to the isolation hospital for infectious diseases where all the nurses were hidden behind masks and gloves and overalls. I couldn't even see their faces.

When I first went into hospital, I hardly knew where I was. I felt sick and hot and achy all over. But the worst thing was that I couldn't move. My neck was as stiff as a plank and, although I kept trying to lift my arms or shift my legs, they wouldn't obey me. I knew they were still there, though, because they hurt all the time.

The Sister of the Children's Polio Ward was horribly

unsympathetic. She kept telling me that I was lucky not to have died, and that I'd be even luckier if I ever managed to walk again. She'd scrape a brush with iron teeth through my mouse-brown hair every morning and tie my plaits so tightly that my scalp would ache for the rest of the day.

The other nurses were kind, I think, but they were afraid to come near me. I heard one whisper to another, 'They ought to transfer you to another ward. You've got children at home, haven't you? What if they catch it?'

I was dreadfully lonely. Visiting hours were half an hour once a week, and only one person was allowed at a time. Visitors weren't even allowed to come near me, but could only wave through a window. When my father came, he wrote messages and held them up to the glass, but I couldn't turn my head to read them properly. It was almost worse than if he hadn't come at all.

I can still remember the pattern of cracks on the ceiling above my hospital bed. I had nothing else to look at, after all. I kept trying not to think about what it would be like if I was paralysed for life, and I would have long conversations with Jesus, explaining to Him how good I would be if He would only make me better.

Sometimes, though, I was too angry to talk to Him at all.

'It's so unfair!' I wanted to shout. 'Why does polio only paralyse children and not grown-ups? And why can't You just stop it happening at all, to anyone?'

*

I don't want to go on thinking about those dreadful days. They did come to an end at last because slowly I started being able to move again. The horrible Sister had to stop telling me I'd never walk again, but ticked me off instead for not doing my exercises enough.

Then, after the worst ten weeks of my entire life, my father, who can't bear to see anyone suffer, came on the weekly visit, took one look at me through the glass window and saw that I was crying. He marched off to the doctors and said he'd checked, and I wasn't infectious any more, and he was taking me home, thank you very much.

Things were quiet at home, because Hope, who was at boarding school in Scotland, wasn't yet back for the Easter holidays, and Faith, my oldest sister, who was training to be a nurse, had decided to move in to the nurses' home in case Dad was wrong and I was still infectious. Only my older brother, Ted, was there. His real name is Theodore, which means 'God's gift', and that's just as well because he thinks he *is* God's gift, to girls, anyway.

I was quite ill, actually, even after Dad brought me home. Sometimes I'd wake up in the night in a panic, thinking I was still completely paralysed. Dad would hear me groaning and he'd pad into my room in his old bedroom slippers. He'd get me some water and make me sip it slowly, then he'd kneel beside my bed and pray, 'Lord Jesus, comfort this child of Thine and heal her for Thy Name's sake.' Then he'd croon the hymn he used to sing to me when I was really little. I sort of liked it, but it was embarrassing too because I was twelve and a half, after all.

It was very boring being at home and having to rest in bed most of the time. Sometimes I wondered what everyone was doing, but not as often as you'd think. After a couple of months in hospital, school had rather faded from my life, which was actually a relief because I'd never enjoyed it much anyway. In fact, not having to go to school was the best thing about still being ill. It's not easy being a Faithful Follower of Christ in a worldly place like a school. None of the other girls worried all the time about whether or not they were being true to Jesus. They just thought I was peculiar. I don't want to sound sorry for myself, but the truth is that I was the girl no one wanted to sit next to, the girl no one picked for teams.

It hadn't been too bad while Faith and Hope were still at home. Sisters can be sort of friends, after all. But I'd been lonely once they'd gone.

You'd think I'd spend my time worrying about whether I'd ever get really better, but I strongly believed that I would. Most of my body worked all right, though my left arm and leg were still weak, and anyway the whole family had prayed so much for me to be better that I reckoned God would just have to listen soon.

The thing I hated most about being stuck in bed was waking up in the morning and hearing Mother and Dad in the kitchen downstairs and thinking they'd forgotten about me. I could practically see them sitting at the kitchen table, passing the toast and marmalade, and Ted rushing in at the last minute, still tying his tie.

A bit later I'd hear the front door close. That would be Dad going off to the station, where he'd be catching the 8.15 train to London. He runs a missionary society, which is good, of course, because he's spreading the Word of the Lord, but it isn't very convenient because they don't pay him.

'The Lord will provide,' I once heard him say to Mother, when she brought up the possibility of us having a fridge. 'We're living by faith, dear. You know that.'

She had to agree with him out loud, of course, because the Bible says that wives should obey their husbands, but later I heard her say to her friend Olive Prendergast, as they buttered sandwiches for the Fellowship Tea, that living by faith was all very well, but actually it meant living off donations from other people who might not have enough for themselves.

Then the front door would go again. Slammed this time. That would be Ted. He'd rev up his bike to annoy the neighbours, then I'd hear it roar all the way down the street till it turned the corner on to the main road.

You can't blame girls for liking Ted. I would if I wasn't his sister because he's really handsome and he's got a motorbike. When he left school, he had to do his two years' National Service in the armed forces. He chose the Navy so he could go off and sail the seven seas. If I'd been a boy, and I'd had to do National Service, I'd have chosen the Air Force. Think about it! What's more exciting than flying? I *bet* Ted only chose the Navy because the uniform made him look so handsome. It was dark blue with a cheeky white cap and the name of his ship embroidered on the front in gold letters. Girls swooned over him when they saw him all dressed up, but none of them knew the secret wickedness of his heart.

Just to give you an example – one day he brought his friend Adam home for tea. Adam is something, I can tell you. Sort of lean and muscular, with one of those faces where the skin is a bit loose so every twitch of the mouth or eyebrows is expressive. Anyway, there I was, going up the stairs, when they came in through the front door, and Ted said, 'That's my little sister, Charity.'

'Not so little,' Adam said, looking straight at me.

And Ted said, '*Are* you still little, Char? Have you got hair growing in your armpits yet?'

I nearly *died*, standing right there on the stairs, then I fled to my bedroom. I shouldn't wonder if it was the stress of living with Ted that made me catch polio. Why me, after all, and not one of the other girls in my class at school?

Anyway, you see what I mean about Ted? Only someone with a cruel heart would say a thing like that to an innocent young girl.

I missed Hope dreadfully when she was away at her boarding school in Scotland. The holidays always passed so quickly. I burned with a sense of injustice that I hadn't been sent there too. If I had, I pointed out to Mother, on more than one occasion, I'd have been in the depths of the countryside, miles away from infection, and I'd never have caught polio in the first place. You can see why I felt jealous, when I tell you that Hope was living in a great big old mansion with lots of girls who had posh names like Anastasia and Griselda, and half of them had their own ponies! She'd learned Scottish dancing and how to hold her teacup with her little finger crooked up.

The reason she was there was because Dad's older sister, Aunt Josephine, was the headmistress, and she paid for Hope's fees and her uniform and everything. She didn't offer to pay for Faith or me. She said she'd picked Hope because Hope's health was delicate and she needed lots of country air. In my opinion, it was pure favouritism. Aren't I delicate too? Who had polio, after all?

You might have thought that a boarding school would be too worldly for a girl from our Lucasite church, but it's all right because the school is a very Christian one, and Aunt Josephine goes to a Baptist church, which is better than nothing. She takes Hope there every Sunday.

Anyway, over the slow weeks and months at home, I did gradually get better. I managed to get out of bed without being helped, and then, when my hands were strong enough, I was able to dress myself. Slowly, I learned to take more than a few steps at a time, and at last I was able to go up and down the stairs. By the time Hope came home at the end of the summer term, I was nearly well again, although I still got tired quickly. Also, my left leg and left arm weren't right. I could walk with only a tiny limp, which didn't really show, but when I tried to run I had to hobble along, which was really embarrassing. And my left arm was irritatingly weak. There was no question of me going back to school till after the summer holidays.

*

I was so used to Faith and Hope being away that when they *did* come home our small house felt rather cramped. I didn't mind that. Home was just home. I'd lived in it since I was two, after all, and it was all I'd ever known. But I'm sure Mother prayed every day for God to give us something bigger. She must have done, because the only possible explanation for what happened next is that it was an answer to prayer. It came in the form of an envelope from a solicitor on the first Saturday morning in July, after Hope had come home for the holidays.

Dad had just taken a mouthful of porridge when he opened the letter, and as he read it he nearly choked. He passed it down the table to Mother, via Ted and Faith, who were sitting on his right, while Hope and I, on the other side of the table, watched.

Mother read it and went pale.

'Is this a joke?' she said.

'No, it's an answer to prayer!' said Dad with a shining, holy look on his face.

'What? What's happened?' begged Hope. 'Are we going to get a pony?'

Everyone stared at her.

'Don't be ridiculous,' said Faith. 'What on earth would we do with a pony?'

'Pass the letter back,' said Dad. 'Let me read it again.'

We waited, holding our breath.

'It seems real enough,' said Dad at last. 'Pringle and Pringle are a well-known firm of solicitors.'

'Yes, but what does it *say*?' I burst out.

'It seems,' said Dad, 'that old Mr Spendlove has very kindly—'

'Mr Spendlove's dead,' I interrupted. 'You preached at his funeral.'

'Don't interrupt, dear,' said Mother with a frown.

'. . . that Reg Spendlove has left us his house in his will, including all the contents and furniture!' continued Dad.

Everyone started talking at once.

'It's that big old place up Badger Hill, isn't it?'

'Hasn't it got a peculiar name? Gospel Bells or something?'

'Gospel Fields, silly.'

'It's not the one with the tennis court, is it?'

'The garden's enormous!'

'There's even a garage! Has he left us his car too?'

Faith hadn't joined in with all this. She has a suspicious mind.

'But why?' she asked Dad, fixing him with a piercing look. 'Did you perform some secret service for him? Was he a long-lost relative we never knew about? Did he cast his own children off without a shilling? In which case it wouldn't be fair.'

'Mr Spendlove had no children and no living relatives,' Mother said, 'and anyway it's not up to us to question the will of the Lord.' But she spoke automatically. She was clearly as astonished as the rest of us.

'Does this mean we're going to *move*?' My voice ended on a squeak.

Mother was recovering.

'It's very kind of Mr Spendlove,' she said, 'but it's out of the question for us to live there. We couldn't possibly afford it.

The place is huge. It would cost a fortune in cleaning materials alone!'

Dad wasn't listening. He pushed his plate aside, beamed round at us and said, 'Clear the table, girls – and you, Ted, do the washing-up. Then I suggest that we take a walk up the hill to look at our new home.'

CHAPTER TWO

That beautiful July morning, when we walked up Badger Hill to Gospel Fields for the first time, was the most exciting day of my entire life. Up to then, anyway.

The house had its back to the road and was behind a line of crusty old pine trees. You had to crunch your way embarrassingly loudly up a gravel drive to get round to the front door.

Mother stopped before we'd reached the corner of the house.

'Are you quite sure about this, Iver?' she said. 'Aren't we being a bit premature?'

'Not at all! Have faith!' Dad said, striding ahead. 'This is the day that the Lord has made. Let us rejoice and be glad in it!'

He'd hardly finished speaking when a voice behind us said, 'Excuse me! Can I help you? You're on private property, you know.'

We spun round. A man with long thin legs and thick grey hair combed back from his face was hurrying up the drive after us.

Dad marched back towards him, beaming and holding out his hand.

'How do you do? Are you our new neighbour? So glad to meet you! I'm Iver Brown.'

The man took Dad's hand then dropped it quickly. He didn't say his own name and he wasn't smiling back.

'The house is not up for sale. Not yet, anyway. Once it's on the market, viewings will no doubt be—'

He spoke precisely, but with an accent, and was looking coldly at us through thick-lensed glasses.

Dad laughed.

'Oh, it won't be going on sale. We heard this morning from Reg Spendlove's solicitors, Pringle and Pringle. The most remarkable thing! Reg has left us his house in his will!'

The man looked astonished, as well he might, but he was beginning to go soft round the edges like a bowl of ice cream when it starts to melt. Dad has that effect on people. It's called charm. Aunt Josephine says that if you've got charm, you can manage without anything useful like common sense or money, but then she'll add darkly, 'Having too much of it is bad for the character.'

Dad pulled the lawyer's letter out of his pocket, but the other man waved it away. A smile was curling up the corners of his mouth.

'You are Mr Spendlove's relative, then?' When he said *r*, it made a sort of rolling sound in his throat. 'He told me he had no living family.'

'We were brothers in the Lord!' Dad said enthusiastically.

'Ah! I see.' The man's smile faded, but he put his hand out to shake Dad's again. 'Leo,' he said. 'Leo Stern. I hope you will find happiness in your new home.'

Then he turned on his long, thin legs and retreated down the drive.

'A warm welcome from the neighbours!' said Dad delightedly. 'What could be better!'

'He's got a foreign accent,' said Mother. 'Isn't Stern a German name?'

'Or Austrian. A refugee perhaps . . .'

The rest of us didn't stop to listen to any more. Ted, Faith and Hope dashed on down the drive, with me trailing after them, and a moment later we were looking up at the front of the house. There were big windows on either side of the door, and a covered veranda along two sides with pink roses climbing up its pillars.

Hope had her nose pressed up against a window.

'This looks like a dining room,' she said. 'There's a long table and . . .'

I ignored her. I'd pushed open the letterbox and was kneeling on the red tiled floor of the veranda to peer into the hall.

It was vast! Big enough for a fireplace all of its own! A wide wooden staircase lined with dark wood panelling curved up and out of sight. I had a beautiful vision of myself descending the steps into a crowd of admirers, delicately holding up my long skirt in one hand, while resting the other on the banister, my fingers rosily tipped with forbidden nail varnish.

13

'Look, you two,' Faith said disapprovingly, 'I really don't think you ought——' But a shout from Ted interrupted her.

'Hey! Come and see! There's a Rover in the garage!'

Dad had taken Mother's arm and was walking her down the lawn, which sloped in a huge sweep of green past an ancient spreading yew on one side and a flower bed full of dazzlingly colourful dahlias on the other. There was what looked like a wood of tall beech trees at the bottom, their glossy leaves waving in the breeze.

'She'll be trying to talk him out of it,' I said to Hope.

'She won't manage it,' said Hope, laughing. 'You know Dad. Come on, let's explore.'

It was just as well that it was a lovely summer morning when we first saw that enormous garden. Mr Spendlove's gardener must have mown the lawn the week before, weeded the long flower bed and rolled the grass of the tennis court (a tennis court!) to a perfect flat green. Blackcurrants and raspberries dangled temptingly in a fruit cage and half-ripe apples and plums were sprouting from a line of trees behind the vegetable plot. There was birdsong in the air.

I caught up with Faith and Hope, who had run down the slope to the bottom of the lawn, and we stood together looking back up at the house. Dad and Mother walked towards us.

'What do you think, girls?' said Dad.

'It's wonderful!' said Hope. 'Not as big as Evelyn Drummond's place, but even she hasn't got a tennis court.'

Faith and I raised our eyebrows at each other. We were sick of hearing about Hope's grand schoolfriends.

'I'll only be here when I'm not on duty at the hospital,' said Faith, 'so it's not up to me, but how you'll keep up the garden, I can't imagine.'

Dad turned to me.

'What about you, Charity?'

'It's very nice,' I said, but inside I felt a bit wobbly. I'd just realized that moving into Gospel Fields meant moving out of 24 Old Manor Road, away from our familiar narrow street and our own proper house, and starting all over again up here on the posh side of town. It meant losing the hidden place behind the laurel bush where Hope and I used to play houses when we were little, and the rickety old toy cupboard in the bedroom we'd always shared (we hadn't played with the toys for years, but still), and on top of all that it would mean a last final break with my oldest friend, Robert-next-door.

All these thoughts rushed through my head as I looked up the endless length of Gospel Fields' lawn, trying to take in its beauteous magnificence. But then another idea took their place. Perhaps 24 Old Manor Road, with its laurel bushes, daisy-strewn lawn, toy cupboard and Robert-next-door were childish things. And here was St Paul, speaking in my head: *When I was a child, I thought as a child, but when I became a man, I put away childish things.*

Or, in my case, *woman*, I reminded St Paul, who, between you and me, needs a lot of reminding that women exist too.

While I was standing there, wondering if it *was* time to put away childish things, Hope and Faith hurried off to inspect the tennis court and Mother and Dad moved slowly off towards

15

the beech wood beyond. Mother's back was stiff, and Dad was leaning in towards her, talking earnestly.

'A retreat!' I heard him say. 'Imagine it, Jeanie. A haven of peace and beauty for the weary and heavy-laden. A home for—'

'Iver!' Mother had stopped walking and was turning to face him. 'Just look around you. This garden! We can't possibly manage it on our own.'

'You're a wonderful gardener, dear. You've always wanted a big place,' Dad said coaxingly. 'And I'd help.'

Mother crossed her arms.

'You? Help in the garden? You don't know a daisy from a . . . from a . . .'

'Daffodil?' Dad asked helpfully.

'Exactly.'

Dad thrust his hands into his pockets. He was looking thoughtful now. I could see that the gears in his brain were shifting.

The only way I can describe what goes on inside my father's head is to compare his brain to a packet of Liquorice Allsorts. You know the ones I mean. There's pink and yellow and white sugary stuff striped with no-nonsense black liquorice in each sweet. Dad is easily inspired by visionary new ideas, but sooner or later his mind works through the fluffy stuff and then he starts making proper, sensible plans. He is Scottish, after all. You might find it confusing, imagining my dad as a Liquorice Allsort, but that's the only way I can explain him.

The thing is that once Dad hits the planning stage, Mother's brain, which is no-nonsense, practical and without a shred of sentiment, clicks into gear too.

'A gardener, two days a week,' she said crisply.

'Ideally, yes,' conceded Dad.

'Not ideally. *Actually.*'

'All right.'

'Help in the house.'

'The girls—'

'Faith has moved into the nurses' home. Hope's only here in the holidays, and Charity's still not strong. She needs plenty of rest.'

'We'll find a way,' said Dad.

'That's only part of it,' Mother said. 'Maintenance, heating — running this place will cost a fortune!' But she hadn't shaken his arm off, and I could hear in her voice that she was half won over. 'Where on earth will we find the money?'

'If this is the Lord's doing,' Dad said, 'then He will open the way. Look up there, Jeanie. Look at the house. Think of the great things we could do with it! If money is the only bar, then I believe that it's time we resurrected Moses.'

'Now, Iver, I thought we'd agreed . . .' said Mother, but then they began to walk on and I couldn't hear what they were saying.

Faith came back from inspecting the tennis court.

'What's happened?' said Faith. 'You look as if you've been hit by a truck.'

'I might as well have been,' I said. 'Dad's gone completely barmy. He's promised Mother a gardener two days a week

17

and someone to help in the house, and now he's talking about resurrecting the dead.'

'I'm not surprised,' said Hope, coming up behind Faith. 'The shock of all this is enough to unhinge anyone. I bet there's a net for the tennis court in the garage. You never know, there might even be rackets and balls.'

Faith refused to be deflected by tennis nets.

'What do you mean, resurrecting the dead?' she asked me. 'Which dead?'

'Moses, of all people,' I said gloomily.

Ted had joined us now. He was wiping grease off his hands with an old rag.

'I got into the garage. The Rover's a beauty. Had a look inside the engine and . . . What's the matter with you lot?'

I explained.

Ted roared with laughter.

'You silly girls! Don't you know about Moses?'

'Of course we do!' I said, offended. 'His mother put him in a basket and hid him in the bulrushes, and Pharaoh's daughter—'

'Not *that* Moses,' scoffed Ted. 'Our great-grandfather.'

'We had a great-grandfather called Moses?' said Hope, astonished.

'Yes! He was a whisky distiller.'

'*What?*'

A thrill of horror ran through me. Whisky is alcohol, and alcohol is Sin in liquid form.

'Why didn't anyone tell us?' said Faith crossly. 'How come you know and we don't?'

'Because,' said Ted, in a revoltingly lordly way, 'it's to do with the family finances, which are a man's business. Women don't have the minds for it.'

I tried to kick him on the shins, which wasn't easy, given the fact that only one of my legs was working properly, but he dodged out of the way, laughing.

'What do you mean, finances?' said Faith, not wishing to be deflected by insults.

I was circling round Ted, looking for a chance to get in another kick.

'Well?' demanded Faith.

'Call this human terrier off me and I'll tell you,' said Ted.

My sisters grabbed my arms and hauled me away.

'Our great-grandfather, old Moses McIver, died of alcoholism,' Ted said, with ghoulish pleasure. 'The whisky business was sold after he copped it and the money went to his grandchildren.'

'So some of it came to Dad?' Hope asked.

Faith was nodding. 'I get it,' she said. 'Dad refused to accept it because it was the wages of sin.'

'Exactly,' said Ted.

'So what happened to the money?' I asked, shaking my sisters off me.

'It went to our aunts, Josephine and Violet,' said Ted, 'but they nobly decided not to take Dad's share. They put it in a special bank account and it's been quietly growing there ever since. There's quite a lot of it, apparently.'

'Do you mean to say,' demanded Hope, 'that all this time

we've been living on scraps and not being allowed to get new shoes and have riding lessons when there's a heap of money that should be ours?'

'Typical of Dad,' said Faith. 'You've got to admire him. If you're going to have principles, you ought to stick with them whatever the cost.'

We ignored her.

'So, when Dad talked about "resurrecting Moses",' breathed Hope, 'he must have meant that he's planning to take the money. And that means we'll live in this gorgeous house *and* we'll be rich!'

'Yes and no,' I said, pulling the three of them back down to earth. 'If Dad takes the money, it'll be because he's giving Gospel Fields to the Lord.'

'Ah,' said Ted.

'Oh,' said Hope.

'Of course,' said Faith, nodding approvingly. 'But how?'

So I told them about the retreat for the weary and heavy-laden. That sobered us up, and we walked slowly back up the long sweep of lawn to the house.

CHAPTER THREE

The next day was Sunday, and before I explain what that meant for the Brown family, you might need to know a bit more about why we're the way we are.

In the Scottish village where Dad grew up, there was no pub, cinema or football team, but there *were* an awful lot of churches.

If you'd been a bird flying over the village's slate-roofed houses on a Sunday morning, you'd have seen rivulets of people walking in different directions. There were Presbyterians in the village's historic old church (most people went there), the Episcopalians had a nice stone building up the hill (they were the posh ones), a chapel made of sheets of corrugated iron was for the Wee Frees (too complicated to explain), another tiny tin church was for the Roman Catholics and then there was our place, the Meeting Hall of the Lucasites.

I used to think that everyone in the world knew about the Lucasites, and, what's more, that they all secretly wished they were members, but I now realize that hardly anyone has heard of us and, if they have, they think we're rather odd.

The Lucasites are followers of a man called Jeremiah Lucas, who lived in the nineteenth century. He was a Scottish lawyer with sprouty side whiskers and thick, fleshy lips. He thought that churches had become too fancy, with their enormous old cathedrals, stained-glass windows, priests, bishops and choir boys dressed up in long robes. He wanted to sweep all that away. The first Christians, way back in the Bible, had just got together in an upstairs room in someone's house. He thought we should be simple, like them.

I'm supposed to be a Lucasite, so I've got to think he was right, but actually he made us be rather boring. Our Meeting Hall is just plain ugly! It's a square old room full of rows of chairs, and the walls are a sort of beige colour. A stained-glass window would brighten it up nicely. Proper music would be good too, with an organ or a piano. As it is we have to sing without one, and things get out of tune and slow right down to a sort of dreary dirge.

At our Sunday morning Meeting, anyone who is moved by the Holy Spirit (any man, that is) stands up and prays or reads out a bit of the Bible or starts everyone off singing a hymn. And then one of the Elders (who all have to be men too) goes to the table in the middle of the room, breaks open the loaf of bread lying on it and hands the pieces out, then passes round a goblet of wine, which everyone who's been properly baptised (by being plunged three times under water, head, hair and all) sips from.

It was our duty, Jeremiah Lucas said, to read the Bible every day and to try to persuade other people to give their hearts to

Jesus. Also, we had to pay strict attention to the commandments in the Bible, especially the one about not doing any work, or anything much at all, on a Sunday, apart from going to the Hall for the Breaking of Bread. And we had to look after each other when we were ill (that was good), and stop each other being sinful (that sounds all right, but it turned the Lucasites into the most dreadful Nosey Parkers, if I'm honest). Of course, we weren't allowed to smoke or drink alcohol (tiny sips of wine during the Breaking of Bread are holy and don't count), and we had to avoid places where the Devil might lurk, like cinemas, or those coffee bars with juke boxes that play wickedly sinful pop music.

Above all, we had to be Sexually Pure in thought, word and deed. (Lucasites *can* have sex, obviously. We'd die off if we didn't! But you have to be properly married first, with babies in mind.)

I know it's unfair that women aren't allowed to speak or do anything in the Meeting except sit quietly and listen, but actually I didn't mind. Ted was starting to get anxious knowing that eyes were on him, waiting for him to stand up and say something, announce a hymn or read from the Bible. He never did it, but I knew he hated the feeling that sooner or later he'd be expected to. I had the freedom to switch off, think my own thoughts and generally daydream if I felt like it. Which I usually did.

There are other things too, like women not being allowed to cut their hair, and having to wear hats to the Meeting, but they're just details, really.

Which brings me back to the Sunday after we first went to inspect Gospel Fields.

In our family, if you like sleeping in late at the weekends, you have to do it on Saturdays, because we always have breakfast together on Sundays. It's a good one too, with porridge, boiled eggs, toast and Mother's home-made marmalade. It doesn't go on for too long, though, because afterwards we have family worship, and then it's time to get ready to go to the Meeting at the Lucasite Hall.

Family worship used to be just a chapter from the Bible and a prayer, but then Dad started reading more and more dreadful accounts in the newspapers of what was going on in other countries. The Second World War had finished a whole ten years earlier, but terrible stories were still coming out about the concentration camps in Germany, where millions of Jewish people had been killed. Hitler was dead, of course, but, thought Dad, what was to stop a wicked dictator sweeping to power in Britain? The Nazis had come out of the blue in Germany, after all. And you never know with politics. Anything can happen.

Dad's nightmare was that we might end up in dungeons somewhere, in solitary confinement, or in a labour camp, like the millions who were still being marched off to be worked to death in Russia. And, worst of all, we would be *without our Bibles*!

The answer was obvious, at least to him. We needed to learn as much of the Bible as possible so that we would carry it with us in our hearts. His method was to get us to repeat Bible chapters again and again, after breakfast, until we knew them off by heart. Then we'd recite them by memory until he was sure we'd never forget them.

I like doing this. My favourite chapter has a bit about the mountains and the hills breaking forth into singing and all the trees of the fields clapping their hands. Now that's something I'd like to see! Hope likes the one about the seraphim putting hot coals on the prophet's mouth. Sometimes, behind those innocent big blue eyes and long blonde hair, she displays a sadistic streak. Mother prefers the description of Heaven. When we get to the bit 'and there shall be no more death, neither sorrow, nor crying, neither shall there be any more pain', she spoils it by crying herself.

Ted usually remembers something urgent he has to do as soon as breakfast is over, and he disappears before Dad gets out his Bible, while Faith deliberately asks for the most embarrassing chapter, which ends 'And now abideth faith, hope and charity, these three, and the greatest of these is charity', and then she and Hope look sideways at me to make sure that I'm not getting above myself.

After we've done the reciting, we always kneel with our faces bowed over the cracked leather seats of our ancient old chairs, which smell of all the bottoms that have sat on them for years and years, while Dad prays. Then it's time to get ready to go to our Lucasite Sunday morning Meeting.

So there we were, setting off for the Meeting on a hot July morning, knowing that soon we'd be striding down posh

Badger Hill instead of dreary Old Manor Road. It would have been wrong, of course, to take the bus to the Hall, as that would have given work to the bus driver and conductor on the Sabbath day so, come rain or shine, the six of us always walked to the Sunday morning Meeting. I'd had a special dispensation to take the bus on account of my weak legs since I'd come out of hospital, but the doctor had told Mother that gentle exercise was good for me, so from now on I had to walk too.

Dad and Ted, in their Sunday-best suits, marched ahead.

'It looks like a good, solid car, Dad,' Ted was enthusing. 'Not a scrap of rust on the bodywork and low mileage on the clock.'

I might have told him to save his breath. Dad didn't know one end of a car from the other, and anyway his mind was on higher things. At the same time, I was cheering Ted on. If only he could get Dad to drive the car, he might actually agree to drive us to the Meeting Hall, thus saving us from the long, boring plod along the main road.

A bus went sailing past, the dust-filled wind it kicked up making Faith, Hope and me clutch our summer straw hats in our white-gloved hands to stop them blowing away. Mother marched stoically on. She couldn't afford a summer hat, so she wore the same green felt one all year round, which she pinned to her hair with two long, scary-looking hatpins. The grimace on her face was caused by the pain of her bunions. Her shoes didn't fit properly, but up till now there had never been enough money to buy new ones.

She looked Lucasite born and bred, although until Dad

had scooped her up out of the ruins of an earthquake in New Zealand (a story I'll tell another time), married her and bore her back to Britain, she had been a Presbyterian. Since it was her firm belief that the man should be the head of the family and it was her duty to obey him, she had turned herself into a perfect Lucasite wife, though never a meek one.

I'd been looking forward to the Meeting for once. I'd been rehearsing how I'd show off to the super-annoying Tabitha Stebbins, the only other girl there my age, about how we'd soon be moving into Gospel Fields, a house of legendary splendour to all the Lucasites.

I must have you over to tea, I planned to say, when I'd imparted the incredible news. *As soon as we've settled in.*

But it didn't work out like that. Miss Rhys-Jones, one of the Lucasite faithful, was a secretary in the lawyer's office, and she'd been unable to resist telling Mrs Gill and Mrs Glass the staggering news of Mr Spendlove's bequest. By the time we arrived, a little later than usual, everyone knew all about it.

As we came into the Hall, people were settling into their chairs, which were arranged as usual round a table covered with a plain white linen cloth, with a loaf of bread and a carafe of wine set out on it. At the sight of us, people nudged each other and whispered. They were alert with curiosity, disbelief and jealousy. Tabitha, sitting opposite us on the far side of the table, looked quickly at me then ostentatiously turned her head away.

As usual, the Breaking of Bread seemed to drag on for hours

while the hands of the clock, which had *It is time to meet the Lord* inscribed on its face, crawled slowly round, but as soon as the last prayer was said there was a clatter of chairs being pushed back and the Lucasites hurried outside to stand in knots in the forecourt and discuss our astonishing legacy.

I stood uneasily, not knowing what to do. Tabitha had turned her back on me. Faith and Hope had been swallowed up by a crowd of inquisitive women. Mother ought to have been discussing next Sunday's Fellowship Tea with the other women, but she'd been waylaid by smarmy Mrs Glass, who was trying to oil out of her an invitation to Gospel Fields.

Only Dad was doing well. Flanked by Ted, he was in earnest discussion with a group of Elders, whose initial wariness was giving way to smiles and nods.

'Well,' I overheard Horace Tubbs wheeze out. 'I'd been wondering what on earth Reg Spendlove thought he was doing, singling your family out like that, but now you've explained your plans I see the hand of the Lord wonderfully revealed.'

I wasn't the only one who'd heard him. There was a relaxation all round. Mrs Prendergast went to rescue Mother from Mrs Glass, the knot round Faith and Hope dissolved and regathered round Dad and Tabitha started coming towards me.

I couldn't cope any longer.

'Quick!' I hissed to Hope. 'Let's go.'

She nodded.

'All right. You go on. I'll just tell Mother we're going home to put the soup on.'

I hurried out of the Hall forecourt, stuffing my cotton gloves into the pocket of my dress and ripping off my hat to let it swing from my hand by its elastic strap.

The rest of that Sunday was normal, I suppose. Mother had made everything for lunch and tea the day before so she didn't have to work on the Lord's Day. We played Scrabble in the afternoon (on Sundays we could only use the names of people and places in the Bible, which is really difficult, actually) and we sang hymns round the piano in the evening. But we were fizzing with questions all day.

Once Dad makes up his mind to do something, he doesn't stop for anything. The next day he signed the forms at the lawyers' office, handed our notice in to the landlord of 24 Old Manor Road and booked the removal company. We moved a month later, at the beginning of August, which was just as well, because I was so wound up with excitement that I'd have burst if the wait had gone on much longer.

It was a shame that I was the only one at home on the day we moved. Faith was on duty at the hospital, Hope was at a Christian camp for young musicians in Devon and Ted was on a Mission sailing week on the Norfolk Broads. He was skippering a boat filled with juvenile delinquents and was supposed to be persuading them to give their hearts to the Lord. I guessed they were probably trying to get him to give his heart to a life of crime, and frankly I thought it was a toss-up who would win.

I was supposed to be away too, on a girls' Bible camp, and I'd longed for it all year because the team leader I'd had at last year's summer camp had been thrillingly muscular and mannish and I'd had a wild crush on her. It was a dreadful disappointment when Dad had decided it would be too strenuous for me. He was right, I suppose. I was still horribly weak after the polio. The pain had gone, but I felt tired all the time and, although I could walk almost normally, I still couldn't run or do anything sporty at all. Anyway, I hadn't been allowed to go.

On our last morning in Old Manor Road, I felt a creeping loneliness settling on me. I hadn't realized that the shabby old tables and chairs being loaded into one of the vans, which had pulled up early in front of our house, were in fact my friends. They looked unloved sitting outside on the pavement. They were on their way to be auctioned, and it was a sad thought that I'd never see them again. Gospel Fields was already stuffed with Mr Spendlove's much grander furniture, so we were only taking a few favourite things with us: Mother's battered old armchair, Dad's sagging bookshelves and a Chinese table with carved legs, which a missionary cousin had sent back from Java.

I wandered round the empty rooms for the last time.

'You won't even know we've gone,' I told them. 'You don't care about us at all. No one will ever know that I made that crack in the window when I threw a book at Hope, or that the stain on the wall is my very own life blood, from the day when Ted accidentally-on-purpose shot me with an arrow from the bow he'd made.'

I mooched out into the garden and peered over the fence, half wanting and half dreading to see Robert-next-door. Then

I remembered that he and his family were on a caravan holiday in Wales, so there was no chance of seeing him anyway.

Robert and I had started being friends when we were really small. He used to knock on the back door every Saturday and almost every day in the school holidays.

'Can I come and play, Mrs Brown?' he'd say, and Mother would silently open the door and stand aside to let him in.

Quite frankly, the best thing about Robert was that he was younger than me, without too many ideas of his own, and he'd liked me telling him what to do. He was an only child and used to being bossed around at home.

Robert's dad was very strict. The patch of grass in our back garden was for playing on, or sprawling on with rugs and books, but Robert's father never let anyone set foot on his lawn, which was mown in stripes and didn't have a single daisy to spoil the effect.

'How does he get it so green?' I'd heard Mother ask Robert's mum one day. She'd blushed and said, 'Bedroom water.' Which, Mother later told me, meant wee. Next door's lawn looked sinister to me after that. And it wasn't the only sinister thing, because Robert's mum was a medium. When her customers came to visit her, she'd go off into a trance. Robert said that strange white stuff came out of her mouth, and the spirits of her customers' dead relations spoke to them through her. I kept on at him to tell me more, but he said he'd only watched once and hadn't been allowed to again in case he disturbed the spirits.

Mother thought all that was dreadfully wicked and wouldn't have let me go next door even if I'd wanted to. I tried to explain to Robert that it was dangerous calling up spirits because an evil one might enter you and take up a place in your heart. You could even be possessed by the Devil himself!

'Is the Devil really real, then?' he'd asked me anxiously.

'Of course he is,' I said, shocked that he could doubt it. '*He walketh about like a roaring lion, seeking whom he may devour.*'

Then I was afraid I'd been tactless, implying that Robert's mum was possessed by an evil spirit.

It was a whole week before he came back to visit and neither of us ever mentioned the Devil or spirits or mediums again. Or bedroom water, for that matter.

It was never the same after that. Robert was changing, anyway. Over the past year he'd gradually got bigger and taller than me, and one day last summer, before I'd gone down with polio, he'd said, 'You know what, I'm sick of your silly games and you telling me what to do all the time. I'm going home.'

I'd been upset, but only a bit because I was tired of our childish games too, only I hadn't known how to tell him.

I thought that would be the end of it, but the next day he'd jumped up and stuck his head over the garden wall.

'Anyway, I'm fed up with you telling me all the time to give my heart to Jesus,' he said in a squeaky voice. 'It's my heart, and I'll do what I like with it, thank you very much. As a matter of fact, I'm an ag-agnosteric.'

'I think you mean agnostic,' I'd said coldly. Then I'd added kindly, 'The Lord will wait for you, Robert. His mercy is infinite and . . .'

He'd jumped down then, but he bobbed up again to stick

out his tongue before he went down for the last time.

Remembering this, I searched around for dandelion clocks in our flower beds, and I blew the seeds over the fence to land on his dad's nasty stripy lawn, in the hope that they'd grow into infuriating big weeds with long roots after I'd gone.

I'm doing this for you, Robert, I silently said. *It's a final act of friendship. To punish your dad for not letting you go on his lawn.*

Then I headed off to say a last farewell to the grave of our old cat, Naboth, until Mother called out, 'Come on, Charity! We're going now.'

Dad pulled the front door shut behind us and double-locked it with a flourish. The first van had gone, but a second, smaller one had been loaded with things to be taken to Gospel Fields. There were a few seats beside and behind the driver.

'Get in, Charity,' said Mother, holding open the van door.

But at that moment I badly needed to be alone.

'No thanks,' I said. 'I'll walk.'

'If you're sure, dear,' said Dad absently. He was clearly anxious to be off.

'The walk'll do you good,' Mother said crisply. 'It's only down to the main road and up the hill on the other side. Not much more than a mile. Don't dawdle, mind.'

I wandered slowly down the road, feeling sorry for myself.

There's no one alive in the entire world who truly understands me, I thought. *Dad's too busy doing the Lord's work, Mother's always run off her feet, Ted hasn't noticed that I exist and Faith and Hope just think I'm a nuisance.*

33

I turned the corner out of Old Manor Road. Something was happening inside me, but I didn't know what it was.

Without thinking, I started drifting across the main road. A bus, hooting furiously, swerved to avoid me and the driver leaned out of his cab. Hot words poured out of his mouth. I'd never heard most of them before, but I could tell they were rude.

I stood trembling on the pavement.

I've just nearly died! I thought.

'You all right, lovey?' said a woman. 'You need to take more care.'

I hardly heard her.

If you'd died, I told myself, *you'd be face to face with Jesus right now! You'd be standing beside the river of the water of life, clear as crystal!*

The thought should have filled me with rapture, but I felt nothing but horror.

'Actually, God,' I muttered out loud. 'I'd rather be at Gospel Fields for the time being, if you don't mind.'

The woman was still looking at me.

'Are you sure you're all right? You've gone a funny colour.'

'No, honestly, I'm fine,' I said, and, taking a careful look both ways, I hurried over the road. As the gap in the traffic closed behind me, I felt as if I'd crossed a frontier into a different country. Old Manor Road really was behind me now, and Gospel Fields, up there on Badger Hill, beckoned.

They'll be unloading the van already! I thought, and, suddenly desperate to be there, I hurried the rest of the way.

CHAPTER FOUR

This has probably never happened to you, but I can tell you that it's the weirdest thing to walk round an enormous house filled with elegant furniture, where pictures in heavy gilt frames, which are probably priceless masterpieces, crowd the walls, where there are curtains and carpets of sumptuous opulence and cupboards crammed with beautiful objects, not to mention hosts of random things like clocks and lamps and umbrella stands. To know that everything now belongs to you and your family! To open cabinets full of china! To pull out drawers with silver spoons and forks in them! To find, in the pigeonholes of desks, neat piles of writing paper and envelopes with your address embossed on them, cupboards piled high with blankets and eiderdowns, shelves lined with old books, an actual grand piano in the drawing room – a drawing room! – chiming clocks on mantelpieces, a row of Wellington boots by the back door, stacks of terracotta flower pots in the potting shed and, most unsettling of all, the old coats of the previous owner (Mr Spendlove in this case) hanging up on pegs in the cloakroom, his suits and shirts in his wardrobe, and his razor and toothbrush still in the bathroom.

I went a bit crazy at first, rushing as fast as my weak legs would let me from room to room, while Dad directed the removal men, who were carrying boxes of our own old things into the hall. I had the maddest urge to mess everything up, to pull all Mr Spendlove's things around and somehow stamp my mark on the place, but I came down to earth when I reached the kitchen and found Mother inspecting the larder.

'Goodness knows what poor Reg lived on,' she said pityingly. 'There are no decent stores here at all.'

I'd been trying not to think about the old man, living alone in all this splendour. Anyway, there was only one thing I wanted to know.

'Which one's my bedroom?' I asked her.

'Next to ours.'

'Which is yours?'

'The big one over the dining room with the green carpet. No, don't run away, Charity. I need you to help me clear out these old jars.'

But I was out of the room and halfway down the back corridor to the stairs before she could stop me.

I wasn't sure about my new bedroom at first. Why was it much smaller than most of the others? Why was I being put so close to my parents? Was it so that they could keep an eye on me? Didn't they realize that I'd turned thirteen two whole weeks ago? What with the fuss of moving, no one had taken much notice of my birthday. The only presents I'd received on the day were a couple of improving Christian children's novels from my parents and a prayer book from Aunt Josephine, although a pretty brooch from Auntie Vi had arrived a week later and, to be fair, Mother had made a pavlova for tea.

I was trying to open the window to let in some fresh air when Dad came in behind me, carrying a heavy box in his arms.

'Your clothes,' he panted, lowering it on to the unmade bed.

I'd been about to ask him, in a dignified way, to knock from now on before he entered my room, but I couldn't very well after he'd puffed up the stairs with my things.

He came to stand beside me and we looked out across the garden together.

'Well, Charity? What do you think? Do you like your new bedroom?'

'It's smaller than the others.'

'Yes, but it won't be so cold in the winter. Look, it's even got a gas fire that you can light yourself.'

I could see his point, but I didn't want to give in too soon.

'To tell you the truth, Dad, I'd have preferred one of those two big ones down the end of the corridor.'

'Those are the guest rooms,' said Dad.

'For the weary and heavy-laden?' I was trying not to sound sarcastic.

'For whoever the Lord sees fit to send us,' he corrected me gently. 'Now, dear, your mother needs you in the kitchen. We've got to pull together, you know.'

It wasn't until late that afternoon that I was able to escape into the garden. I'd started to feel stifled in the house, tiptoeing around in all that magnificence. Not that I'd had the chance to explore it for long because Mother had whirled me into a cleaning frenzy in the kitchen and my arms ached with scrubbing.

Free at last, I wandered down the slope past the flower border. It still felt wrong being there, as if I'd broken into someone else's property, but part of me felt grand and sort of aristocratic. I could see myself in a flowing white dress, sitting on an elegant garden chair beside a picturesque table covered in a lace cloth, watching the butler walk towards me in a stately way bearing tea and cakes on a silver tray, while—

Voices close by made me jump.

'How annoying!' a girl was saying. 'You mean new people have moved in already? Have you asked them yet?'

'Of course not,' another girl replied. 'Mutti won't hear of it. It was different with Mr Spendlove. He hardly ever went into the garden and he practically begged us to use the court. This lot's a big family. Four children. Well, not children. The youngest looks a bit younger than me, Papa said, and the older ones are practically grown up.'

Their voices were coming from behind the privet hedge, which sloped away from the house behind the long flower border. I spotted a thinner patch through which I could see daylight and crept towards it, tiptoeing across the soft soil round a clump of lilies. Carefully parting the twigs, I looked through.

'There's no harm in asking, surely.' The speaker's mouth was pinched with irritation. Her flowery dress looked new and her blonde hair was set in careful curls. 'They'd probably *like* more people to make up sets.'

The other, taller girl impatiently tossed her thick black hair away from her face.

'I told you, Susi. Mutti won't hear of it. We don't know anything about them.' She bent to gently remove a wasp, which had settled on her crumpled shorts.

'Yes, you do,' said Susi. 'They belong to the same crackpot religious sect as old Spendlove. Your mother said so.'

I reared back away from the hedge, feeling as if I'd been kicked in the heart. Then I heard the taller girl say, 'I know he had weird beliefs, but it didn't mean that I didn't like him. I was really sad when he died. He was the kindest person ever. They might be nice too, but you know what Mutti's like. *Ach, Rachel, Rachel, don't be so trusting! You think this country's safe? For us nowhere is safe! From now on we stick to our own!*'

Susi laughed.

'My mother's just as bad. But couldn't you just – you know, go round there and—'

'No,' the girl called Rachel said shortly. 'Look, I've got to go. Dentist.'

'Oh.' Susi sounded sulky. 'I'll come over tomorrow then, shall I?'

'Not sure. I'll call you.'

Their voices faded away towards the house.

I hadn't known there was a girl my age next door. I needed to see more.

The privet hedge ended where it ran into a large old yew

39

tree whose spreading branches swept the ground. I'd peered through them on our first visit to the garden. The space under the tree was like a shady room, carpeted with dead yew needles. I worked my way through the low branches into the middle. I was quite hidden here. Half the tree was inside our garden, but the other half led out into the Sterns's.

Someone had been in here, but not for a long time. There was a crude doll's house, the wood cracked and rotted by rain, and a toy pram, its wheels rusting, lying on its side.

That girl, Rachel, I thought. *I bet she used to play in here when she was little.*

It was easy to see out from inside the tree while staying completely hidden. The Sterns's garden was much smaller than ours. There wasn't room for a proper lawn. A winding path of old red bricks led between shrubs and clumps of flowers. A couple of chairs stood on a patch of gravel, and a book lay on the round metal table between them. There was a wooden arch, which was covered with a mass of white and yellow roses. Beyond it I could just make out the corner of the house and an open window with a blue-painted frame. Someone was playing the piano.

But what caught my eye was a statue of a woman. She was standing on a stone under what seemed to be a pear tree. She didn't have any clothes on, but she didn't look at all indecent. I was a bit shocked for a moment, then I remembered the pictures of the Venus de Milo we'd been shown in primary school when we'd been doing the Ancient Greeks. We'd all sniggered, but Mrs Finch had told us that naked people carved in stone weren't rude. They were art.

I'd never seen anything like this woman, though. She looked lonely and strong and noble all at the same time, and her head was lifted as if she was trying to see something far away. She made me feel curious about the family next door. Lucasites didn't usually go in for works of art, either in their houses or in their gardens. Some of the pictures in Gospel Fields looked like actual art, but I couldn't be sure if they were or not. But I was sure about this statue. It was the real thing.

For the rest of the day I couldn't get the Rachel girl out of my mind, so after supper (baked beans on toast) I followed Dad into his study, where he was unpacking boxes of books.

'You know the people next door?' I began.

'The Sterns? What about them?'

'When we came, that first time, Mother thought they might be German. Are they?'

He'd opened a book and was starting to read it.

'Hm? The Sterns? I expect so. Or Austrian. Jewish refugees probably.'

'Oh!'

That shook me. There had been a Jewish boy from Austria at Ted's school. Ted had come home one day blazing with anger as he told us what had happened to the people in the boy's family who hadn't managed to get out of Austria in time.

'That's enough, Ted,' Mother had said at last. 'You'll give Charity nightmares.'

I'd only been eight at the time, but I'd never forgotten

the horror. The thought that the Sterns, our actual next-door neighbours, might themselves have escaped from such a terrible fate made me shiver. Why would a girl who had been through so much have time for me – plain old Charity Brown?

But before I could even think of trying to make friends with Rachel, there was a hurdle to cross. Dad had gone back to his book and he barely looked up when I said, 'Did you know that the Sterns have got a daughter? I think her name's Rachel.'

'That's nice.'

He wasn't listening – I could tell.

'The thing is, Dad, supposing I get to know Rachel, is it all right for us to be friends? It's just that I know I'm really only supposed to be best friends with Lucasites. And if she's Jewish she's not even a Christian.'

He looked up at me, surprised.

'I thought your best friend was the Stebbins girl? Tabitha.'

I tried not to groan out loud.

'I keep *telling* you. Tabitha Stebbins is *boring*. She doesn't read books. She only cares about getting boys to look at her. Honestly, Dad, I can't stand her.'

'Ah. That's a pity. A friendship based on a shared commitment to Christ is the best kind. But we can't always stay safe in the fellowship of God's people. The important thing, Charity, as you go forth into the World, is to remain ever faithful to Christ in all you say and do.'

'So I can make friends with Rachel, then?'

He was reading his book again.

'Yes, dear, of course. Put the light on, will you? It's getting too dark to read.'

I hadn't realized how late it was. A mighty yawn broke from me. My legs felt almost too heavy to take me up the stairs, but all I wanted to do was climb into my strange new bed in my strange new room and go to sleep.

I didn't sleep, though, not for a long time. Gospel Fields didn't feel like home at all. The floorboards creaked when anyone went past my room, and from time to time I heard a train whistling on the far side of the valley. I imagined that I was on it, tucked up in my berth on the night sleeper, rocking north to Scotland, on the way to visit my Aunt Josephine.

Dad's got two older sisters, Josephine and Violet. His mother had spent ages thinking of boys' names before he was born, in case she got a son at last, and she'd whispered all her favourite ones in my grandfather's ear as she looked down fondly at her baby lying in her arms, but it was the last thing she did, because a moment later she closed her eyes and died. My poor grandfather didn't know which name she'd have chosen, so he took them all. Dad's whole name is Archibald Hector Malcolm McIver Brown, but everyone calls him Iver.

Grandfather had marched off to war in 1916 with his kilt swinging and his bonnet at a jaunty angle, but he'd come home from the trenches silent and depressed. He was just beginning to recover when his wife died, and then he sort of closed down altogether. He went on going to Lucasite Meetings on Sundays and took the train into Glasgow every day to the office where

43

he worked, but at home he became a ghost.

Aunt Josephine was fourteen when her mother died. Since the family was more or less without any acting parents, she took charge of six-year-old Violet and baby Iver, and ruled tyrannically over them with the help of Mrs Cameron, the cook. It can't have been much fun for her, I suppose, but it was good practice for being a headmistress later on.

As soon as he could walk, Dad started trying to escape, and he became so good at it that Josephine and Mrs Cameron gave up chasing him and left him to roam the moors and hills around the village for as long as he liked. He would come home at sunset with scratched knees and torn shirts.

'Where have you *been*?' Aunt Josephine would say. 'Where's your belt? Your cap? Your bootlaces?'

'Lost them,' he'd answer helpfully. 'I'm hungry.'

It was Violet who always said, 'What did you find today, Iver? What have you got?'

'No, don't let him open it!' Josephine would shriek, but Violet watched with interest as Iver took the lid off his battered specimen box to reveal a hoard of bugs and beetles, centipedes and spiders.

One evening, when Dad was eleven, his father noticed him drawing a picture of a woodlouse on a scrap of torn-off paper. He was astonished by how accurate it was, and it suddenly occurred to him that young Iver had outgrown the village school and needed to get a secondary education. He enrolled him in a school in Glasgow, and from then on Dad and his father took the 8 a.m. train from the small station in the heart of the village and travelled into the city together, where Grandfather would go to work in his accountants' office, and Dad would run off to school.

During these journeys, Grandfather realized that Dad knew practically nothing about the Bible. Since their earliest childhood he and his sisters had yawned their way through long Meetings in the stuffy little Lucasite Hall on the edge of the village, but Dad had barely taken in a word. Grandfather, looking at his grubby, skinny, long-legged twelve-year-old son, as if for the first time, discovered that he loved him deeply and yearned for him to find the path to salvation. Warmth came into his pale cheeks, his eyes lit up and he began to enthuse Iver with the glorious poetry of the Bible. They became so excited as they recited whole passages of scripture together that the other regular travellers learned to avoid the carriage they were in, choosing to stand in corridors where at least they could read their newspapers in peace.

To his sisters' surprise, Dad passed his school-leaving exam with brilliant marks and embarked on a degree in Biology, in order, as he explained to anyone who would listen, to learn more about God's wondrous creation.

'There was a tricky moment, Charity, when your dad read about Darwin's theory of evolution,' Auntie Vi told me on one of her rare visits to Old Manor Road. (Violet was my favourite aunt. Way out in front, although there wasn't much competition from Josephine, quite frankly.)

'Oh, you mean that thing about evolution contradicting the Book of Genesis,' I said, trying to look bored and knowledgeable.

45

'Dad explained it to me. The Bible is basically true, because God did create the heavens and the earth, the seas and all that is in them, of course He did, but in the Lord's eyes one day is as a thousand years, and a thousand years is as one day. He did all the creating in what seemed like days to Him when it was actually ages and ages, and if He chose evolution as His method, who are we to question Him? Problem solved.'

Auntie Vi laughed.

'Well done, Charity. Iver has trained you well.'

'But don't you believe in God the Creator?' I asked anxiously. I couldn't bear to think that Auntie Vi might have been ensnared by the Devil.

'Oh, believe! Believe! What do we all believe?' she said vaguely. 'Don't tempt me to corrupt your innocent young mind, darling.'

She'd wandered out into the garden after that, and I had a dreadful suspicion that she was going to smoke a cigarette. It wouldn't have surprised me. When Violet was nineteen, she'd scandalized her family, the Lucasites, and the whole village, by cutting off her hair, dressing like a man and striding off to London to work in the theatre.

'No, I'm *not* an actress,' I'd overheard her tell Aunt Josephine. 'A theatre director is a very different thing. And you needn't think I'm a scarlet woman. I've got excellent morals, as a matter of fact, even if I am just the teeniest bit pink.'

No one was surprised when Dad decided to study entomology. He spent his student years in the labs of Glasgow University peering down microscopes and gasping with wonder at the exquisite bodies of tiny bugs and beetles, and filling notebooks with his drawings and observations. He discovered, too, that he had a terrific gift for preaching, and he spent his evenings in mission halls in the poorest parts of Glasgow, persuading people to give their hearts to Jesus.

As soon as he'd graduated, his professor called him into his office.

'We're sending an expedition to New Zealand,' he'd told him, as he inspected Dad over his glasses. 'To study wildlife. We need an insect man. Are you interested?'

Dad stared back at him. Could this be a call from the Lord, or was Satan talking out of the professor's mouth?

'Well, sir,' he said at last, 'I'll need time to pray about it.'

The professor's eyebrows rose.

'I see. Well, please ask the Almighty to inform you of his decision soon, because I need to know by Friday. And I might as well tell you, Brown, that taking part in this expedition will be a big step up in your career, if, as I hope, you are considering applying for a research post at this university with a view to becoming a lecturer in the future.'

Dad sailed for New Zealand a week later.

The next part of Dad's story obviously shows the guiding hand of God because the moment he arrived off the coast of New Zealand, and his ship dropped anchor off a small town called Napier, the water started shuddering violently, there was a terrifying boom as the sea bed rose and hit the keel and the whole ship tilted over. Meanwhile, on land, the hills were shaking as if they were made of jelly and the town of Napier burst into flames.

'If the Lord hadn't sent that earthquake, I would never have met your dear mother,' Dad used to say, looking revoltingly sentimental. This was true, but it gave me a strange opinion of the Lord because a lot of people died or were injured in that earthquake, not to mention animals, and it seemed a big price to pay just so that my parents could meet each other.

Anyway, the ship's captain mustered a team of volunteers to go ashore and Dad went with them. He would never tell us what he did exactly, but I expect it was terrifically heroic. I imagine him pulling children out of burning buildings, tearing at smouldering rafters with his bare hands, then striding off to the hospital with the wounded hoisted up on to his skinny shoulders.

I know the bit about the hospital is true because the doctor in charge was the man who would become my other grandfather. He'd got his daughter, my future mother, to put up stretchers for the wounded on the lawn outside the building, which looked as if it would collapse at any moment. When Dad first set eyes on Mother, her right eye was swollen and half closed because a brick had fallen on her head, and her face was covered with soot, but he took one look at her and that was it. It makes me feel peculiar to imagine my parents in love, so I'll leave it there.

Dad left his ship and the bug-and-beetle expedition and married Mother. Of course, he wouldn't have done so if she hadn't been a true believer too, but she was, just as much as

48

Dad, which proves again that God must have willed it all, or how would two such souls have found each other on the diametrically opposite sides of the world?

There was no question that they would devote themselves from then on to the Lord's work, which in Dad's case meant leaving New Zealand's insects to themselves, and being employed on a tiny salary by a Christian organization to travel round New Zealand preaching, and in Mother's case meant staying at home, having babies and managing on almost no money. (And I just want to make it absolutely clear that that sort of life is not going to be for *me*!)

Which brings me back to my arrival on the world stage.

Mother is the most practical person I've ever met. She was even super-efficient at having babies, which popped out in no time at all. She knew what to expect, so when she realized that I was on the way, she called a taxi to take her to the hospital. But it was a close-run thing because she'd nearly left it too late and I might have been born right there on the pavement if a passing sailor hadn't picked her (us) up in his arms and rushed her (us) into the hospital.

'Go on, tell me more about the sailor,' I used to beg her.

'Nothing to tell, dear,' she'd say crisply. 'Except that he was wearing a pink vest.'

It's my belief, though of course I can't prove it, that being (virtually) born in the arms of a sailor instilled in me a great desire to travel and to see the world, which, when I've grown up and left home, I fully intend to do.

*

Our family was in New Zealand all the way through the Second World War, and Dad was never called up to fight, which is just as well because he would have made a useless soldier. He's so tender-hearted he'd step out of the way of a snail rather than crush it underfoot. All through the war, he went on spreading the gospel round New Zealand and persuading people to learn long passages of the Bible in case they ever found themselves with nothing to read in prison camps. He did it so brilliantly that when the war ended sales of Bibles in New Zealand had rocketed and the missionary society in London sent him a telegram:

DIRECTOR NEEDED TAKE OVER SOCIETY
WORLDWIDE STOP ARE YOU INTERESTED STOP

A few months later we were standing in the drizzle on the quayside of the London Docks, being inspected by Aunt Josephine, who had come down from Scotland to meet us. I was only two, and I don't remember it at all, but Faith told me that when Aunt Josephine heard Ted speak, she said, 'Oh dear me, what a shocking accent. We'll have to see about *that*,' which dreadfully offended Mother. It got them off on the wrong foot and they never really got on to the right one. Aunt Josephine tries to boss Mother around, and Mother won't have it. It's quite fun watching them go head to head, actually.

The reason why I'm telling you all this about Dad, the aunts, the earthquake, Mother and New Zealand, is that I think it explains things about our family.

'Do you know who you are?' I said to Faith a few days after we'd moved. I was in the middle of sloughing off Old Manor Road and becoming the new me in Gospel Fields, and I think I must have been rather confused.

'What are you on about now, Char? Of course I do. I'm Faith Brown.'

'No, but are you English?'

'I am *not*,' she said, frowning. 'And neither are you.'

'Well, are we Scottish, then? Or New Zealand-ish?'

She pushed her long hair out of her eyes.

'Inside, I'm a New Zealander. I always will be.'

She seemed caught up for a moment in memories of our lost and golden land, where the sun always shone, fruit dripped off the trees and children didn't have to wear shoes and socks. She was nine when we came to London, after all.

'I wish I felt the same,' I said sadly. 'But I can't remember a thing about it.'

'Who do you think you are, then?'

'Scottish, I suppose. I don't know.'

'The important thing to remember,' she said, in a revoltingly older-sister, superior way, 'is that we are first and foremost a Christian family. Scotland, New Zealand, England — it doesn't matter where you're from.' Then she put on her Bible-quoting voice. '*There is neither Jew nor Greek, for ye are all one in Christ Jesus.*'

And that's what's so irritating in the Brown family. The minute someone quotes the Bible, it shuts everyone else up, because they can't argue back against Holy Writ. Faith was already halfway out of the door.

'That's another thing,' I said, trying to catch her out. 'Jews and Greeks. What does that mean, *There is neither Jew nor Greek*? There are lots of Greeks in Greece, and there might be Jews living right next door.'

'You know what it means, Charity,' sighed Faith, who was ostentatiously looking at her watch. 'Followers of Christ are all brothers and sisters in the Lord, no matter where they come from.'

'Yes, but are they brothers and sisters if they're not followers of Christ?' I persisted. 'That doesn't seem very fair. I need to know this, Faith. I desperately want to be friends with Rachel Stern next door, and she's probably Jewish. As far as we know, anyway.'

Faith had had enough.

'Oh, leave me alone, Charity. I'm on nights this week. I've got to get back to the hospital.'

CHAPTER FIVE

Ted came home from his sailing week in a bad mood. His face was tight, and I knew he'd snap at me like an angry dog if I got in his way, but I'd been so fed up with having no siblings around to share the excitement of the move that I couldn't stop myself bouncing round him like a yapping puppy as I tried to show him the wonders of the house.

'Go *away*, Char,' he kept snarling. 'Leave me alone.'

'Yes, but you haven't seen this!' I'd say, opening cupboards to reveal exquisite hand-painted tea sets, and pulling out drawers to display piles of snowy lace-edged tablecloths.

He wouldn't look at anything.

'You're being maximum irritating,' he said, after I'd pointed out the picture of a field of poppies over the fireplace in the drawing room. 'Just tell me where my room's supposed to be, then scram.'

I hurried up the stairs ahead of him.

'They put your stuff in here,' I said, opening the door of the small room over the kitchen.

He looked round silently, then turned his scowling face to me.

'Out,' he said. 'Now.'

'All right, you beast,' I said, allowing myself to be offended at last, and I slouched back to my own room and slammed the door behind me. Then I wished I hadn't because after a moment I heard him come out of his room again. I was dying to see what he was doing, so I gently opened my door a crack to look.

He was standing at the other end of the corridor, tugging at the handle of a low, narrow door. It was painted the same creamy sort of colour as the walls and was quite hard to notice.

'It's stuck!' I called out before I could stop myself. 'I've tried it millions of times.'

'Stop spying on me, you little horror,' he said, but he didn't sound so angry now. He ran past me down the stairs, and I heard him open the front door. I dashed over to my window to watch him crunch over the gravel round the side of the house to the garage. He appeared again with a screwdriver in his hand, and a moment later was back up the stairs working at the little door. It gave with a rusty creak, and I caught a glimpse of a bare, narrow staircase. He went inside, shutting the door with a snap behind him, then I heard his feet clumping around overhead.

He came down at last, brushing cobwebs off his clothes. He was looking pleased with himself.

'What's up there?' I dared ask.

He actually grinned at me.

'There's a great big attic, crammed with stuff. And one end's blocked off to make a decent-sized room with a window under the gable end.'

He pushed past me.

'Where are you going?'

'I'm moving my stuff up there. You can help me if you like.'

'But Mother——'

'Never mind about Ma. She'll be glad to have an extra bedroom for the weary. Are you going to help me or not?'

'In a minute. Let me have a look round the attic first.'

I limped up the stairs and Ted came after me. There was a window at the far end of the attic and an electric light bulb dangled on a long cord from the rafters. Ted found a switch and turned it on.

I shrieked with fright.

'Ted, look! A person! Without a head!'

He laughed.

'It's only a tailor's dummy, silly.'

He picked his way towards it across the cluttered floorboards and pulled the white wrapper off. Underneath was what looked like a woman dressed in a tweed skirt and jacket with a purple felt hat balanced on the neck where a head should have been. There was something horribly wrong about it.

'Wrap it up again,' I begged Ted. 'It's creepy. Who could have worn that stuff? Mr Spendlove wasn't even married.'

'He was, actually. His wife died years ago. You wouldn't remember. Funny old girl. A least thirty years older than Mr S. More like his mother than his wife.'

'So they didn't have any children?'

Ted smiled.

'I don't think it was that kind of marriage.'

'What's that supposed to mean?'

'Never you mind.'

Normally, I'd have been infuriated, but I was so happy to be exploring the attic with Ted that I let it go.

'Come to think of it,' I said, 'if they'd had children, the house would have gone to them and we wouldn't have got it, would we? Why do you think he left it to us, Ted?'

Ted shrugged.

'How should I know? Perhaps he'd been lonely and liked the thought of a big family filling the place up. Hey, look at that enormous rocking horse! There must have been a child here once.'

The attic was so dusty and full of old furniture, trunks, suitcases and boxes that it was hard to explore. Ted soon lost interest, and went back to take another look at the bare, uncarpeted room on the far side of the staircase. The late afternoon sun was flooding in through the window tucked under the gable-end of the roof. Ted walked round it, examining everything through narrowed eyes, as if he was measuring it up.

'It's so unfair,' I said. 'I wish I'd found it first.'

'You need to be near Ma and Pa,' he said absent-mindedly, 'in case you're ill again and need them in the night.'

'It's still not fair,' I said, kicking out at the wall and raising a cloud of dust. 'And I'm not going to be ill again. Ever.'

'Charity? Where are you? Charity!'

'Ma's calling you,' Ted said unnecessarily.

'I know. I've got ears, haven't I?'

'Where on earth have you been?' Mother said crossly when I went into the kitchen. 'Your face is filthy and you've got cobwebs in your hair.'

'With Ted, in the attic.'

'What attic?'

'You mean you didn't know? It's brilliant, Mother! It's crammed with stuff and there's a separate room up there that Ted wants for his bedroom.'

I waited for her to purse her lips and say there was no question of it, but she only said, 'Set the table, Charity. It's nearly supper-time. Your father will be home any minute now.'

I started laying things out on the kitchen table, where we'd been having our meals up till then, but she shook her head.

'In the dining room. We'd better get used to being in there before anyone else joins us.'

It was lovely eating in the dining room. I sat opposite the big bay window. The August evening sun poured through it, making the wood panelling gleam and the faded red carpet glow. It was only our typical high tea (grilled herrings, bread and butter, oatcakes, early apples from the garden and cups of tea), but I lost myself in imagining a footman behind me, murmuring, 'More caviar, miss?' while I rebalanced the tiara on my head.

'Charity, wake up! Clear away the herring bones,' Mother said, and when I'd done it and sat down again I realized I'd been missing an important conversation.

'You know, Ted, it's never good to make a hasty decision,' Dad was saying.

I now wished I was sitting on the other side of the table with my back to the window, because Ted's face was against the light and I couldn't read his expression.

'I know, but I've been thinking about it for a long time, and it all came to a head last week.' He sounded nervous, as if he was braced for trouble. 'I did my best, honestly, on the sailing camp. I tried to talk to the lads, but they just – I couldn't make any impression on them.'

'You can't be sure, dear,' Mother said, pouring Ted another cup of tea. 'You might have planted a seed in the heart of one of those boys, which will—'

Ted clenched his jaw and I knew he was trying not to snap at her.

'I'm quite sure I didn't, Ma. The truth is that I haven't got Dad's gift for – for converting people, and – well, I haven't got his conviction, either. I know you want me to go to Bible College next term, but I've realized I just – I can't.'

There was a painful silence. My heart lurched. Had Ted lost his faith? Was he bound for the fires of Hell, where there would be weeping and wailing and gnashing of teeth?

Mother cleared her throat.

'This is very sudden, Ted. Term starts in a matter of weeks. Have you thought about what you want to do instead?'

Ted leaned forward eagerly.

'Yes! I've thought and thought about this. It started in the navy. Two years in and out of ships, on land and at sea.'

'And we were so proud of you, Ted,' interrupted Dad, leaning forward. 'It's not easy to be out in the world, to keep your faith burning like a flame of fire when all around you—'

'Yes, well,' Ted said shortly, 'the thing is, Dad, I'm going to study marine engineering.'

'Boat building?' said Mother, looking confused.

'Among other things. There's so much that's new since the war! New techniques, new materials, new ideas . . . I'll be able to get a good job at the end of my degree. Well paid!'

'A degree?' said Dad. 'Where?'

'Here in London,' said Ted. 'I applied before I went away. The letter from the polytechnic was waiting for me when I got back today. They've offered me a place, with a grant to pay the fees. I thought, if it's all right, I could stay here at home and travel up for lectures and . . .'

His voice faltered into the general silence.

'You seem to have thought it all out,' Mother said, a touch of acid in her voice.

'Ma, I'm twenty-one!' Ted sounded exasperated. 'Of course I've thought it out!'

'Well,' said Dad, making a brave recovery, 'this is exciting news, Ted. Of course you can stay at home while you study. It's what I did when I was a student in Glasgow. But, before you make a final decision to give up your place at the Bible College, perhaps we should take it to the Lord in prayer? And what better time than now, when we are all together?'

I was about to obediently shut my eyes and drop my head when I caught Ted's eye. Even though I couldn't see his face very well, I was almost sure he winked at me.

*

59

It was wonderful, of course, suddenly finding myself in a great big house on top of a hill in the middle of a huge garden, but actually it was rather lonely. I wished I could ask a school friend round to visit, but the sad truth was that I didn't have any. I'd only been at the grammar for one whole term, then I'd got polio in January and now I wouldn't be going back till after the summer holidays. Everyone would have sorted out their friendships by now. I was no good with girls my age, anyway. Things would start off well enough, but they'd always stray into worldly talk about films and boys and make-up, and when I'd try to be a witness to the Lord and attempt the holy work of bringing their souls to Christ they'd walk away, or, worse still, laugh at me and tell me I was weird. I was rather dreading the start of the new term, in fact.

I missed Hope dreadfully, but she was still at her music camp and there'd be only two weeks after she got home before she had to go back to school in Scotland. Sometimes, I was so desperate for company that I was tempted to sneak back to Old Manor Road on the other side of the valley and try to make it up with Robert-next-door.

But I put that thought sternly aside. I had a new neighbour now. A girl of my own age. A girl with a work of art in her garden. I hadn't even talked to Rachel Stern yet, but I knew for sure, in my bones, that we were destined to be great friends. I was worried, though, that my chance of meeting her properly was drifting by. We were halfway through the summer holidays, and school would start in a few weeks' time. I needed to meet her soon.

The Sterns's garden, so small and overgrown and interesting, constantly drew me back. Every day I would creep inside the yew tree and peer through the branches on the Sterns's side, hoping to catch sight of Rachel, but although I heard music pouring through the open windows of the house, and sometimes voices speaking in another language, she didn't appear.

Until, one morning, she did. She was sitting at the little green metal table, her long bare legs propped up on the second chair, reading a book. I could only see her back, so I crept out from under the yew tree and tiptoed up to the thin place in the hedge, through which I'd heard her talking to her friend Susi. I was parting the twigs to look through when a gruff voice behind me said, 'Watch out for them lilies. Flower beds ain't for treading on.'

I spun round. A crusty old man was glaring at me.

'Who are you?' I said in as dignified a voice as I could manage.

'Arthur Barlow, the gardener, that's who I am, and I'll trouble you to remember it.'

'Oh, sorry. I thought you were on holiday.'

'Well, I'm back. Hey! Don't trample about like that! There's daffodil bulbs planted right there!'

'Sorry,' I said again, hopping back clumsily on to the grass. 'I'm Charity Brown, by the way.'

If we'd been in a book, he'd have said, *Beg your pardon, miss, I didn't realize you was the daughter of the house*, but he just scowled at me, grunted and stalked off.

I was standing there, staring crossly at his back, when I

heard a giggle from the other side of the fence.

She must have heard everything! I thought, my face flaming with embarrassment, and I fled back to the house.

The postman was wheeling his bicycle away down the drive when I reached the open front door. He'd left a handful of letters on the doormat. I picked them up and put them on the table beside the grandfather clock.

Mother came out of the kitchen and riffled through them.

'One for the Sterns, mixed up with ours,' she said. 'Why don't you take it round to them?'

My heart thumped. This was my chance! I took the letter from her and was halfway out of the house when she said, 'And please ask Mrs Stern if she'd like some apples. We've got more windfalls than we can use.'

The Sterns's small front garden was so crammed with shrubs that you couldn't see much of the house. The front door was shut and looked like it wanted to stay that way.

I screwed up my courage and knocked. Professor Stern opened the door almost immediately.

'Yes?'

'I – I'm Charity Brown from next door. The postman left this letter with us by mistake.'

'That's kind. Thank you.'

He took the letter and started shutting the door.

'And – and Mother said that if you'd like some apples we have more than we can use.'

Someone came through from the back of the house. It

was Rachel. Her thick dark hair bushed out untidily from her face, and her eyes were the greeny-blue colour of the sea on a cloudy day.

'Ah, Rachel,' said Professor Stern. 'Charity's mother is kindly offering us some apples. Why don't you go next door with her and fetch them?'

Rachel was about to answer when Mrs Stern appeared.

'I heard you, my dear,' she said, looking flustered. 'Please tell your mother, thank you, but we have enough apples for now.'

A frown flashed across Professor Stern's face before he turned back to me.

'Thank your mother, Charity,' he said apologetically. 'Another time maybe.'

Did I see a tinge of regret in Rachel's face before he shut the door? I couldn't be sure, but I hoped so.

CHAPTER SIX

Ted had found himself a summer job working at London Zoo. Every evening at supper he had a new story to tell. An elephant had sneezed all over an old woman's hat. A sad lion did nothing but pace backwards and forwards in his cage all day long. A gorilla threw nutshells at people when they laughed at him.

'Have you worked in the insect house yet?' Dad asked him every evening.

But Ted never had.

When he wasn't at work or at meals with us, Ted was either in the garage tinkering with the car, which needed a lot of work as it hadn't been used for so long, or he was up in his attic room. From my bedroom I could hear bumps and scrapes and hammering noises, and I'd watch him walk round to the garage and come back into the house carrying bits of wood, tools and pots of old paint.

I longed to know what he was doing and kept hovering by my bedroom door looking hopeful whenever he passed in case he wanted me to help. Of course he always ignored me. I had to wait till he was out at work before I could creep upstairs and look.

There wasn't much to see at first. His bed was in a corner under the sloping eaves, and unpacked boxes and stacks of books were piled on the floor. There was an old desk too, which he'd dragged in from the attic. One of the drawers had been broken but he'd mended it and put new knobs on all the others. Soon a shelf appeared, running along the wall above the desk with a record player and his model yacht on it. The day after that there was a neat rack for all his records. Next there'd be a rail for his clothes suspended from the ceiling; a bookcase (also from the attic) by his bed; and a row of pegs holding an array of peculiar hats: a sailing cap, an old panama with a hole in the brim, a conjuror's black top hat and, at the end of the row, Mrs Spendlove's felt hat with its feather straightened, which he'd taken off the dummy.

I was sitting at his desk one day, admiring the way he'd sorted his pens from his pencils into a pair of enamel mugs, and wondering if I dared open the drawers and look through them, when I heard the attic staircase creak. I jumped up. Where could I hide? I was about to crawl under the bed when Ted came into the room.

'Caught you at last, you little snooper!'

'I – I was just—'

'Snooping.' To my relief, he laughed. 'It's all right. I'm not cross with you. I know you come in here every day.' Then he wagged his finger at me. 'Look as much as you like, but don't ever, *ever*, open my drawers and look inside them.'

'I wouldn't!' I said, trying to look offended and not blush at the same time. 'How did you know I've been in here, anyway?'

'Not very observant, are you?' He pointed to a dusting of powder just inside the door. 'My little trap. You tread in it every time.'

I felt indignant.

'That's — that's sneaky!'

'And spying on me isn't, I suppose?'

'I'm not spying! It's just that — that I get so bored, and there's nothing to do, and your room's so interesting! It's all so complicated and funny and neat and tidy.'

He looked pleased.

'You learn to be tidy in the navy. No room for mess on board ship.' He pulled a record out of the rack and showed me the pink-and-black label. 'Bill Haley and His Comets. Want to hear it?'

I wasn't sure. It didn't look like a Christian song to me. Tabitha Stebbins's mother said that modern pop music was the work of the Devil because the beat was a bit faster than your natural pulse rate and it made you think dirty thoughts.

'Mrs Stebbins says——' I muttered.

'Mrs S is a narrow-minded old bag,' Ted said cheerfully, putting the record on the turntable and lowering the needle. 'Listen to this.'

I stood, transfixed. 'Rock Around the Clock' was the most sensational thing I'd heard in my whole life. Ever. It made my head buzz and my skin tingle and I couldn't stop myself from jigging around to the beat.

'Well?' Ted said with a grin when it was finished. 'Did that make you feel all sexy?'

I went scarlet.

'I don't know what you mean,' I said stiffly. 'And I don't think you ought to—'

'. . . lead you astray.' I jerked my head away as he reached out to pull one of my plaits. I hated him doing that. 'I suppose you're right. I've got classical stuff too. Mozart mainly. And some military marches. Even Mother approves of those.'

Mozart and marches sounded reassuring, but I couldn't help wishing that Ted would put 'Rock Around the Clock' on again.

I looked up to see that he was watching me. This was actually an unusual event. Ted normally took no notice of me, except to tease.

'You feeling all right these days, Char?'

'I suppose so. What do you mean?'

'The polio and all that.'

I wasn't used to sympathy from Ted. It made me feel warm inside.

'Can't have been much fun.'

'I can't bear to even *think* about the hospital, but I'm nearly better now. It's just that it's so annoying getting puffed out all the time, and my left leg and arm are sort of weak. They don't work properly. I'm going to get teased, I know I am, when people see me trying to run.'

'Looking forward to going back to school?'

'No! There's this girl, Monica, the queen of the bullies. I think she hates me. She's turned all the others against me.'

He nodded.

'I don't blame you for hating school,' he said. 'I did. It's such a strain feeling that you've got to . . .' He stopped.

'Witness to the Lord all the time.'

'Quite.'

We stood there, grinning at each other, and he was about to say more when a mellow clanging sound rolled up the stairs. Mother had got so tired of shouting for us all over the house when meals were ready that she'd started using the old Burmese gong, which hung from dragon-shaped brackets in the hall.

'Lunch,' said Ted.

I followed him out of the room.

'Why aren't you at the zoo, anyway?' I asked his back, as I tried to keep up with the way he leaped down the stairs.

'My day off. To make up for working on Saturdays. And, in case you're wondering, I get a different day off every week, so you'll never know when I'll creep up on you nosing round my room.'

It was just Mother, Ted and me for lunch, so we ate it in the kitchen. It had been getting hotter all morning, and she'd opened the windows wide to let in a cool breeze.

'What about old Barlow?' said Ted.

'He brings his own sandwiches,' said Mother with a sniff. 'Just as well, really. I can do without mud all over the kitchen floor.'

I hadn't seen the gardener since he'd caught me looking

through the hedge. I shot Mother a quick look, but she seemed to have forgotten him already.

He hasn't told her about me treading on the lilies, I thought. That was a relief.

I was hoping that Ted would let me back into his room after lunch, but as soon as we'd cleared up, Mother held out a shopping bag and a pound note.

'Lamb chops and streaky bacon,' she said. 'I've phoned the butcher. He'll have them ready for you.'

I groaned.

'It's so hot, Mother. I'll roast.'

'No you won't. The walk will do you good. You've got to build up your muscles again. And there's a lot to do today. Your father's bringing a guest home with him tonight. He'll be staying for a while.'

'What guest? Who?'

'Mr Fischer. He's from Germany.'

'Which is he, then — weary or heavy-laden?' said Ted, sidling towards the door before Mother could think up a job for him. She pursed her lips and didn't answer.

I was puffing up the hill on my way back from the butcher's when I heard footsteps behind me. I turned to see Rachel Stern. My heart quickened. This was my chance!

'Hello!' I said. 'You're Rachel, aren't you? You live next door to us. I'm Charity Brown.'

She fell into step beside me.

'I know who you are. You offered us some apples.' I shot a

sideways look at her. She seemed embarrassed. 'You must have thought . . . I mean . . . it was a bit rude, not—'

'Not at all! It's a pain having too many apples. Better than not enough, obviously, but we've got three trees and they're all fruiting like mad, and we don't know what to do with them, and now the plums are ripening, and . . .'

I stopped. I was talking too much. I'd made that mistake with the girls at school.

'It's just that, you know,' she went on, 'my parents – well, my mother – she doesn't know you, and . . .'

Her voice tailed off.

'You don't have to explain a *thing*,' I said happily, 'because as a matter of fact I know exactly what you mean.'

We'd reached our gate.

'Would you like to look round the garden?' I said, desperate to hang on to her. 'I could show you . . .'

She smiled.

'I've been in it lots of times, thank you. Mr Spendlove used to let me and my friend Susi come in and play tennis whenever we liked.'

'Oh. Right,' I said, disappointed.

She flashed me a quick smile.

'Look, you haven't been here long and I bet you haven't discovered everything. Why don't I show *you* some of *my* favourite places?'

For a moment, I thought, *That's cheeky, seeing as this garden's mine*, but I didn't want to lose this chance. I hurried into the kitchen and put the meat away in the fridge (we now had a

70

fridge!), and by the time I came out Rachel had walked down the lawn and was heading for the gnarled old oak tree on the bank above the tennis court. She grabbed hold of a low branch, pulled herself up with practised ease and sat on it, swinging her long, tanned legs and waiting for me to join her.

'This is bad,' I muttered to myself. I hadn't tried climbing anything since I'd been ill and I wasn't sure if my arms would be strong enough to pull me up.

Rachel was too busy watching a squirrel scamper about in the upper branches to notice that I was hesitating. I took a deep breath and attacked the tree with everything I'd got. Though I grazed my knees, it was easier than I'd thought, and a moment later I was sitting unsteadily beside her, clinging to the trunk and trying not to let her see that I was out of breath.

She said, 'Your family must have been really close to Mr Spendlove for him to leave you all this.'

I was just about to give her the usual answer about him wanting to support Dad in doing the Lord's work, but I stopped myself. Was that the real reason? Did I know? If Rachel was going to be a great friend, I would have to be honest with her.

'Actually,' I said, 'we didn't know him very well. You probably knew more about him than we did, living right next door.'

'We hardly knew him at all! Only that he was kind about letting Susi and me play tennis, and that he belonged to a weird little religious sect.'

She must have felt me stiffen because her hand flew up to cover her mouth.

'Oh! I've gone and put my foot in it, haven't I?'

'No,' I said, but my voice had gone tight. 'It's what lots of people think who don't know – who don't understand.' I was going to say, *who haven't accepted the Lord Jesus Christ as their own personal Saviour*, but once again something stopped me. It would be my duty, I knew, to try to bring Rachel to the Lord, but after making such a mess of it with Robert-next-door I realized that it might be better to take things slowly.

I hate these moments, when I feel called upon to witness. My heart starts pounding and my hands go clammy. I know it's not as tough for me as it was for those early Christian martyrs, trying to stand still and pray while drooling lions padded forward to eat them – although, honestly, I knew how they felt.

But Rachel said something no one had said to me before.

'I do understand, actually.'

I was so surprised that my head whipped round and I nearly lost my balance. I had to grip the oak tree's thick trunk to stop myself toppling off the branch.

'I'm Jewish, in case you didn't know,' she went on. 'Lots of people think we're crazy. My family isn't even religious, but that hasn't stopped some people thinking that we're actually wicked.'

'Crazy? Wicked? What do you mean?'

'There have always been awful stories made up about Jewish people. Really weird, sick things. You can't imagine anyone believing them, but lots of people do. They did in Germany, anyway. And even here in Britain quite respectable people can be nice on the surface, but say horrible things behind our backs. And not always behind our backs. Susi and her mother wanted to join a tennis club, but they told her straight out to her face that they "didn't accept Jews". Look I don't want to talk about all that. Papa and Mutti don't discuss it in front of me in case I get too upset.'

'Papa and . . . ?'

'Mutti. It's what I call my mother.'

'But I don't see how anyone can think those things about Jewish people,' I said, my slow mind trying to catch up with her. 'They – you're – the Chosen People. It says so in the Bible. Though actually I've never understood what that means.'

Rachel's lips twitched into a little smile. 'Neither have I, really. Something about being chosen to be close to God?' Her smile dropped. 'Anyway, sometimes it feels like we were chosen to be murdered.'

This sounded a bit blasphemous to me, and dreadfully sad too, but I was totally out of my depth, so I didn't answer.

'Look, Charity,' she said after a short silence. 'You can be as Christian as you like. But please don't try to convert me or anything.'

'No, no of course not! I wouldn't dream of it,' I said.

I wasn't sure if that was a sort of lie, because, after all, it was my duty to try, but it was a weight off my mind, quite frankly.

To fill the awkward silence I said, 'Thanks for showing me this great perching place. Would you like to look round the house? It's full of incredible stuff. The attic . . .'

She was already climbing down the tree.

'Love to! I was afraid you'd never ask. I'll race you to the house.'

'Don't try too hard,' I called after her. 'You'll win anyway.'

It had been my dream to show off Gospel Fields and all its treasures to a friend, but when we'd almost reached the open front door, a taxi came round the corner of the drive and pulled up in a scatter of gravel. Mother must have been listening out for it because she hurried outside.

Dad got out first and fished in his pocket to pay the driver. He was followed by a tall man, almost as thin as a skeleton.

'Who's that?' whispered Rachel.

'I don't know,' I whispered back. 'It might be the first of the weary.'

'Who's weary? What do you mean?'

'I think he's one of the people who are going to stay with us. Dad said we could only accept the house if we made it into a refuge for the weary and heavy-laden, to give them rest.'

Rachel turned a shining face to me.

'That's – well, I think that's lovely!'

'Yes, I suppose it is,' I said unwillingly, but I'd realized that actually I didn't think it was lovely at all. I felt invaded, as if Gospel Fields wasn't really ours any more, when I'd only just got used to it being home.

Mother bent to pick up the man's suitcase, but he stepped in quickly to prevent her. He said something that sounded like, 'Bitter . . .' in an unfamiliar accent. It was only one word, but it was enough to make Rachel gasp and take a step backwards.

'He's German!' she hissed. 'What's he doing here? Why have you invited a Nazi to your house?'

And before I could stop her, she'd run off round the corner of the house and disappeared.

I marched inside after Mother and the German man, feeling furiously resentful. Finally I'd started to actually make a friend and she'd been snatched away almost at once. I tried to slip past them to go upstairs to my room, but Mother said, 'Charity, come and meet Mr Fischer.'

The man put out a bony hand to shake mine. I stuck it out unwillingly. He bowed over it and said, 'Good morning, Fräulein.'

'Hello,' I said rudely. Then I wrenched my hand back and stormed out of the house again.

I was by the back door whacking a clump of weeds with a stick, sweating with heat and fury, when Mother appeared at the kitchen window.

'Come inside,' she commanded.

'Why?' I said rebelliously.

'Just do as you're told.'

There was an ominous snap in her voice.

'Sit down,' she said, pointing to a chair by the table.

I sat. She sat too.

'How could you be so rude to Mr Fischer?' she demanded. 'I was ashamed, Charity. *Ashamed.*'

'He's German.' I scowled. 'He shouldn't be here. You can't expect me to be polite to a *German*.'

'It's why the Stern girl ran off, I suppose,' said Mother.

'Of course she did! Do you blame her?' I was nearly shouting.

'Calm down, Charity. You know nothing about Mr Fischer. He's our guest. The Lord has sent him to us. I was afraid this would happen. You've been filling your head with ridiculous fantasies ever since we moved into this house, imagining you're now a rich, grand lady, and the minute we start putting Gospel Fields – which is not ours but *the Lord's* – to its proper use, you—'

I leaped to my feet, scarlet with fury.

'That's so unfair! You don't know what you've done! Rachel was going to be my friend, the first proper one I've ever had. You've got no idea what it's like, trying to be a Lucasite at school! The others think I'm peculiar because I'm not allowed to go the cinema and I can't go on about all the films I've seen, and when I told them that I wasn't allowed to cut my hair and that it's sinful to wear make-up, they all laughed at me. I tried to persuade a girl called Monica to give her heart to Jesus, but she was so mean, so – *hateful* . . .'

I bolted back out into the garden, wiping my eyes on my sleeve. I hobbled to the oak tree, struggled up it awkwardly and perched on Rachel's favourite branch. Mother's words were poison in my ears.

And, anyway, I wasn't rude! I shouted at her in my head. *You were rude to bring a wicked German into our house! And I haven't had fantasies about being rich and grand. Not much. Not really. Not . . .*

A quiet voice near my foot made me start.

'Charity, get down. I want to talk to you.'

76

Dad was looking up at me. I knew that quiet tone. It was scarier than Mother's anger. I slid down out of the tree, painfully scraping the backs of my legs, and stood in front of him, feeling stupid and small and furious, as if I was five years old again.

Dad sat down on the grass and leaned against the tree trunk.

'Sit beside me, Charity. Here in the shade. I'm going to tell you about Mr Fischer.'

'What about him?' I said, sitting opposite him, as far away as I dared.

'Karl Fischer is German,' Dad began.

'Exactly!' I burst out. 'That's why—'

He put his hand up to silence me.

'Please, Charity. Just listen.'

I took in a deep breath and let it out again with exaggerated patience.

'He comes from a town in East Germany. It was bombed by the Royal Air Force, *our* Air Force. Karl Fischer was out at a meeting when the attack happened. A bomb fell on his house and his wife and only daughter were killed. His little girl was two. She would have been about your age now.'

'Oh, but—'

'Karl was a Christian pastor. I'm ashamed to say that most pastors went along with the Nazis. They even welcomed them! Karl didn't. He dared to preach against Hitler in his church. He was arrested by the Gestapo and forced to join the army. He was sent to the eastern front, the most dangerous place for German soldiers, where he was captured by the Russians. He spent years in a Russian prisoner-of-war camp, forced to do heavy labour, and almost starved to death. Are you listening, Charity?'

I gave a very small nod. I wasn't enjoying this at all.

'He was sent back to Germany,' went on Dad, 'and tried to rebuild his old church, preaching the gospel in the open air, but he was arrested and imprisoned by the communist East German government on charges of sedition. He was extremely ill in prison and was released only a few weeks ago. He's the bravest man I know and one who has suffered terribly.'

I sat in silence, trying to take this in.

'What's he doing staying with *us*, though, Dad?' I said at last, knowing even as I spoke that I sounded like a spoilt child.

'I've asked him to set up a branch of our International Bible Mission in Germany,' Dad said. 'In West Germany, first, and then, God willing, in the communist east. He arrived in London yesterday to discuss it, but the journey was too much for him. He almost fainted in my office. He's come to us for a time of rest, to eat your mother's good food, to meditate in this lovely garden and let God do His healing work on his mind and body. He'll be with us for quite a while, I should think.'

'I'm sorry,' I said at last. 'I wasn't nice to him. But Rachel—'

'I know. Your mother told me. But Karl Fischer is not a Nazi. He's a hero, who spoke against Hitler's tyranny. And helping to heal him is the Lord's work, Charity. Nothing must come in its way. But —' and then he gave me one of his most winning smiles, the one that makes cats purr and old ladies giggle with delight — 'your mother told me, too, about the difficulties you have had at school, and how much you want Rachel to be your friend. Why don't you explain to her that Karl Fischer isn't her enemy? That he put his life at risk to help the Jewish people in Germany? If she's a friend worth having, she'll understand.'

After he'd gone, I climbed the tree again and sat leaning against the trunk. There was a lot to think about and I didn't like my thoughts at all.

CHAPTER SEVEN

Mr Fischer wasn't the only person to arrive that day. Just before dinner a tiny Baby Austin car pulled up in front of the house, driven by a young man with a moustache. Hope, looking maddeningly cool, unfurled her long legs from the front seat, flicked back her blonde ponytail, dragged her suitcase out of the boot and waved the car and its driver away with a flick of her wrist.

'Hope!' I squealed. 'I thought you weren't coming till next week! Who's that man?'

'Oh, no one,' she said. 'Someone's brother. I made him bring me back early from music camp. Where's Mother? Do you think she saw him? She's bound to make a fuss.'

'Don't worry. She's in the kitchen. It's on the other side of the house. Why are you worried, anyway? Isn't he a Lucasite?'

'No, though I don't see why it should matter. He only gave me a lift. What's it like here anyway? I've been dying to come home and see it all.'

I took her arm and dragged her in through the front door.

'Incredible! Every cupboard and drawer is full of marvellous things – and the attic! It's . . . oh, you should see Ted's room! I can't even describe it. And there's a girl next door called Rachel Stern. She's . . .'

Hope wasn't interested in Rachel Stern. She shook off my arm and stood quite still, taking in the glories of the hall.

'Come on, I'll show you your room,' I said. 'You'll like it. It's got a view of—'

Mother came out of the kitchen.

'Hope!' she said. 'We weren't expecting you today. Is everything all right? Why didn't you ring? I'd have ordered more chops for dinner.'

I always longed for Hope to come home, but when she did I was usually disappointed. We'd played together all the time when were younger and I sort of forgot, every time she went away, that she was three years older than me. I'd plan all kinds of things to do together, but once she was back I wouldn't even bother suggesting them.

Hope was growing up much faster than me. Those three years between us seemed to stretch out further and further, until she seemed impossibly old and sophisticated. Annoyingly, she kept getting slimmer and prettier. She was brilliant at sewing, and the flowery summer dresses she made for herself looked elegant on her, while the hand-me-downs that came to me went limp whenever I put them on. Men had started noticing Hope. Lenny Bissel, at the Meeting, went red and swallowed nervously whenever he saw her, making his Adam's apple bob up and down in his scrawny neck.

I was dying to take Hope upstairs so I could show her her bedroom, but she'd run into the drawing room and had seen the grand piano. I didn't have a chance after that. She lifted the lid of the piano stool (I hadn't even realized you could) and started taking out sheets of music.

'Beethoven sonatas! A whole book of them!'

She set the book on the stand, opened the keyboard and started playing.

'Do that later,' I said. 'Come and—'

Too late. Mother had heard us. She was standing at the door, pink with heat.

'For goodness' sake, girls. There's the table to set and the lettuce to wash and—'

'Coming, Mother,' we chanted together, in the way we'd always done.

Once again, showing off the house would have to wait.

Mr Fischer was very quiet at dinner, and after a while we all stopped trying to make him talk. We had nearly finished our pudding (stewed apples, of course) when everything went weirdly dark. Mother was offering seconds of custard as the first streak of lightning lit the room, and a second later a deafening thunder clap made the windows rattle. I love thunderstorms, so I'd twisted round to look out of the window behind me, hoping to see another bolt of spectacular lightning. I didn't notice what was going on until a clattering noise made me turn round. Mr Fischer had dropped his spoon into his pudding bowl, splashing custard over the table. He'd gone a horrible green colour and his hands were shaking.

Ted knew what to do. He put a hand on Mr Fischer's arm.

'Quite a storm, isn't it?' he said, in a calm voice. 'Thunder like that – we don't get it very often.'

Mr Fischer didn't seem to hear him. A second crack had made him start so violently I thought he might dive under the table.

'Nice meal, Ma, thanks,' said Ted, getting up. 'Do you mind if Mr Fischer and I go into the drawing room? It might be quieter in there, on the other side of the house.'

He crooked his hand under Mr Fischer's elbow to encourage him to stand and they went out of the room, with Dad following on behind.

'Well!' said Mother. 'How unfortunate. Shell shock, I suppose.'

'But shell shock was from the war,' I objected. 'That finished years ago.'

The thunderstorm was moving away, the rumbles getting quieter.

'The after-effects of war go on and on,' said Mother. She gave me a meaningful look. 'Mr Fischer is going to need a lot of understanding from us all.'

She was pressing one hand against the side of her head as if she had a headache. I was too irritated to feel sympathetic.

'I *know*, Mother,' I burst out hotly. 'I said I'm sorry. And I will extend to Mr Fischer –' I searched round for the right phrase – 'the hand of Christian fellowship.'

'Good,' said Mother. 'Mind you do. Clear the table, girls.

The washing-up won't do itself. You too, Hope. You're not at school now, being waited on hand and foot.'

Hope gave Mother a puzzled look, surprised by her snappy tone, then picked up a pile of plates.

'Wasn't Ted *wonderful*?' she breathed. 'He knew just what to do.'

I'd thought the same, but I wasn't going to encourage Hope by saying so. She hero-worshipped Ted because she'd never been around long enough to discover the dark recesses of his soul.

'I suppose they had people like Mr Fischer in the veterans' home where he had that last holiday job,' I said. 'Just think what it's like in a thunderstorm with all of them sitting in a row and shaking like jellies.'

I was trying to be funny, and it was only when I'd said it that I realized how horrible it sounded, but I got away with it because Hope didn't seem to have heard and Mother had already gone out of the room.

'Why's Mother so cross?' Hope asked as we carried the dirty dishes through to the kitchen.

'I don't know. She's always like that now. Since we moved, anyway.'

'She looks exhausted,' said Hope. 'Not surprising, I suppose, trying to run this place on her own.'

That's another irritating thing about Hope. She's truly kind and notices how other people are feeling. She makes me feel like a selfish, insensitive beast.

I'll show her, I thought, so I pushed past her into the kitchen and said, 'Mother, Hope and I'll do the dishes. Why don't you go and sit down?'

Mother looked at me, surprised.

'That's very thoughtful of you, Charity. Thank you. Be careful with the glasses. They're the best ones.'

We'd nearly finished washing up when Dad came into the kitchen.

'Hope, dear, can you come and play the piano? We're going to have a time of hymn singing.'

I didn't like the idea of Hope stealing all the limelight.

'What about Mother?' I said. 'She usually plays for the hymns.'

'She has a bad headache. I've sent her off to bed,' said Dad.

'Oh. She didn't say,' I said.

'You know your mother. Never complains. Leave those dishes to drain, Charity.'

Mr Fischer looked better when we went into the drawing room. Now that the storm was over, Ted had opened the windows. Soft, moist air filled the room, bringing with it the scents of the wet garden. Mr Fischer smiled at me and I gave him the widest possible smile back, trying to look really friendly, then was afraid I'd looked insincere and anyway was showing my gums.

I love family hymn singing. We take turns to choose our favourites, and Hope and Ted sing the alto and tenor parts.

Dad handed out the family's hymnbooks, and Hope sat down on the piano stool trying out a couple of scales.

'It's a bit out of tune,' she said.

'Never mind that!' I was eager to get going. 'Why don't we start with . . .' I stopped myself just in time. I'd been about to say 'Onward, Christian Soldiers' (which, if you don't know it, is a terrific hymn with a sort of *thump, thump* marching rhythm), but I realized just in time that it might be tactless to sing about going to war, even if it *was* war against the Devil.

'Forgotten what I was going to say,' I mumbled, hiding my red face in my hymn book.

Mr Fischer looked happier and happier as we sang together, and when Hope at last stood up from the piano, he went across to it himself.

'Is it all right if I play now?' he asked.

He sat down and ran his fingers lovingly over the keys.

'Only a little out of tune, and just the top notes,' he said, and then he began to play.

'But I know this one!' said Hope. 'It's Schubert! The "Good Night" song!' And just like that, without looking at all embarrassed, she stood by the piano and started to sing. In German too.

I'd heard my sister sing before, of course, but I'd never heard her sing like that. Her voice soared and trembled over the notes, and Mr Fischer made the piano talk back to her, the music rising and falling, quieter, then louder, folding round her voice.

When they'd finished, we all sat still for a moment, then Ted started clapping. Mr Fischer turned to face us and I saw that his face was wet with tears.

As I went up to bed, I heard Ted say to Dad, 'I hadn't quite understood what you planned to do with Gospel Fields. I do now, and I'm behind you all the way.'

As a matter of fact, so am I, I thought, and my head was full of noble resolutions as I brushed my teeth and put on my pyjamas.

I got up early the next morning and was downstairs in time to see Dad halfway out of the door on his way to catch the 8.15 to London. Ted had already left for the zoo.

'Your mother's headache's still bad,' Dad said. 'She needs to rest in bed today. Can you girls manage?'

'You can rely on me, Dad,' I said, my chest swelling with determination. 'Is she awake? I'll take her a cup of tea.'

Mother was looking dreadfully pale when I went upstairs. She struggled to sit up when she saw me.

'Is Mr Fischer down yet?' she said wearily. 'I need to—'

'You don't need to do a thing,' I said triumphantly. 'We'll manage. Mr Fischer's still getting up. I heard him. I've set the breakfast out, and Hope and I'll do lunch.'

'Cold ham and beetroot salad,' whispered Mother. 'Get a lettuce from the garden. Everything else is in—'

'. . . the fridge. I know. Look, I've brought you a cup of tea.'

'Oh!' Mother laid her head back on the pillow. 'That's lovely, darling. A bit of a rest, that's all I need.'

She called me darling! I thought, as I tiptoed out of her room. It was unusually gushy for Mother. I felt worried. Was she seriously ill? Did she have a brain tumour? Would I have to nurse her to the end, then run Gospel Fields for the weary on my own?

I met Hope on her way to the bathroom. She was still in her pyjamas.

'Hurry up!' I hissed at her. 'Mother's ill in bed and we've got to do breakfast and lunch and everything!'

She gave me a sleepy smile.

'Don't panic. It'll be fine.'

I wanted to kick her, but to be fair she was dressed and down in the kitchen in double-quick time.

She ran an eye over the breakfast table.

'Well done, Char. Cornflakes, milk, marmalade – here, pass me the butter.'

'What for? What about toast and tea – and should we do eggs?'

She'd taken the butter over to the draining board and was bending over it, too busy to answer.

'I'll put water on for eggs in case,' I said. 'What on earth are you doing?'

She turned to show me the butter transformed into delicate curls, rising in a pyramid from the butter dish.

'We have to curl butter at school when visitors come to tea,' she explained.

'Well, good for you,' I said sharply. 'But do you know how to boil eggs?'

'Not really.'

'Just as well that I do, then, isn't it?' A floorboard creaked in the kitchen corridor. 'Quick! Mr Fischer's coming! Put the kettle on!'

*

Mr Fischer didn't seem to mind about the toast being a bit burned and the eggs being nearly hard. He was quiet and seemed shy, and after breakfast he took a book and wandered out into the garden. I watched as he walked slowly down the slope towards the wood, pausing to look up at a bird perched in one of the two old cherry trees that made islands of shade in the enormous expanse of lawn. He stood for a moment at the top of the bank and gazed down across the tennis court, then walked slowly back and settled himself on the old stone seat beside an arch of soft pink roses. He opened his book at last, but instead of bending his head to read, he just stared straight ahead. Every now and then I looked out to check if he'd moved. He hadn't, and never seemed to be reading either, but just sat there, as still as a statue.

'Do you think he's all right?' I asked Hope when the morning was half gone and he was still there. 'What'll we do if he starts shaking again?'

'Goodness knows,' said Hope. 'Look, Char, we don't need to do any more housework. You've dusted the dining room and I've swept the kitchen floor. Can you manage the lunch on your own? I thought I'd ask him if he'd play for me again.'

I nearly felt cross, then remembered about being noble.

'If you want to,' I said.

She gave me a hug.

'You're lovely! Call me if you need me.'

Hope takes after Dad in being a hugging kind of person. I nearly like being hugged, but sometimes it's too much and I wish people would stop.

I hadn't realized, till I started getting the lunch ready, that I still didn't know what was in all the drawers in the kitchen. I'd never had the chance to poke around on my own without Mother being there. I found china jelly moulds and strange spoons with holes in them, measuring jugs, three sizes of grater and things that didn't seem to have any purpose at all.

I went out to the vegetable garden to pick a lettuce, relieved that it wasn't one of Mr Barlow's days. Most of the lettuces had gone to seed, but a couple of good ones were left. It took me ages to wash the leaves, checking for slugs and bits of dirt. I was feeling pleased with myself when I remembered about pudding. Mother hadn't said anything about that.

I crept upstairs to ask her, but when I peeped in to her bedroom she was asleep.

Blancmange! I thought. *I can do that. No! Plums! They're sure to be ripe by now. We can just eat them as they are.*

I was in the kitchen fetching a bowl when the doorbell rang. Hope was singing too loudly to hear it, so I went through to the hall and opened the door.

Rachel stood outside. She seemed surprised to see me.

'I thought that was you singing.'

'No. It's my sister Hope.'

She shifted her weight from one foot to the other, looking embarrassed.

'I came to say I was sorry I ran off like that. It was rude.'

The music from the drawing room stopped. At any moment, Mr Fischer and Hope might come out.

'It's all right,' I said. 'Look, will you come and help me pick plums? Mother's in bed with a headache and we've got to do lunch and dinner by ourselves.'

I led her round to the side of the house where purple fruit was dropping off the plum tree.

'The thing is,' I began, 'you got it wrong about Mr Fischer. He's not a Nazi at all. In fact — mind that wasp!'

Rachel didn't say anything for a while after I'd finished explaining. Then she said, 'I didn't know there were decent Germans like that. I was in a muddle about it, actually. Papa had an argument with Mutti when I told them about your Mr Fischer. Papa told her she shouldn't jump to conclusions, and Mutti started crying because she can't forget the men who dragged her parents and her sister away to be murdered.'

I gasped, nearly dropping the bowl of plums.

'Murdered?'

'Yes. In a Nazi death camp. Look, I don't want to talk about it.'

'Rachel, I—'

'No, really. Please. I can't bear to think about them. And there's Papa's family too. We still don't know . . .'

It was my turn to be silent. At last I said, 'I'm not surprised you ran away. Actually I'm surprised you came back. Though I'm *really* glad you did. Do your parents know you're here?'

'Yes. Papa sent me. He heard your sister singing. Who was playing the piano?'

'Mr Fischer.'

'Papa thought so. He said that only a German could play Schubert like that. Then Mutti said, "Lots of Nazis liked music too." I was afraid they'd start arguing again, but instead she said it was a crime to play on an out-of-tune piano and gave me the phone number of a piano tuner to give you. I nearly forgot. It's in my pocket.'

'She loves music too, then, your mother?'

'She lives for it! She teaches piano and singing, when she can get pupils. It's not so easy. Lots of ignorant English people don't like going to a Jewish teacher.'

I was outraged.

'That's disgusting!' The bowl of plums was overflowing, so I led the way back to the house. 'I know it's not nearly as bad, but I understand a bit what it's like. The girls at school call me weird and won't sit next to me because I'm a Lucasite, and I — well, it's my duty to try to bring them to the Lord.'

She looked alarmed.

'You said you wouldn't!'

'I won't! Not you. It's different anyway. You're Jewish.'

'Don't *say* that!' Her anger startled me. 'Being Jewish *doesn't* make me different.'

'I didn't mean it that way. Only, well, you've got a religion already, and it's sort of the older brother to Christianity, so there's no point in trying.'

She laughed.

'You're wrong about that. My family aren't religious at all.' We were nearly at the back door. 'But that doesn't mean you can try to convert me,' she added hastily.

I was still trying to digest the idea that you could be Jewish without being religious when she said, 'Do you — I mean, have you – played tennis on the court yet?'

That girl Susi's been getting at her again, I thought, then my heart quickened as I realized that this was the moment for an uncomfortable confession.

'Faith and Hope are going to, when Faith comes home. Ted too, I expect. But I can't – yet.'

'Why not?'

I opened the back door and she followed me into the kitchen. I turned my back to her as I put the plums down. I didn't want to see her face.

'I've had polio,' I said.

I knew she'd gasp and step away from me, and she did.

'It was ages ago!' I went on. 'In January. I'm not infectious any more. Haven't been for months and months. I promise you, Rachel, I'm really not.'

I heard a panicked shuffle, as though she was backing even further away, and I stared resolutely down at the bowl of plums.

'What was it like?'

'It was . . .' I wanted to brush her question off, but I had to be truthful with Rachel. 'It was like – I can't describe it. I was paralysed all over for a while. That was so frightening. I thought I'd never be able to move again. It hurt a lot too. I haven't been to school for months and months. I don't mind that. I hate school anyway. None of the girls like me. It's not only because of trying to convert them. There's this girl, Monica, she's got them all to call me Charity Girl because Mother knitted my school jumper instead of buying it from the uniform people.'

'But – are you all right now?'

'Nearly. I still get puffed out when I try to run. My left leg's a bit weak, and I can't do as much as I used to with my left arm. It'll probably get better eventually. I was quite pleased with myself, actually, for managing to climb your favourite tree. I've done it again lots of times and it's getting easier. It's my favourite tree now too.'

I still hadn't dared look at her.

Someone came into the kitchen. Out of the corner of my eye, I saw that it was Hope.

'Rachel's from next door,' I muttered. 'I've just told her I had polio.'

There was a short silence. I squeezed my eyes tight shut, imagining Rachel, her back to the wall, as far away from me as possible. Hope must have understood at once, because she came up to me and put her arm round my shoulders.

'Lovely to meet you, Rachel. I hope Char's told you how brave she's been? She'll soon be right back to normal. The best thing is that you're less likely to catch polio from her than from anyone else because she had it ages ago and isn't infectious any more, not like someone sitting next to you on the bus who may not even know they've got it.'

I turned at last to look at Rachel. I wasn't sure if she'd believe Hope or not. She was biting her lip, but not looking as scared as I'd feared. When she saw me looking at her, she tried to smile.

'That's awful, Charity. Everyone's terrified at school. We're not allowed to have swimming lessons any more in case we catch it at the pool. I'm really glad you're better.'

There was an awkward silence.

'What lovely plums!' said Hope, picking one out of the bowl and biting into it. 'Would you like to take some home with you, Rachel?'

She'll say no, I thought, *like her mother did with the apples.*

She must have read my mind because she said, 'Yes, please. They're not apples, after all, are they?'

I was so relieved I burst into giggles, and she burst out laughing too.

'What's the matter with you two?' said Hope.

'Nothing,' said Rachel. 'I'd love to take some plums home, if you're sure.'

CHAPTER EIGHT

Mother insisted on getting up in the afternoon, but she still looked pale. When Dad came home, he was shocked to see her out of bed.

'Mother needs proper help in the house, Daddy,' Hope said firmly. She was the only one of us who still called him Daddy. 'You did say, when we moved here—'

'Yes, of course!' Dad ran a hand through his hair. 'But who?'

'I've prayed about this,' said Mother. 'And I discussed it with Olive Prendergast before they went off to Bognor for their holiday. She says that Doris Stebbins is hard up and might welcome the chance to earn some money. Olive said she'd sound her out when she gets back.'

'No!' I shouted before I could stop myself. The thought of prune-faced Ma Stebbins poking her disapproving nose into every corner of our house, snooping in *my bedroom*, was too horrible to be borne.

'She can bring Tabitha with her in the school holidays,' Mother went on. 'She'll be good company for Charity.'

This was dreadful!

'She won't! I can't stand Tabitha!' I protested. 'Why doesn't anyone ever *listen* to me?'

Everyone ignored me. Again.

'I'd need her twice a week,' Mother went on. 'Mondays to help with the laundry and ironing and Thursdays to vacuum.'

'I'll leave it to you to settle it,' said Dad cheerfully. 'Now, girls, let your mother sit down while you sort out the supper. Where's Mr Fischer?'

'In the garden.' I was trying not to scowl. 'He's been out there more or less all day.'

The thought of having Tabitha Stebbins foisted on me for days on end in every school holiday was so awful that I grumbled out loud at any opportunity. In fact, I was almost reconciled to term starting again, even though I'd been dreading it for weeks, so that I wouldn't be at home when Mrs Stebbins came to spy on us.

Mother had been putting off driving the car as she'd been out of practice for so long, but Ted had loudly proclaimed that it was now roadworthy, so on the first day of term she bravely backed it out of the garage, ready to drive me to school.

'Don't get used to me driving you around,' she said as I climbed into the passenger seat. 'This is just till you get your energy back.' She looked me over critically. 'Where's your school jumper?'

'I won't need it. I'll be too hot,' I mumbled.

I had no intention of parading my despised hand-knitted jumper in front of the bullies until I absolutely had to, but there was an autumn nip in the air and I had to make an effort not to shiver.

My heart thumped as I went into the school grounds through the tall Victorian pillars. In my polio-fevered nightmares Monica and her minions had swooped on me, shrieking like vampires, their claws out, ready to rip me to shreds. I wanted to turn tail and run, but Monica, bully-in-chief, had already caught sight of me.

'It's Holy Charity!' she shouted across the playground. 'We thought you'd died and gone to Heaven! Where's your halo, Charity Girl? Left it at home with Mummy?'

To my surprise, several of the other girls turned on her.

'Shut up, Monica,' one said.

Another came up to me.

'It's nice to see you, Charity. Was it awful, having polio? Mrs Pearcey told us you'd been really bad with it. She sent a letter to all our parents saying you're not infectious any more and we've got to be understanding.'

I didn't exactly enjoy being patronised, but at least there were no claws in sight. Girls clustered round me, eager to know what polio was really like.

Maybe school won't be so bad, after all, I thought.

I felt like a celebrity that first day back, and it was only as I walked out after the last bell had rung that I realized I hadn't mentioned to anyone about giving their heart to Jesus. In fact, I hadn't witnessed to the Lord at all.

Mother was parked a little way along the road. I took my

time getting to the car. I needed to think.

I'm not going to try and convert people at school again, I told myself. *It doesn't work and it just irritates everyone.*

It might have been a wicked decision, but once I'd made it a great weight rolled off my shoulders. I actually felt taller and lighter.

I'll witness through doing good deeds instead of words, I explained to Jesus. *I'll just be kind and honest and things like that.*

'How was it?' asked Mother as I opened the car door.

'All right. I've got loads of homework. I'll never catch up with everything I've missed.'

A few days later, Faith phoned. Hope got to the phone first, but I could just hear Faith's voice through the crackle.

'I've only been at Gospel Fields for a night or two since we moved in,' I heard her say. 'I'm off duty this weekend. Tell Mother I'll be home tomorrow.'

'Oh goody,' said Hope. 'I've got to go back to school on Monday. I was afraid I wouldn't see you again.'

There was a short silence, then Faith said, 'I'm bringing a friend home for supper.'

'Are you?' said Hope. 'What's her name?'

Another short silence.

'It's a him.'

Hope's eyes locked on to mine.

'Faith's got a boyfriend!' I shrieked, then clamped my hand over my mouth so I could hear more.

'Sorry,' Hope said hurriedly. 'There's a – a cat or something that's got into the house and it's making an awful noise.'

I made a superhuman effort to control myself.

'His name's Justin. Justin Fraser,' I heard Faith say. 'He's a doctor. Tell Mother not to make a fuss. Look, I've got to go. And you can inform Charity, or whatever that cat's called, that if she embarrasses me in front of Justin I'll never talk to her again.'

Faith's news set Mother whirling off in an anxious spin.

'A doctor!' I overheard her say to Dad. 'I wonder if he's thinking about Africa? The mission hospitals are crying out for staff.'

She started at once on a major programme of housework. To my relief there had been no more talk of Mrs Stebbins. I was secretly hoping that she'd turned down the offer of a job, after all, and that Mother would find someone else.

'You'd have thought this Justin fellow was the Admiral of the Fleet coming to carry out an inspection,' grumbled Ted, who had had to spend the evening polishing the brass fender in the drawing room.

I couldn't wait to get home from school the next day in case Faith and Justin arrived home early.

Mother was in the kitchen, looking flustered.

'The soup's gone off,' she said. 'I left it out accidentally overnight. What'll we do for a first course?'

'Something with fish,' suggested Hope, coming in behind me. 'We always have fish on Fridays at school.'

'Fish?' Mother looked round wildly. 'We've only got tinned sardines!'

'Sardines on toast!' said Hope triumphantly. 'Little fingers of toast with mashed sardines and a sliver of lemon on top. I had them at the Dalrymples. They looked awfully smart. But you don't need a starter. Faith said not to fuss.'

'What's that smell?' I asked.

'The Hawaiian roast!' cried Mother, making a dash for the oven. 'Hope, have you polished the glasses? And where are you going with those scissors?'

Hope smiled sweetly at her.

'Into the garden. I've cut roses for the table. I left them outside.'

Mother turned to me.

'Upstairs with you, Charity. Put on your Sunday dress. They might be here any minute.'

I pulled a face. My Sunday dress was a hideous lurid tartan. It had looked pretty on Faith, who'd had it first, and lovely on Hope, but by the time it had come down to me it was limp and faded, and the gaudy colours didn't suit me at all. Anyway, before I had time to move, the doorbell went.

'They're here!' said Mother, whipping off her apron and tucking a strand of hair into the bun at the back of her head.

I pushed past her down the kitchen corridor and into the hall. Through the open front door I glimpsed Hope with an armful of roses talking charmingly to a tall young man with a lock of dark hair falling over his forehead. But my eyes were riveted on Faith, who had come inside.

'You've cut off your hair!' I wailed. 'And it's gone all curly! But that's – that's unscriptural, Faith! How could you?'

She ignored me. Her eyes were on Mother.

'Hello, dear,' said Mother. 'Well. Quite a surprise. I suppose short hair is more practical for nursing.'

I swivelled round to stare at her. Was she going to condone this lapse in godly behaviour?

Justin came into the hall with Hope behind him.

'How do you do, Mrs Brown?'

His smile showed his even, white teeth. His eyes were a deep, glowing brown and I saw that he was dreadfully handsome. I mean 'dreadfully' too, because it's my belief that you can't trust handsome men. Aunt Josephine says that good looks are a serious temptation. They make a man think too much of himself and be all puffed up with vanity. Every time.

Ted came whistling down the stairs with his hands in his pockets.

'Hello,' he said to Justin. 'Are you the boyfriend?'

Faith went scarlet and shot Ted a look that would have struck anyone less thick-skinned dead on the spot. Justin only smiled his wicked smile again and said, 'I suppose I am. Are you the brother?'

I don't know why that made me giggle. It just did. And once it started I couldn't stop. It happens sometimes. A bubble starts inside me and it grows and grows until I'm gasping and my eyes are streaming and I'm laughing so hard I can hardly breathe.

'Take no notice of Charity,' said Ted. 'She's thirteen.

Adolesc-ing all over the place.'

Hope grasped my arm and dragged me away into the kitchen. She shut the door behind us and shook me.

'Stop it! Stop! Or you'll set me off too!'

'Did you see . . . Faith's . . . face when Ted said "boyfriend"?' I gasped out.

'No. But poor Faith. Ted's so embarrassing. What did you think of Justin, anyway?'

The giggles had gone, leaving only hiccups behind.

'I don't like him,' I said.

'Why ever not?'

'He's too handsome. And he's made Faith cut off her hair.'

'You don't know he made her do it. She might have decided herself. Anyway, I think it suits her. It curls round her head really nicely.'

'But it's *wrong*, Hope! It says in the Bible—'

'It says lots of things in the Bible we don't worry about any more. It actually says that you're not supposed to plant more than one kind of seed in the same place. So according to the Bible, we should be growing all lettuces or all cabbages in the vegetable garden and not a few of each. But that's just ridiculous, isn't it?'

I felt the ground heave under my feet. What was wrong with my family? Ted was refusing to go to the Bible College and was listening to sinful music in the attic, Faith had cut off her hair and Hope was doubting the Bible! Was I the only member of our family to stay true to the Lord? Then I remembered how I'd decided not to talk about Jesus at school. My brain was spinning in confusion.

Hope was trimming the stems of the roses.

'Aren't there any vases in this house?' she asked.

I opened a cupboard to reveal three rows of them.

'Goodness! What beauties!' she said.

She lifted out a midnight-blue one and began to arrange the flowers.

'Anyway,' I said, 'if Faith marries Justin, it won't be just us any more. She'll go away and everything will be different. She'll even stop being a Brown. Faith Fraser. It sounds silly!'

'At least it's Scottish,' said Hope. 'Like Dad.'

'All right,' I conceded, 'but . . .'

I stopped. There were more voices in the hall.

'Dad's home,' said Hope, picking up the vase and setting off for the dining room. 'Someone's with him too.'

The new visitor was tall and broad-shouldered with a weather-beaten face.

'This is very kind of you, Mrs Brown,' he was saying, grasping Mother's hand and pumping it vigorously up and down.

I saw Mother wince as she pulled her hand away.

'I met Dr Sturges at Waterloo station,' Dad said breezily. 'His ship from South Africa docked at Southampton this morning, and the people who were supposed to meet him off the boat train had got the date wrong. They're not expecting him till tomorrow. He stopped me to ask if I knew of a cheap hotel, so of course I invited him home to stay. Such a wonderful example of God's providence! Dr Sturges is a missionary in Natal! He's very familiar with our Bible mission work!'

He watched, beaming, as Dr Sturges shook our hands one after the other. I couldn't understand the look of pain on everyone's face until my own hand was crushed in such a fierce grip that I was afraid half my fingers had been broken.

Mr Fischer came wandering in from the garden.

'Who on earth is that?' Faith whispered in my ear.

'He's German. The first of the weary. He's got shell shock.'

Faith rolled her eyes.

'I can't cope. I'm going to show Justin round the garden.'

There was no time to do sardine toast, after all, because Mother had to cut the burned bits off the Hawaiian roast and cut up more pineapple, which had got shrivelled in the oven. She'd made me go upstairs to change into my Sunday dress, and by the time I came down again everyone was sitting round the table.

'So good to have you all with us this evening,' said Dad, after he'd finished saying grace. He lifted the carving knife to start on the ham. 'Where do you worship, Justin? Which is your home Meeting?'

Faith took a deep breath.

'Justin isn't a Lucasite, Dad. He's Church of England.'

To do our father justice, the knife only stopped moving for a couple of seconds.

'His uncle's the Bishop of Khartoum,' added Faith nervously.

Dr Sturges's face had closed at the mention of the Church of England, and the mention of a bishop made him scowl.

'Well, young man,' he boomed, 'so you're going to be a

doctor? Bound for the mission field, I hope?'

Who does he think he is? I thought furiously. *He's acting as if he owns the place.*

Justin took the plate offered to him and passed the roast potatoes to Mr Fischer.

'No,' he said calmly.

'Justin's specializing in anaesthetics,' said Faith.

'Good, good,' said Dad. 'Relieving pain! Helping the suffering! Such a noble—'

'Not much call for anaesthetics in our mission hospital,' interrupted Dr Sturges. 'The natives don't feel pain like we do.'

Mr Fischer, who had said nothing until now, dropped his fork with a clatter on to his plate.

'You can't mean—' began Mother.

Dr Sturges put up a hand to silence her.

'I've lived in Natal for thirty years. I know the African.'

'Which African would that be?' asked Justin, looking deceptively innocent. 'If you've lived in Natal for a while, I should imagine you know quite a few. Is this person a particular friend of yours? Or a patient? Why doesn't he – or is it a she – feel pain? Surely there's something wrong. Shouldn't you investigate the cause?'

'Don't be ridiculous.' Dr Sturges's face was going red. 'You know what I mean.'

'But I'm not sure that *I* do,' cut in Faith, copying Justin's innocent manner. 'All human beings are biologically identical. We all feel pain the same way. It's been proved again and again. But you seem to have made a fascinating discovery about Africans! Do explain.'

Dr Sturges recovered himself.

'Generally speaking,' he said, 'the African—'

Mr Fischer's quiet voice cut across the dinner table.

'I believe we have heard enough of your racist theories, Herr Doktor. You speak like a Nazi. I had hoped never to hear such talk again.'

Dr Sturges was reaching across Hope to help himself to the last spoonful of peas, but she deftly pushed the dish out of his way.

He frowned at her, then fixed his eyes on Mr Fischer.

'Oh, you know, the Nazis weren't wrong about everything. They went too far, I suppose, but the Jews brought it upon themselves, with all their—'

Everyone had frozen, their forks halfway to their mouths.

'Dr Sturges, I really must protest . . .' began Dad.

I couldn't keep quiet any longer.

'The Sterns next door are Jewish!' I burst out. 'And the Nazis murdered their family and put Mr Fischer in prison. He's the bravest man Dad's ever met. And I don't believe that African people don't feel pain.' I was so furious that I was almost choking. 'You're just – just cruel! You must *like* hurting people! You nearly broke my fingers when you crushed my hand!'

'That'll do, Charity,' said Mother, but she didn't sound cross at all.

Dr Sturges pushed back his chair. His face had gone red.

'I can see I'm not welcome here. This is not the kind of right-thinking home I expected to find in a worker for the missions. Bishop of Khartoum! It's practically Roman Catholic! No, don't see me out. I noticed a hotel near the station. I'll find my own way there.'

We sat in silence as the front door slammed and Dr Sturges's footsteps died away round the corner of the house.

Ted clapped his hands.

'One last broadside from Charity's guns and the enemy ship was holed below the waterline! Went down with all hands!'

Dad was looking troubled.

'How very — very disappointing,' he said. 'I had heard that some of our South African brethren held views that are, let's say—'

'Disgusting!' I crowed, basking in my triumph.

Dad frowned at me.

'Your feelings do you credit, Charity, but you spoke rudely to a guest.' Then he smiled at me. 'However, in this instance—'

'But I am grateful to Fräulein Charity,' broke in Mr Fischer. 'She is someone who has the courage to tell the truth to a bully.'

'Where *did* you find him, Dad?' demanded Ted. 'Who on earth is he?'

'He was wandering about at Waterloo station,' Dad said unhappily. 'Just off the boat train. He looked rather lost. I felt I ought to show him hospitality.'

'He took you for a sucker,' said Ted, shaking his head.

'Don't speak to your father like that!' scolded Mother. 'Girls, clear the table. Charity, bring in the fruit salad from the kitchen, and, Hope, fetch the cream.'

'You've got to admit,' said Hope as she took the cream out of the fridge, 'that, handsome or not, Justin was brilliant standing up to that awful man.'

'I suppose so,' I said unwillingly. But I had something more important than Justin on my mind. Missionaries had always been heroes to me, noble souls, dedicating their lives to spreading the Word of God. Dr Sturges didn't fit the picture at all.

'Are they all like that?' I asked Hope.

'Who? Like what?'

'Missionaries. Like Dr Sturges.'

She shook her head.

'I don't think they can be. Look at Dad. He's a sort of missionary, isn't he? He's not like that awful man at all.'

There was no answer to that, but as I picked up the crystal bowl of fruit salad and followed Hope out of the kitchen my thoughts were picking their way through the broken fragments of a shattered illusion.

Back in the dining room, it was clear that everyone had done their best to forget about Dr Sturges. Justin was saying politely, 'What a beautiful garden you have, Mrs Brown.'

Mr Fischer smiled at him.

'It is a blessed place of beauty and quietness. I feel its healing power every day.'

'It's only peaceful and quiet on the surface,' said Ted. 'There's a battle royal going on right under our noses in the insect world. Isn't that right, Dad?'

He was trying to make up for calling Dad a sucker, I could tell.

'What did you say?' said Dad. He was still looking shaken.

'Insects. In the garden. What they get up to,' said Ted.

'Ah, yes. I haven't had time to study them closely since we moved here,' said Dad, 'but there will be plenty of activity with the spiders now that it's September. The mating season, you know, when the males are wandering round looking for females.'

Faith choked. She'd gone bright red. Hope smothered a burst of laughter.

'Do your parents have a garden, Justin?' Mother said hastily.

'A small one. They live in Wimbledon,' said Justin.

At least, I think that's what he said, but I can't be sure because an attack of the giggles was rising inside me again.

'Got to go to the lavatory!' I managed to say, and dashed out of the dining room, making it up the stairs and into my bedroom, where I collapsed onto the bed and buried my face in the pillow to muffle my hysterical laughter.

I calmed down at last and met Hope in the hall, carrying the last dishes into the kitchen from the dining room.

'Ted's taken Justin upstairs to see his model yacht,' she said, 'and Faith's crying in the kitchen.'

I went to see for myself.

Faith was marching up and down, her face wet with tears.

'I hate this family!' she was shouting. 'You've ruined everything! How could Dad have brought such a – such a *monster* home? And Ted saying "boyfriend", and Dad going on

110

about mating spiders!' She turned on me. 'And did you *have* to tell everyone you needed the lavatory?'

I was stung.

'That's so unfair. I got rid of Dr Sturges for you, didn't I?'

'Yes, by being terribly rude!' Faith wrenched a handkerchief out of her pocket and blew her nose. 'You don't understand! Justin's family is very – very respectable!'

'And we're not respectable?' I put in hotly.

'His father's a general in the army and his mother does embroidery. He doesn't have any brothers and sisters, and their flat is full of antiques!'

'What matters,' said Mother, 'is not his parents' furniture but his Christian faith. Has he given his heart to Jesus, dear?'

'Yes! He's a true, noble Christian! Just because he doesn't talk about it all the time . . . And, anyway, I thought perhaps he'd given his heart to me, but now he won't want to have anything more to do with me!'

She ended on a wail.

Ted came into the kitchen.

'The boyfriend says he's got to go,' he announced. 'On duty early tomorrow. What's the matter with you, Faith? He's a good chap. I like him. I came to tell you that he's gone into the garden with Mr Fischer to look for you. He said to ask you if you'd walk down to the station with him.'

'He did?' Faith lifted her head out of her handkerchief.

'Quick!' said Hope. 'Wash your face with cold water. You don't want him to know you've been crying.'

It had been raining all day, but it had cleared while we were having supper, and now a golden glow from the setting sun poured in through the windows. Ted went off to the garage to tinker with the Rover, Hope made Mother sit down with a cup of tea, then she and I tackled the clearing up.

I took a tray into the dining room to collect the last of the glasses. Dad and Mr Fischer were standing at the window looking out into the garden.

'I'm sorry to have subjected you to such a man,' Dad was saying. 'I was appalled! To think that a Christian – a *missionary* – could have such views!'

Mr Fischer smiled warmly at him.

'I learned, in our time of suffering in tyranny in Germany, that you cannot tell a good person by the label they bear. I have known saints who have never stepped inside a church, but in whom the love of God is warm, and so-called Christians who welcomed the Nazis.'

Dad's shoulders were hunched.

'I sometimes wonder,' he said in a low voice, 'if I truly understand . . .'

I was desperate to hear more, but I accidentally dropped a spoon. Dad turned round.

'Clearing up, Charity. Good, good,' he said with his usual cheerfulness.

'Iver, the evening is beautiful. Perhaps we could walk around your garden and talk more together,' Mr Fischer suggested diffidently.

They went out into the hall, leaving the dining-room door open.

'What did you think of Faith's young man?' I heard Dad say.

'She loves him, I think. And you, my friend, what did you think? He is not in your community . . .'

They had gone too far for me to hear Dad's answer.

The clearing up took ages, and we'd only just finished when Faith burst into the kitchen through the back door. It was almost dark outside by now, but she seemed to bring light inside with her. Her face was full of colour and her newly cut hair was curling wildly round her head.

'Where's Mother?' she asked breathlessly.

'Faith? What's happened? You've gone all pink, and your hair . . .' began Hope.

'Justin's asked me to marry him!' announced Faith ecstatically. 'Look!'

She thrust out her left hand. A sapphire the colour of the summer sky glinted on her ring finger.

Hope rushed forward to hug her.

'That's so wonderful! Congratulations.'

Faith was watching me over Hope's shoulder.

'Charity?'

'Yes. Lovely.' I was trying to smile, but I couldn't.

'What'll Mother and Dad think?' Faith said anxiously. 'Did they like him? Did they say anything? I know he's not a Lucasite, but . . .'

'I'm sure they'll be fine,' said Hope. 'I mean he's so—'

'Handsome,' I finished for her, trying not to sound gloomy.

Faith was already running out of the kitchen. Now I could hear her excited voice in the hall. Hope darted after her and I was alone.

I felt shaken to my bones. A missionary had turned out to be as bad as a Nazi. Mr Fischer seemed to think that Christians were no better than anyone else. Dad was having doubts about — what? And to cap it all, a vile seducer had invaded our home and was going to carry off my own sister.

My brain was full. I couldn't think about any of it any more. I sneaked up the stairs and took myself off to my room.

CHAPTER NINE

I felt more than ever, as I tossed and turned in bed, trying to get to sleep, that what I needed was a friend. And the one I wanted was Rachel. But how could I get to know her? I wasn't at all sure that she wanted to be friends with me, and now that she knew I'd had polio she'd probably be terrified of catching it too, even though Hope had told her I wasn't infectious any more. After all, who wants to risk spending the rest of their life lying on their back in a hospital inside a huge machine, unable to move a single muscle and breathing through an iron lung?

Quite possibly, God had been eavesdropping on my thoughts because when I woke up the next morning the answer was in my head. Of course! Music lessons! I'd get Mother to ask Mrs Stern to teach me the piano! And once I was in their house I'd have plenty of opportunities to get close to Rachel.

I nearly jumped out of bed and went to find Mother then and there, but I stopped myself just in time. Mother had an uncomfortable way of seeing through me. I was going to have to be subtle.

The problem was that she'd tried to persuade me lots of times to learn the piano and I'd always refused.

'It's such a useful skill,' she'd kept on telling me. 'Pianists are always in demand for accompanying hymns. It would be a service to the Lord, Charity.'

'But we don't have a piano at the Morning Meeting,' I'd objected. 'Mr Tubbs says it would be worldly.'

'That only applies to the Breaking of Bread,' said Mother. 'There are plenty of other occasions, as well you know.'

The thought of plunking away on the piano while the Lucasites ground out hymns hadn't attracted me at all. Hope being so good at music had put me off too. I hated the thought of being compared to her all the time. But since Mr Fischer had come to stay I'd started to feel differently. He played the piano in our drawing room every day, sometimes for hours at a time, and the music was so beautiful that I had to stop and listen whenever I passed through the hall. Perhaps I had an unsuspected talent that Rachel's mother might discover and reveal to an astonished world.

I got dressed and went slowly downstairs, trying to work up my strategy. I'd start by putting Mother off her guard.

She was in the kitchen, slicing bread for breakfast.

'You're up early for a Saturday,' she said.

'What do you think about Faith and Justin?' I said. 'He isn't even a Lucasite. Don't you mind?'

She pulled out a small saucepan and put water on to boil for the eggs.

'Obviously, it's not – I mean, it's easier all round for family members to stay together within our community, but you all have to find your own way in life. The decisions you make, for good or ill, are yours.'

'You think marrying Justin's for ill?' I was trying to work out what she meant.

'I didn't say that, dear. We must pray that Faith and Justin will find true happiness in a Christian marriage. It's our task to support—'

I was getting bored.

'Well, I don't like him,' I interrupted.

That startled her.

'Why not?'

'He's too handsome. And — and she'll go away and our family won't be just us any more.'

She laughed.

'It'll be your turn one day. You'll think differently then. Now, go and get the butter out of the fridge.'

'Mother,' I said, keeping my back to her as I opened the fridge door, 'I've changed my mind about piano lessons. I'd like to have them, after all.'

'What brought this on?' She sounded surprised.

'I like hearing Mr Fischer play. I just — I don't know. It's beautiful, that's all.'

'All right, dear. I'll have a word with Olive Prendergast. She used to teach piano. We'll see if she can fit you in.'

I whipped round, the butter dish nearly falling from my hands. This was awful! The horrible memory of the Prendergasts' sitting room with its sickly-green wallpaper and overstuffed sofa leaped into my mind. I could practically hear Mrs Prendergast's old pug dog wheezing and snuffling round my ankles.

'But – but they live right at the top of Oak Lane,' I said, thinking rapidly. 'I'm not sure I can manage to walk all that way uphill yet. I was just thinking – Mrs Stern's only next door and she's a piano teacher. I thought – I mean, I just – it would be easy, that's all.'

She gave me a sharp look.

'You seem very interested in the family next door.'

I shrugged, trying to look casual.

'If you don't think it's a good idea . . .'

'No, it is a good idea, Charity. I'll write a note to Mrs Stern. On second thoughts, I'll go and see her myself.'

You want to check up on them, I thought. *To see if they're too weird and worldly.*

I wasn't surprised. She'd never got over Robert-next-door's mother calling up the spirits of the dead just over our garden fence.

What with all the fuss over Faith and Justin and the need to get Hope's trunk packed for her return to school, I expected Mother to forget about Mrs Stern, but there was no point in nagging her until things had calmed down.

It was a strange morning. Faith came down to breakfast looking pale. Last night's raptures had worn off and she kept glancing nervously across at Dad.

Family worship was longer than usual. Dad made us recite

three whole chapters of the Bible, then he prayed a lot about guidance and making good decisions. I'd woken up hoping that Faith would see sense and send Justin the Seducer packing, but as Dad droned on I started to worry that he might make her break things off and then she'd be unhappy forever and go into a decline and die of disappointment. Also, I always got a pain in my weak leg when I knelt on it for too long. I hadn't liked to mention this in case everyone thought I was making a fuss.

When it was over at last, Dad said, 'Faith, come into my study. We need to have a chat.'

Faith went even paler and I heard her whisper to Hope, 'Wish me luck.' That made me frown. The Lucasites don't approve of luck. It's superstition. Everything that happens is supposed to be the will of God. No counting magpies or avoiding ladders for us.

The house seemed quiet after that. Ted went back up to the attic. Hope started sorting out her clothes to pack for school. Mr Fischer disappeared as usual to read in the garden, and Mother sent me up to my room to do my homework, which was slightly annoying because I'd intended to do it anyway.

I was beating my brains fruitlessly over some algebra problems when Mother came in.

'I've just been to see Mrs Stern,' she said.

My heart leaped.

'What did she say?'

'I had the feeling she was interviewing *me*,' Mother said, looking rather offended. 'She seemed worried about your polio, in case you were still infectious. I told her that your school would hardly have let you go back if you had been. Then Mr Stern—'

'Professor Stern.'

'Yes, well, Professor Stern came in. He seems nice enough, but I must say the house is peculiar. Some of the pictures on the walls – modern art, I suppose.'

'Yes, but what—'

'Then she wanted to know about Hope, where she'd learned to sing like that. "The voice of an angel," she said. Kind of her, but rather overdramatic. And she started on about how she'd trained in a conservatory in Austria, though what music's got to do with glasshouses I really can't imagine.'

'But did—'

'Anyway, in the end, she told me her fees, which are very reasonable, I must say.'

'So will she—'

'Yes, I suppose so. But, Charity, when you're outside our own community you need to be on your guard. You've only been into Lucasite homes up till now. The Sterns will do things differently and there may be new temptations. This will be a test.'

'What new temptations, Mother? What do you mean?'

'I don't know, exactly. There might be wine in the house, or . . . or Rachel might want to make you try on lipstick or something like that.'

I felt a thrill of excitement, but at the same time told myself sternly that, whatever the temptation, I would remain true to the Lord.

'All right, Mother,' I said, 'but when—'

'Wednesdays, after school. Now, get back to your homework. You have a lot of catching up to do.'

Yes! I thought, punching the air after she'd gone. *Yesss!*

It was impossible to go back to algebra after that. I heard footsteps on the gravel outside and looked out of the window to see Faith and Hope walk round to the road, shopping bags in their hands. There were faint bumps upstairs. Ted must be moving things in his room.

I crept downstairs. Mother was in the kitchen, out of earshot. No one would hear me. In the drawing room I lifted the lid of the piano. The black and white keys grinned back at me like a mouthful of teeth. I wasn't sure if they were smiling or snarling. I played a few notes with my right hand. They sounded nice. Then I tried to make a chord using my left hand too. That was harder. I hadn't realized how weak my fingers still were. Would Mrs Stern refuse to teach me if my hands weren't strong enough to play? I wouldn't worry about that now. The main thing was that I'd managed to find my way into next door.

Back in my room, algebraic puzzles fell into place. Everything seemed easier now.

'So what did Dad say?' I asked Faith as, a while later, we set the table for lunch.

'He just asked lots of questions. About Justin, and how I felt, and whether I'd prayed for guidance.'

'And had you?'

'Goodness, Charity, there's no need to look so fierce. I had, as a matter of fact.'

'So you think it's all right, then, marrying out of the Lucasites? Joining the *Church of England*?'

'You needn't say it like that, as if the Church of England was the work of the Devil. They're Christians too.'

'But Mrs Stebbins says—'

'Oh really! That old biddy! She's as narrow as — as — I can't think of anything narrow enough. Dad's not like that at all. In fact, he's a lot more broad-minded than I thought he'd be. He said he was sorry I hadn't been able to find my life's partner in the Lucasites, and he went on a bit about us being such a close community, and our precious traditions and all that, but he ended up by saying he understood that I needed to spread my wings, and that no doubt it was God's will, after all.'

'He said *that*?'

'Yes! I was surprised too. Mainly, though, he wanted to know more about Justin. He's coming to tea this afternoon, by the way. Did Mother tell you?'

'Yes.'

'Don't look like that, Char. Why don't you like him?'

'How did you know?'

She laughed.

'Your face is an open book. Always has been. Well?'

'It's — he's so handsome.'

'Yes!' She clasped her hands ecstatically. 'Isn't he? But what's wrong with that?'

'He'll take you away!' I burst out. 'You won't even be a

Brown any more! I can't bear to think of our family broken up. I'll *miss* you, Faith! You'll be all married and boring and different and someone else.'

To my surprise, she hugged me.

'Oh, that's sweet. But you're being silly. I'm not leaving the family. I'm bringing in another member. You'll have a new brother. Like Ted.'

'I hope not!' I said, revolted. 'Ted's the most embarrassing person I've ever met.'

'He is, isn't he? But, I promise you, Justin's much too kind to embarrass anyone. Wait till you get to know him. You'll love him, honestly. You'd better make your mind up before the wedding, anyway, because I'm going to need you and Hope to be my bridesmaids.'

A bridesmaid! I wasn't sure what I thought about that. A lovely dress, I suppose, but Hope would be dressed the same, and she'd be bound to look much prettier than me. And where would the wedding be? In the Meeting Hall? Or in Justin's Church of England? If so, it was sure to have a long aisle, and I'd have to walk down it behind Faith, and everyone would see me limp.

But the wedding's sure to be ages away, I told myself, *and my leg'll be completely better by then.*

By the time I was standing outside the Sterns's front door the next Wednesday afternoon, I was almost too nervous to knock. I'd been dreading this moment all day. What if I turned out to be hopeless at playing the piano? Even worse, perhaps

Rachel would be annoyed with me, barging into her house like this. I hadn't seen her, after all, since I'd told her I'd had polio.

In fact, it was Rachel who answered the door. She was wearing the brown skirt and yellow jumper of Dame Ellen Pritchard private school, which was a lot smarter than my navy-blue grammar-school uniform.

'I've been waiting for you,' she said, smiling. 'Mutti's just finishing with someone else. Come into the kitchen.'

There was a delicious smell of cinnamon in the kitchen. Some little cakes were cooling on a rack.

'Help yourself,' said Rachel, picking one up and taking a bite. 'Mutti always bakes on Wednesdays. You chose the right day for lessons.'

The cake was still warm and tasted unlike anything Mother made. It was spicy and sweet at the same time. I liked it.

'I've never had a music lesson,' I confessed. 'Is your mother very strict? Ted says I've got a tin ear and I couldn't tell the difference between a nightingale and a quacking duck.'

'That's mean!' said Rachel indignantly.

'You don't know the half of it. Ted's the bane of my life. Having a brother isn't exactly a bed of roses, I can tell you. And now I'm going to get another one because Faith's gone and got engaged.'

'No!' said Rachel, enthralled. 'Lucky you! Maybe they'll have babies and you'll be an auntie.'

I hadn't thought that far ahead, and frankly I didn't want to.

Outside the kitchen, I could hear Mrs Stern saying goodbye to someone.

'I meant to tell you,' I said quickly. 'If you and your friend Susi want to play tennis on our court, it's fine. Any time. I asked Mother.'

She looked a bit embarrassed.

'Actually, I'm not really friends with Susi any more.'

My heart lifted.

'Why not?'

She shrugged.

'I don't know. She just gets me down. She's always on at me about something. Anyway, we were only friends because Mutti thinks she's suitable. Being Jewish and everything.'

I laughed.

'I've got someone like that. Mother's always trying to get us together just because she's a Lucasite. Her name's Tabitha Stebbins. I can't stand her.'

'Tabitha what?'

'Stebbins.'

'Poor girl! What a name.'

I heard the front door click.

'Go on,' said Rachel. 'Time to face the music. Literally.'

Mrs Stern was tidying some sheets of music. The room stretched from the front to the back of house and was really two small rooms with big double doors between them. A grand piano nearly filled the front room. It only left space for two little armchairs with a round table in between.

'So, Charity,' said Mrs Stern. 'You want to play music? That is good.'

I blushed. What would she think of me if she found out I'd only come because I wanted to be friends with Rachel?

'I'll probably be hopeless,' I said. 'I've never tried to learn music.'

She laughed.

'Today there is no *trying*. We talk. Sit down, my dear. Oh! Books on all the chairs again!'

She darted forward to scoop up the piles of books on the two armchairs and added them to the tower on the table. I sat down on one chair and she pulled up the other till she was right in front of me.

'Show me your hands,' she said.

I put mine unwillingly into her outstretched ones. She turned them over. I'd never noticed before how ragged my nails were. And *why* hadn't I scrubbed away the dark crescents under them?

She closed her own hands over mine.

'Grip me,' she said. 'Good. Now squeeze. Yes.' She let my hands go. 'The right hand is not bad. Quite strong but with too much tension. The left one is different, *hein?*'

I felt ashamed, as if I'd done something wrong.

'Yes. You see—'

'I know, my darling. The polio.' She was stroking my left hand gently now. 'I think you have suffered a lot. There was pain, no? And when you were paralysed, I think you were very frightened?'

To my horror, tears pricked my eyes. No one had talked to me like that before. No one had wondered what it had actually

126

felt like to be so ill. No one had ever understood how terrified I'd been. I knew I ought to say something like, *Yes, but the Lord held me always in His tender care*, but I couldn't. Not to this woman, with her deeply lined face, whose kind brown eyes were fixed so steadily on mine.

'We will see if music will have the power to lift from your soul the burden it has carried,' she said.

That sounded embarrassingly flowery to me, but before I could reply she went on, 'Music, I think, has already set your sister free.'

Hope doesn't need to be set free, thank you very much, I wanted to say. *For a start, I'm the one who had polio, not her.* But a second later I thought, *But it's true. Hope is free. I don't quite know why. She just is.*

Mrs Stern must have sensed the sort of battle going on in my head because she laughed and said, 'Now you will listen and I will play for you, and you will tell me which kind of music you like best.'

That's easy, I thought, settling with relief against the dark yellow velvet cushions of the chair.

She sat down at the piano and began to play. As the music flowed around me I allowed myself to look round the room.

It was quite different from any I'd been in before. For one thing, there was no carpet on the floor, which was made of wooden blocks set in a sort of herringbone pattern and polished to a warm, deep brown. Every other house I'd been into had cream-coloured walls, but in this room the walls were a deep yellow, and pictures were crammed together all over them. I could see what Mother had meant about them being peculiar. Some didn't even have people or buildings in them. They were just lines and patterns and dashes of colour. But one picture kept drawing me back, only it wasn't a painting but a photograph. It showed a huge white-painted house standing on a sweep of grass. It had shutters at the windows and a steep overhanging roof. Rearing up behind it was a mountainside covered in fir trees. In front of the house was a middle-aged couple and a young girl. I wished I could go up to it and look more closely, but I knew, even though the photo was on the far side of the room, that the girl was Mrs Stern.

She had been playing the sort of swirling, sweeping music that Hope and Mr Fischer liked, but now she started on something different. It made me sit up and listen carefully.

'You like that one, I think,' she said, when the piece came to an end.

'Yes! It's sort of strong and steady and it's got a shape and there are things happening below the tune all the time.'

She laughed.

'A good description of Bach, Charity. I see that your sister Hope is the romantic of the family, but Bach is in the end the greatest, the master of them all. One day, perhaps, you will learn to play his music. Now that's enough for today. You will come again next Wednesday, I hope.'

I stood up, too surprised to say anything. Half an hour had passed in a flash.

'Thank you, Mrs—' I began.

'Wait! I haven't given you your homework.'

'I haven't learned anything yet,' I objected.

'But I have.' She picked up a ball of wool that was lying on top of the piano. 'I'm sure your mama has many balls of wool in her work basket. I want you to take one and do exercises with it to strengthen your hand. Watch how I grip, release, grip and release. Do that as often as you can. Then practise stretching out your fingers. Good. Soon perhaps they will be strong enough for Bach.'

We went out into the narrow front hall. Rachel burst out of the kitchen, as if she had been waiting for me. A wonderful aroma of coffee floated out after her. It was much richer and fuller than the smell of the instant Nescafé everyone drank at home.

'Is she a genius then, Mutti?' said Rachel.

'She likes Bach,' said Mrs Stern. 'That is a good start.'

I took my courage in both hands.

'Please, Mrs Stern, would it be all right if Rachel came over on Saturday? I want to show her round our house.'

Professor Stern had appeared behind Rachel. I saw a kind of signal pass between him and his wife, wariness giving way to tiny nods.

'Yes, of course,' said Mrs Stern. 'Off you go, now.'

'Don't get lost on the way home!' Rachel laughed, shutting the door behind me.

My music lesson had been interesting, but I'd found it unsettling too. What had Mrs Stern meant when she'd said that music had 'freed' Hope? Freed her from what? And why had I got upset when she'd been so sympathetic about polio?

Mother had looked after me, of course, but in a matter-of-fact kind of way. Almost every day, when I was ill, she'd told me to trust in the Lord because faith can move mountains (that's what St Paul says, anyway), and I knew that she and Dad were praying non-stop for me to recover. They assumed that their prayers had worked, and that I should be grateful and give thanks to the Lord, but I wasn't so sure. In my heart of hearts I'd wondered why He'd needed to work a miracle when He could just have stopped me from getting ill in the first place.

What with one thing and another, I had a lot on my mind when I went to sleep that night.

CHAPTER TEN

By Saturday, the weather had turned and sharp gusts of wind were blowing leaves all over the garden. Things had quietened down at home. Hope had gone back to school after a last-minute panic over a lost hockey stick, which left Mother even more tense than usual. Mr Fischer — whose cheeks had filled out already so that he now looked less like a walking skeleton — no longer spent hours on his own in the garden. He was so much better that he'd started going off with Dad every morning to spend the day at the missionary headquarters. Faith, of course, was at the hospital, and Ted, whose summer job at the zoo was over, had started his course in Marine Engineering at the polytechnic and was meeting up in the evenings with his old friends from the navy. I always seemed to be the person to pick up the phone when he called as supper-time drew near.

'Tell Mother I'll be home late,' he'd say. 'I'll eat something in town.'

Which was annoying, because I'd be the one to get snapped at when I passed the message on, as if it was all my fault.

I'd started noticing, actually, that Mother had become even

more short-tempered. I found myself circling round her, like you do with an irritable dog. She was always rushing from one thing to another, then she'd be so tired she'd have to go and lie down. It was a relief, that Saturday morning, when I ran downstairs and found Dad alone in the kitchen.

'You're up with the lark today,' he said, 'and it's just as well because your mother needs a rest. I'm keeping her in bed this morning and I'm not quite sure where everything is. The bread knife, for example.'

'You can leave breakfast to me, Dad,' I said grandly. 'But you'll have to move your things off the table if I'm to set it.'

'Of course, my dear.' He made a pile of the books he'd spread out and carried them to the green-painted dresser at the end of the kitchen. 'Do you know, there are some remarkable books in this house. I've been making an inventory of what's in the study. Architectural history, a splendid edition of E.B. Ford on butterflies and a whole series on the Old Testament. Look at this! The Prophet Jeremiah! A standard work!'

I wasn't interested in the Prophet Jeremiah.

'I keep making new discoveries too,' I said, 'and I haven't even looked in all the cupboards and drawers yet. It's sort of like living in a museum, but everything belongs to us.'

A shadow crossed his face. I bit my lip. I knew what he was thinking.

'Only not really ours, of course,' I said hastily. 'To – to use for the Lord's work.'

He looked at me over his glasses.

'That's our duty, yes, Charity, and our privilege too. Legally, of course, everything *is* ours. But possessions are dangerous things. They can make other people envious, and we have to worry about looking after them. Worst of all, they can distract us from what really—'

He was interrupted by the whistle of the kettle boiling furiously on the stove. I'd stopped listening to him, anyway.

'What I don't understand,' I said, 'is that all this belonged to old Mr Spendlove. I mean, he didn't seem to be the sort of person to have lace tablecloths and tea sets with roses on them and little silver forks for eating cakes.'

Dad laughed.

'Reg? No, but then this house was his wife's.'

'Was it? I didn't know. What was she like?'

'I never met her,' he said as he fetched the milk out of the fridge. 'She died before the war. Her father was a well-known architect – Jacob Austen. He designed this house. Margery was his only child. Where are the egg cups?'

'Behind you. On that shelf. In the corner.' The breakfast china, displayed on the dresser, was a marvel to me. The plates, cups and saucers were cream with green rims, and yellow chickens were painted all over them. 'Go on about Margery.'

'There's not much to tell. She lived here alone after her parents died. She was very well off, but she must have been lonely. She became – well, eccentric, you might say.'

'Poor girl!'

'Not exactly a girl. She was sixty by the time Reg Spendlove came along.'

'He was much younger than her, wasn't he?'

'Yes, he was only thirty. But he was very shy. He lived alone too. He ran a small building company and called in sometimes to fix things for her. That's how he got to know her. After a year or two he led her to the Lord, and brought her into the Lucasites.'

'They must have looked a bit funny, him being so much younger,' I said, trying and failing to imagine Mr Spendlove as a young man. 'Like she was his mother or something. And she must have been a lot posher than him too. I bet she didn't have a London accent, like he did. Were they actually – you know – in love?'

'I think they were,' Dad said. 'It's a mistake to judge on appearances. They were very happy together. Reg cared for her tenderly through her old age when she was nearly blind. She lived till she was ninety. He was lost without her when she died.'

'It's sort of sweet, isn't it?' I said. 'But sad too. They didn't have any family. Only each other.'

I'd been making the toast while we talked. It had finished browning on one side, so I pulled out the grill pan and flipped it over to do the other side.

'Very expert,' Dad said admiringly. 'You're becoming a good housekeeper, Charity, dear. Your mother's finding things a bit much at the moment and she needs your help. Today, for example . . .'

Danger loomed. I needed to head it off.

'I know, Dad, and I will this afternoon, honestly, but Rachel's coming over this morning.'

'Rachel . . . ?'

'Stern. From next door. I'm going to show her round the house.'

'But your homework, Charity . . .'

'I did nearly all of it last night. Anyway, Rachel can help me with my French irregular verbs. We can learn them together.'

The kitchen door opened.

'Good morning!' said Mr Fischer heartily. 'Ah, Fräulein Charity, the maker of breakfast! Today you will please to let me clear the table. I insist. For too long I have been idle.'

It was still only half past nine by the time breakfast was over, and I could hardly expect Rachel to come so early. I ran upstairs to my bedroom and looked round critically. What would Rachel think of it? Most of the furniture had been brought from Old Manor Road. I hadn't realized how shabby it was. The dog-eared books in a row on the windowsill suddenly looked childish. I scooped them up and hid them under the bed. The hated tartan dress was lying in a crumpled heap on the chair, so I hung it in the wardrobe. I couldn't do much about the picture of Jesus being the good shepherd with a flock of sheep all round Him, so I left it where it was. I picked up Susanna, the doll I'd adored when I was younger and still kept on my desk to keep me company while I did my homework, and I hid her in a drawer.

The grandfather clock in the hall downstairs chimed the hour. Ten o'clock! Suddenly I couldn't bear to wait any longer.

I'll go round and fetch her, I thought, *in case she's forgotten.*

I hurried out through the front door and round the side

of the house to the road. I was just about to open the Sterns's garden gate when I heard voices. Mrs Stern and Rachel were at their front door. I stepped back out of sight.

'She's an interesting girl,' Mrs Stern was saying. 'I like her. She has a strong personality and she has suffered – but, Rachel, what do we know of the family?' Rachel had her back to me, and I didn't hear her answer. 'All we know is that they belong to the same crazy religion as the old man.'

'I didn't think he was crazy,' Rachel said rebelliously. 'He was nice.'

There was a pause.

'It's up to you, darling. You have to make these decisions yourself. But you know how it ended with that girl you were so fond of at your primary school? *Jews are this, Jews are that, of course we don't mean* you, *Rachel.*'

My heart fluttered in panic. What if Mother said something like that in front of Rachel?

'You have to make these decisions yourself,' Mrs Stern went on. 'But, *Liebling*, in the end, it's safest to stick with our own people. By all means go today. It would be rude not to, but you should be on your guard.'

I nearly laughed out loud. Mother had said exactly the same thing to me.

'Mutti, please, I—' Rachel sounded exasperated.

'Why don't you call Susi later? She's left two messages for you. She wants to find out what you're going to wear for her brother's barmitzvah.'

Bar what? I thought. *What's she talking about?*

I was so busy trying to work it out that I missed Rachel's reply.

'She doesn't only think about clothes and hairstyles!' Mrs Stern was saying now. 'And her brother, Rafael, he's handsome, no?'

'Mutti! Stop it!' said Rachel, then came her footsteps, running down her garden path.

I had no time to run away, so I walked out on to the street and tried to look surprised to see her.

'I was just coming to see if you'd forgotten,' I said.

She gave me a searching look. I smiled back at her innocently.

'Of course I haven't forgotten! I'm dying to see the house. You'll show me everything, won't you?'

'We picked the right day,' I said, ushering Rachel in through the front hall. 'We've got the house to ourselves, nearly. Dad's taken Mr Fischer to buy some new shoes, Ted didn't come home last night, and Mother's in bed.'

'In bed? Why?'

I shrugged.

'She's tired. Dad says she's been overdoing it.'

Rachel was staring round at the big entrance hall.

'You could fit our whole ground floor in here, easily,' she said. She ran across to the fireplace and looked up at a picture of yellow roses in a gilded frame that hung above the mantelpiece.

'That's lovely. Who painted it?'

'I've no idea,' I said. 'Let's go into the study before Dad comes back.'

The study was to the left of the front door and had

windows on two sides, but the other two walls were covered in bookshelves. The books looked old and boring to me. Two deep leather armchairs flanked the fireplace. I hadn't tried them out yet, so I plumped myself down in one of them. It was lovely and soft and deep. I could imagine myself curling up in it with a favourite book in front of the fire. Rachel was studying the picture above the mantelpiece. I got up and looked at it too.

It was a portrait of a little girl, perhaps six or seven years old. She was wearing a white dress with a lace collar and a big blue sash and she was holding a porcelain doll dressed in identical clothes. Wisps of limp brown hair hung round her face. You wouldn't really have called her pretty, but she looked quite strong, as if she knew how to get her own way.

'Who is it?' asked Rachel.

'I think it must be Mrs Spendlove, when she was a little girl. Her name was Margery Austen.'

'Margery who?'

So I told her what Dad had told me, about how Mrs Spendlove's father, Jacob Austen, had designed this house and left it to his daughter. Perhaps I exaggerated a bit. Well, I know I did, but the more I looked at the little girl, the sadder her story seemed to be. What had it been like, being an only child with a famous father, living in this big house?

'Her mother had died, I think,' I found myself saying, improvising freely. 'And there was only a cruel servant to look after her. She became a recluse when her father died, and then along came Reginald Spendlove, who was a nobody, really, but a man with a heart of gold, and—'

'Mr Spendlove wasn't exactly a nobody,' objected Rachel. 'He was really, really nice.'

'Once they got married, she took him in hand and educated him,' I said firmly.

I was getting myself into deep water and was quite glad when Rachel lost interest in the picture and walked round to the far side of the enormous desk that stood in the middle of the room. A long cabinet stood against the front of it. It had tiers of wide, shallow drawers.

'Can we look?' asked Rachel.

I glanced out of the window. There was no sign of Dad yet.

'Yes, let's. It's all new to me. I've hardly ever been in here.'

Rachel pulled out the top drawer.

'Architects' drawings,' she said, holding up a huge piece of paper covered with faint geometric lines. 'What did you say Margery's father was called?'

'Jacob Austen.'

I was starting to feel restless. The drawings looked boring and I was dying to show Rachel my favourite things in the rest of the house. I think she would have opened one drawer after another if I hadn't dragged her back into the hall.

I was about to take her into the drawing room when I remembered the piano. *I bet she plays brilliantly*, I thought. *She'll probably get stuck trying it out.* So I veered sideways and opened the door into the dining room.

Even on a grey day like today, the room was filled with light from the long, curved bay window. Padded cushions covered the window seat. The material matched the curtains, which were cream and blue, patterned with a complex design of leaves.

'They're lovely,' said Rachel, fingering the material.

I didn't care about the curtains.

'Come and see this!' I said, opening one of the drawers in the long, ornate sideboard.

I'd been dying to show off the ranks of silver forks and spoons, each one cradled in its own velvet holder. I picked out a big serving spoon to show her. She turned it over and back again, then peered closely at the handle.

'Look. There's an initial. *A*.'

'I know,' I said, though actually I'd never tried to decipher the squiggles on the cutlery. '*A* for Austen.'

I took the spoon back from her and replaced it. The thought of those *A*s stamped all over our wonderful new cutlery was giving me a funny feeling.

Rachel wandered across to the tall glass-fronted cabinet near the window.

'Look at all this china! It's Art Nouveau!'

'Art what?'

'Nouveau. It's a style they had before the First World War.'

'Mother thinks it's hideous. Anyway, how do you know what it's called?'

'Because I'm going to study art when I leave school. I'm going to be a designer. My grandfather was a famous one, in Vienna, before . . . before . . . Papa's got books showing some of the things he made. I'm going to make the world sit up and notice the Sterns again. I'm going to prove that Hitler hasn't won. We're still here, doing great things!'

She looked proud and noble. Beside her I felt small and ignorant.

'I thought you'd be a musician, like your mother,' I said.

She laughed.

'Mutti's tried. She says I'm unteachable. I can't tell one note from another.'

'Does she mind?'

'I don't know. She likes me thinking about art, anyway. She and Papa are always taking me to art galleries and exhibitions and everything.'

I felt smaller than ever. I'd never been to an art gallery in my life.

'What are *you* going to do, then?' she asked suddenly. 'When you leave school, I mean?'

'I've always sort of assumed that I'd be a missionary,' I said slowly. 'In Africa or somewhere.' Rachel was forcing me to think clearly again and I wasn't sure if I liked it. 'But . . .'

'But what?'

I looked past her into the garden. It was only the middle of September, but it was beginning already to feel like autumn. A brisk, gusting wind was tapping a last pink rose against the window, blowing off the petals.

'I've just realized – honestly, just this very minute – that it's really the travelling bit I want. I'm no good at witnessing to the Lord. I only put people off.' I knew I was making an important discovery. 'I can only just remember the ship we came on from New Zealand. It had dropped anchor somewhere off the coast of Africa. Hope and I were on the deck. She was holding my hand and we could smell the land. Sort of earthy and green and tropical – so different from the salty smell of the sea. And there were white houses going up a hillside and crowds of people wearing beautiful, bright clothes. I wanted to jump off the ship and go and explore.'

Rachel shuddered.

'I never want to leave England. It's safe for us here. Safe-ish, anyway.'

I hardly heard her.

'And I want to learn new languages. I love doing French at school. I want to understand people, and, and know what they're like.'

'You're so brave, Charity,' Rachel said. 'I don't want to go anywhere where there are snakes and great big spiders.'

'Well, you just have to mind where you put your feet,' I said. 'I mean, wouldn't you love to go into a rainforest, you know, with trailing vines and monkeys and parrots, and be able to talk to the people who live there in their own language? They know the most amazing things. I've seen these pictures, in a book . . .'

But Rachel was vehemently shaking her head.

'No, thank you. What if something with lots of legs fell out of a tree onto my head? I'd rather stay right here in London and just look at pictures.'

I'd been carried away with my own vision. Brought down to earth, I stared at her, disappointed. She was looking at me too, a bit warily.

Oh well, I thought. *It's all right for us to be different, I suppose.*

There was nothing more to be said, so I went back to the sideboard and pulled out another drawer. A faint musty smell tinged with lavender wafted out of it. Why had I never noticed it before?

'Look at these napkins!' Rachel said, pulling one out. 'There's an *A* embroidered in the corner. The same design as on the spoons.'

She began to explore the other drawers, finding salt cellars and tea cosies and mats edged in deep, cream-coloured lace.

'It's all so perfect!' she said. 'Like in a museum. Everything must have been bought or made for the house.'

Her words struck me like a blow.

She's right, I thought. *The house is like a museum and it doesn't belong to us at all. It's still Margery Austen's and it always will be.*

I had an insane urge to rip a tablecloth in half, or take a teacup out of the cabinet and smash it on the floor. Why had I shown Rachel that portrait of the child with her perfect porcelain doll? I'd never get her out of my mind again.

'Let's go up to my bedroom,' I said.

She followed me unwillingly, but I wouldn't let her even open the drawing-room door.

'Later, I promise you, I'll show you everything.'

'It's nice,' Rachel said, looking round at my small bedroom, but I could tell she was disappointed. What had she been expecting? There weren't many Austen things in here, only my bed and the table under the window. Why had I insisted on keeping that wonky old wardrobe from Old Manor Road?

I was suddenly conscious of how plain and lopsided it looked.

I sat down on my bed. Rachel perched beside me.

'That chest of drawers and the wardrobe are from our old house,' I said, feeling defensive. 'I know they're battered, but they make me feel at home.'

Rachel nodded.

'I know what you mean. Our house is full of old stuff too. When Mutti and Papa came to live in England, my grandmother couldn't bear the thought of them not having furniture or beautiful things. So she bundled up pictures, books, photographs — all sorts of family treasures — put them in a truck and sent them over.' She shivered. 'It was before the Nazis took over Austria. If only they'd known then what would happen! They wouldn't have bothered with a whole lot of chairs and tables. They'd have brought out the rest of the family and every other Jewish person they knew.'

'Why?' I asked.

I knew it was a stupid question as soon as I'd said it.

'You know why! Because as soon as the Nazis took over they arrested all the Jewish people — including my grandparents — and a whole lot of other people too, and sent them off to the camps to be murdered!'

I didn't know what to say. I was finding it hard to take everything in.

'Why did your parents come to England anyway?' I asked.

'Papa had written his first book,' she said, 'and—'

'Your father's written a *book*?' I was so impressed that my voice came out as a squeak. 'What was it about?'

'Physics. It was full of new ideas and the University of London offered him a job. He could see things might get difficult in Austria so he took it.'

It was my turn to shiver. 'I'm really, really glad he did.'

Neither of us spoke for a minute or two. Then I said, 'That photo, above your piano, the one of a big house. Is the girl in it your mother?'

'Yes. With my grandparents.'

'Were they on holiday or something? It looks like a place in the country.'

She tossed her hair back in a careless way, looking suddenly grand and distant.

'That was their country home. They spent the summers there.'

'You mean they owned it?'

'Of course. In the winter they lived in their house in Vienna.'

'Oh.'

I felt smaller than ever. I could see now why the Sterns's house was crammed with so many beautiful old things.

Gospel Fields really ought to belong to them, I thought. *They'd know how to live in it.*

'You are lucky,' Rachel said, breaking into my thoughts.

'Me? What do you mean?'

'You've got a lovely big family. A brother and sisters. We don't have anyone else. There's only us three. Everyone else is dead.'

There was no answer to that. At last I said cautiously, 'Well, a big family is lovely up to a point, but brothers and sisters can be a real pain too. Brothers especially.'

'Yes, but you haven't got your parents breathing down your neck all the time.'

I thought of the way Mrs Stern had held my hands.

'Sometimes,' I said, 'it would be nice to have them notice me a bit more. In a good way, I mean.'

Rachel moved to the window. She stood looking down the sweep of lawn, her face partly hidden by the fall of her hair. I had a horrible feeling that things were going wrong.

She must think I'm an ignorant idiot, I thought. *A sort of fraud too, living in this great big house.*

My heart pumped a bit faster.

Don't pretend to be something you're not, I told myself fiercely. *Show her who you really are.*

'You were right,' I said, 'about the house being a museum. I hadn't really thought like that before. And it makes me feel peculiar.'

'I didn't mean—'

'No, it wasn't you. It was looking at that portrait of Margery. It's made me see that we don't belong here at all. That we're — I don't know — fakes or something.'

'That's daft. You do belong here. Mr Spendlove left it all to you so—'

'Legally, I know. But it doesn't *feel* real. I'll show you what's real.' I jumped up, wrenched open the groaning drawer in my chest of drawers and pulled out my poor old Susanna. Her clothes were torn and grubby, and the glaze on her china face was crazed with little cracks. 'This is me. She's really mine. I've had her since I was three. And look.' I bent down and pulled my tatty old books out from under the bed. 'I hid them because I felt ashamed that we'd been poor. I wanted to impress you with all the stuff in the house, but I can't do it. Susanna and these old books, they're really me. You see?' I threw open the wardrobe door and pulled out my tartan Sunday dress. 'This is my best dress. It was Faith's and then Hope's, and now I've got to wear it.'

I couldn't look at Rachel.

She'll despise me now, I thought.

But she threw back her head and laughed.

'You're the most amazing person, Charity. I've never met anyone so honest.' She picked up Susanna and stroked her matted hair. 'You should see my Mitzi! She's much tattier than Susanna.' She laid the doll back carefully on the bed and bent to look at the books, which I'd spread out on the floor.

'*The Secret Garden*! I loved that one. And *Little Women*! Who's your favourite character?'

'Jo, of course.'

'Mine too.'

When we'd stopped laughing, she said, 'Do your brother and sisters feel the same as you?'

'I don't think they've thought about it. Faith doesn't live here any more, and Hope sort of floats about over everything. And Ted – well, he doesn't bother with anything at home except the car and the tools in the garage and his room up in the attic. I'll show you that if you like. He's made it all himself.'

'Won't he mind?'

'He's not here, is he? Anyway, he said I could look if I don't touch his things.'

We went out on to the landing, but before we started down the corridor that led to the attic stairs, I heard a cough from Mother and Dad's bedroom.

'Isn't that your mother?' said Rachel. 'Do you want to see if she needs anything?'

'Oh yes, yes, I'd better.' I bit my lip. I'd promised Dad that I'd bring her up a cup of tea, but I'd forgotten all about it.

Mother was out of bed and had started putting on her clothes. Her long loose hair, falling over her shoulders, made her look oddly girlish. I suddenly noticed, as she picked up her hairbrush, how thin she'd become.

'Are you all right, Mother?' I said. 'I meant to bring you up a cup of tea, but Rachel's here and I forgot.'

'It doesn't matter. I've been trying to sleep. Has Faith called? She's bringing Justin home for supper. He hasn't asked your father's permission yet.'

'Permission for what?'

'To marry Faith, of course.'

'Oh. Is Dad going to say yes?'

'That's between them,' Mother said repressively as she twisted her hair into a rope, coiled it and pinned it into a bun on the back of her head.

'Do you need me to do anything? Only I'm showing Rachel the house.'

'Not now. I'll need you this afternoon.'

'Are you really all right, Mother? You look, I don't know . . .'

148

'I'm perfectly all right. Now off you go. Don't keep Rachel waiting.'

I surprised us both by darting forward and giving her a hug.

'Thank you, Mother, and I will help later, I promise.'

Rachel hung back at the door of Ted's room as if she didn't dare go in.

'It's all right, really,' I urged her, going in first.

It felt good showing Ted's room off to Rachel. There was nothing museum-y in there, and the only bit of Margery was her old hat perched with the others on the row of hooks.

Rachel looked round with astonishment at the diagrams of ships pinned up on the walls and the complicated arrangement of shelves and cabinets.

'It's all so tidy,' she said. 'I thought boys' rooms were always a mess.'

'His used to be awful,' I told her. 'He learned to be tidy in the navy and he's never stopped.'

She was staring at the hats.

'They're so funny,' she said. 'Where did he get that felt one with the feather?'

'It was Mrs Spendlove's. He found it in the attic. Come on. I'll show you.'

Rachel loved the attic. She laughed at the tailor's dummy with the clothes still on it. She darted about, picking up torn cushions and broken ornaments, opening a trunk to pull out a top hat, a velvet cape and a feathered fan.

The things in the attic felt different from the ones in the

house. They'd been unwanted, cast aside as unworthy of the museum downstairs. I felt I could make them mine.

Rachel pounced on a china lamp and held it up for me to see. Its deep blue gaze gleamed in the poor light of the attic. There was only a little chip off the base, and its cream silk shade was only a bit frayed round the edge.

'This would be lovely in your room,' she said.

She thrust it into my hands and edged round the enormous rocking horse to pull out some rolled-up rugs.

'These look interesting,' she said.

There was a clatter on the stairs and Ted appeared.

'I saw the light was on,' he said. 'Are you treasure hunting?' Then he caught sight of Rachel. 'Who are you?'

'She's my friend Rachel. From next door,' I said. 'I'm showing her the house. She likes your room, by the way.'

'I charge extra for tourists. Especially nosy girls,' Ted said. He gave a mighty yawn. 'Hop it, you two. I've been up half the night and I need a kip before Ma drags me downstairs to be nice to the boyfriend.'

'Fiancé,' I corrected him.

'Whatever you say, Captain.' Ted made a mock salute. 'Go on. Get out of here. I need some peace and quiet.'

Rachel ran down the attic stairs, and as I followed her out of the little door at the bottom I saw a look on her face that I'd seen countless times before.

'Don't tell me you've fallen for Ted,' I groaned. 'That would be so – so banal.'

'Of course I haven't!' She sounded too indignant, and

anyway her blushing gave her away. 'Is he — I mean, does he often stay out all night?'

'Only since he started seeing his old navy friends.'

'But don't your parents mind? His friends aren't all from your church, are they?'

She was pressing on a sore spot and I didn't want to answer. Mother and Dad were worried about Ted, I knew. I'd heard snatches of conversation from their bedroom at night and then the murmurs of their prayers. But I didn't want to discuss Ted with Rachel. It would have felt disloyal.

Downstairs, the grandfather clock struck.

'Twelve!' said Rachel. 'I'd better go before Mutti starts fussing.'

CHAPTER ELEVEN

I was surprised to find that I was relieved when I shut the front door after Rachel. She had a sort of authority about her, the confidence of someone who knew about art and furniture and china. If we'd stayed in the attic any longer, she'd have picked out rugs and ornaments and bits of furniture and reorganized my whole bedroom. I was grateful to her for finding the lamp, but I wanted to choose other things for my room myself.

Rachel was giving me a lot to live up to, but I'd show her what I could do. And I was more determined than ever that we'd be friends. Great, great friends.

Mother needed more help that afternoon than I'd expected. Normally she could throw a cake together in a few minutes and slice vegetables faster than a machine, while giving out orders to her daughters as if she was running a canteen. This afternoon, though, she sat at the kitchen table looking helplessly at the open recipe book in front of her.

'I was going to do pineapple upside-down cake,' she said, 'but I used the last tin of pineapple on the Hawaiian roast.'

'What about trifle?' I suggested.

'Too late. No time for the jelly to set.'

'Crumble?' I liked offering her ideas. Usually she just told me what to do. 'I could see if there are any apples or plums left in the garden. And you showed me how to make it, Mother. I'm sure I can do it.'

To my horror she dropped her face into her hands and her shoulders started heaving.

'Mother? You're — you're crying!'

I'd never seen her cry before, not once in my whole life. It felt as if an abyss had opened up in the floor in front of me.

'I'm — I'm perfectly all right,' she said shakily, groping for the handkerchief she kept up her sleeve. 'I don't know what's come over me. You really think you can manage a crumble?'

'I know I can.' I was trying to sound more confident than I felt.

She made a visible effort to pull herself together.

'Lamb casserole,' she said. 'The lamb's already diced. While you're looking for apples and plums, pick some parsley, Charity.'

I made a dash for the back door.

'And — and . . .'

I waited, expecting another instruction.

'We'll manage,' she said, with a watery smile. 'We'll do it together, won't we?'

Her words warmed my heart as I reached up to pick the last few apples. She'd almost sounded as if she was talking to a friend! But then I started to worry. It wasn't like Mother to say things like that. Was she seriously ill? Might she even die?

I was in a panic by the time I got back into the kitchen, but Mother was more like her old self. She had cut up the onions for the stew and started on the carrots.

'Look,' I said, showing her the bowl full of apples. 'These'll do, won't they?'

If I'd hoped for another moment of softness, I wasn't going to get it. She didn't look at the apples.

'I'm sure they're fine.' She took out her hanky again and wiped her forehead. 'Goodness, I do feel rather dizzy. Get your crumble done quickly, dear, and start peeling the potatoes.'

Dad and Mr Fischer arrived home first, and Faith and Justin were a few minutes behind them.

'Is he here yet?' Faith said, when I answered the doorbell.

'Who?'

'Dad, of course.'

'Yes, he's in the study.'

Behind her I could see Justin pulling the knot of his tie away from his neck as if he was suddenly too hot. Dad opened the study door, making Justin start. Seeing him look nervous made me like him a bit better. He was still too handsome, but at least he didn't look so snooty.

'Splendid,' said Dad. 'Now, Justin, let's take a turn round the garden. Always a good idea to walk while you talk, don't you agree?'

Justin threw Faith a look over his shoulder. She mouthed, '*I love you*,' which made me feel a bit peculiar, then he followed Dad outside.

'You don't think Dad's going to tell him he can't marry you, do you?' I asked Faith. 'I mean, he can't. You're grown up!'

'There's such a thing as *acceptance*. As welcoming someone into a *family*,' Faith said passionately. 'Oh, what do you know about anything?'

Stifling a sob, she ran upstairs and I heard her bedroom door slam.

So now I had Mother in the kitchen being ill and strange, Faith being emotional upstairs, Dad deciding Justin's fate in the garden, Ted presumably fast asleep in his attic room, while Mr Fischer could be heard quietly playing the piano in the drawing room. The entire success of the dinner rested on my shoulders. I was going to make sure that the honour of the Browns was upheld.

And it was. Upheld, I mean. I urged Mother to go upstairs to rest (she didn't resist much, which was worrying), took over the lamb casserole, boiled the potatoes and the cabbage, kept a check on the crumble in the oven, made the custard (though I had to strain out the lumps), set the table *perfectly*, then waited till exactly half past six and banged on the gong.

'What are you doing?' Faith said, running down the stairs. 'You mustn't hurry them. What if Dad — what if — oh!'

I turned to see Dad and Justin walking in from the garden. I couldn't read the expression on Dad's face, but Justin was smiling, in a triumphant sort of way. Faith ran up to him and they held hands and stared at each other. *Please, please don't start kissing*, I silently begged them. They didn't. Ted came yawning down the stairs. Mr Fischer came out of the drawing room. I couldn't bear to witness Justin's brazen triumph. I fled to the kitchen.

I was trying not to burn myself while dishing up the potatoes when Ted sauntered in.

'Where's Ma?'

'I made her go and rest. She was being really strange. She said she felt dizzy and kept dropping things.'

He raised an eyebrow.

'You got Ma to lie down? That's quite an achievement.'

He sounded sort of casual but he looked a bit worried.

'She might be really ill, Ted.' I handed him the bowl of potatoes to take into the dining room. 'What if . . .'

Before I could go on, Mother came in. She had changed into her Sunday dress and tidied her hair. She looked normal again.

'You all right, Ma?' Ted asked her. 'Char says you're feeling peaky.'

'I'm perfectly all right,' said Mother. 'Charity can take in the dishes. Ted, get out two bottles of grape juice. Pour them into a jug and add a little vinegar and bicarbonate of soda to make it sparkle. A celebration is in order.'

'Ma Brown's best champagne, eh?' Ted murmured in my ear. 'If that doesn't show Justin what he's in for, nothing will.'

I frowned. What was wrong with Ted these days? I hated him saying disloyal things. Surely he didn't expect us to drink actual, evil alcohol? This was yet more proof that he was backsliding from the Lucasite path. I hurried after him into the dining room with the boiled cabbage. It had gone a sort of grey colour and I was afraid I'd overcooked it. Too late to worry about that now.

All through Dad's long grace I tried to pray for Mother, but I couldn't stop thinking about Justin and Faith kissing and all the other things they would do once they were married. I knew the facts of life, of course, but nothing about what was actually involved. It was doubly wrong to think about it while I was supposed to be praying, but I couldn't help it, and I started to feel hot all over. It was a relief, quite frankly, when Dad said his final Amen.

The meal started. Ted went round filling everyone's glasses with fizzy grape juice, the vegetables were passed round, Dad was dishing out the casserole and still no one had realized that I'd cooked the entire dinner myself.

I was just about to say, *Oh, I do hope the potatoes are done. And you might find the casserole needs a bit more salt*, when Mother said, 'We have Charity to thank for dinner tonight. She cooked everything herself.'

But the effect was entirely lost because Faith and Justin had just taken their first sips of grape juice. Justin's face went red and he started coughing, and Faith screwed up her face and said, 'Ted, how much vinegar did you put in this?'

By the time the grape juice had been poured away and everyone had been given orange squash, no one remembered about me cooking the dinner and, anyway, they were too busy talking about weddings and asking Justin how many uncles and aunts he had. I could just as well have slapped mouldy cheese sandwiches in front of them. They wouldn't have noticed a thing.

I was proud of the crumble, I must say. The top was nicely browned, and a little apple juice was bubbling up round the edges.

'I do hope I've cooked the apples long enough,' I said pointedly, 'and tell me if you need more sugar.'

But once again no one noticed. Everyone was watching Mother, who had picked up the jug of custard to pass it to Justin. Her hand was trembling so much she could barely hold on to it, then she let it go with a crash. The jug broke. Yellow custard poured out in a thick stream over the white tablecloth.

For a moment, no one moved. Then Faith and Ted dashed into the kitchen to get bowls and cloths while Mr Fischer began moving the plates and glasses off the table and piling them on the sideboard. I sat frozen to the spot, watching Mother, my heart falling into my stomach. She was crying again.

Dad rushed round from the other end of the table and put his arm round her shoulders.

'Jeanie, Jeanie, it's only custard! My dear, oh don't, oh . . .'

Justin gently moved him aside.

'I don't think she's well, Mr Brown. Can you help me take her up to her room? I'd like to examine her, if you don't mind.'

Everything was odd after that. I was hardly aware of Faith, Ted and Mr Fischer clearing up the mess. I sat glued to my chair, my head filled with dreadful thoughts.

After a while Mr Fischer came to sit beside me. We were

the only two left in the dining room.

'Your mama will be well again soon, Fräulein Charity. Your new brother is an excellent doctor, I am sure. The Lord sent him to you at the right time. And you have been a good daughter today. Such work, to make a meal for so many!'

He had put on the sort of voice people use to children, and I would have been offended if I hadn't been so upset.

'I haven't been a good daughter!' I burst out. 'I knew Mother wasn't well. I kept asking her, and she kept saying, "I'm perfectly all right," but I should have known she was just being brave. I should have told Dad about her having to rest so much and bursting into tears. And anyway, the cabbage was boiled for far too long and the crumble was the best bit of the whole dinner and no one even tasted it!'

Rapid footsteps crossed the hall and there was a ping as the receiver was taken off the telephone. I rushed to open the door. Faith and Ted had already come out of the kitchen and were listening too.

Justin looked calm and doctorly as he spoke into the telephone.

'Yes, this is Dr Fraser. I need an ambulance now. The patient is Mrs Jean Brown. She will need to be admitted. I suspect acute hyperthyroidism. Gospel Fields, Badger Hill.'

'Oh!' Faith, put her hand up to her throat. 'Why didn't I see it? She should have started treatment weeks ago.'

'You should have seen what?' I almost shouted at her. 'What's wrong with her? Is she going to be all right?'

Faith didn't seem to hear.

'No wonder she's been so odd recently. Tense and snappy and tired all the time.'

'Tell me!' I shrieked. 'Is she going to die?'

'What? Oh no, no. But she'll have to be in hospital for a while. She might need an operation.' She pulled her hanky out of her pocket and leaned over to wipe the tears off my cheeks. I hadn't even realized they were there. 'Don't worry, little sister. It's going to be all right. Really it is.'

I jerked my head away. I was quite capable of wiping my own tears, and anyway, as one who had cooked an entire meal, I felt that 'little sister' was rather too patronizing.

While we waited for the ambulance, Ted got the car out of the garage.

'I'll take Dad,' he told Faith. 'I suppose Justin will go in the ambulance with Ma?'

'We need to pack her things,' said Faith. 'Come and help me, Char.'

I let her go first into Mother and Dad's bedroom, afraid of what I'd see. Mother was lying on the bed. She struggled to sit up when she saw us. Dad, sitting beside her on the bed, gently lowered her down again. Justin was holding Mother's wrist in one hand and looking down at his watch with the other.

'Well?' asked Dad.

'Still too fast,' said Justin.

He stood back to let Faith and me come close.

'What a fuss I've caused,' Mother said fretfully. 'It looks as if you'll all have to manage without me for a while.'

'I'll get leave from the hospital,' said Faith.

'You won't need to,' I told her firmly. 'I'll manage fine.'

Mother was looking anxiously from Faith to me.

'Why don't we sort all that out later?' said Justin gently. 'Mr Brown, can you help me get her downstairs? The ambulance should be here soon.'

He and Dad took her arms to help her off the bed.

'I can manage quite well, thank you,' said Mother, sitting on the edge of the bed and feeling about with her feet for her shoes.

I felt a rush of love as I looked at her. She was so small, so thin and brave and determined.

'Don't worry about being in hospital, Mother,' I said. 'It's not too bad when you get used to it.'

She was already on the way to the door, her hand on Dad's arm.

'My small suitcase is under the bed,' she said over her shoulder. 'Clean nightie in the second drawer down.'

The little case was soon nearly full. Mother's Bible, the black leather cover rubbed and worn, lay on the top of her night things, with her prayer list beside it.

Downstairs, the doorbell rang. The ambulance had arrived.

When they'd all gone, Faith and I went into the kitchen. Faith made a pot of tea, and we sat at the table to drink it.

'I blame myself for not seeing how ill she was getting,' Faith said.

'Well, I didn't, either. And I see a lot more of her than you do.'

'I suppose it was the stress of the move that triggered it,' went on Faith. 'That, and having to cope with looking after this enormous house on her own.'

I was offended.

'I do help, you know. I actually cooked dinner on my own tonight, though no one seemed to notice.'

She ignored this.

'I thought she was going to get Mrs Stebbins to come and help with the housework. Why didn't she?'

A bad feeling started curdling my insides.

'I think — well, it might have been my fault,' I mumbled.

'What?'

'I think I sort of persuaded her not to, because Mrs Stebbins is so — so horrible and nosy and disapproving and gossipy, and she'd have to bring Tabitha here in the holidays. I think I might have been rather — loud.'

'You mean you've been having tantrums.'

'No!' I tried to feel offended again, but inside I was crumpling. 'Maybe I have. A bit.'

She stared at me, horrified.

'Char, how could you? Anyway, I thought you and Tabitha were friends.'

'You can't have done! Why does everyone keep on *saying* that? She smells of — of wet dog!' And then I crumpled inside a bit more. 'Oh, Faith, it's not my fault, is it, that Mother got to be so ill?'

She poured herself another cup of tea and took her time to answer. She wasn't going to let me off lightly, I could tell.

'Probably not, but you've got to stop being so selfish and think what's best for Mother.'

'I will! I promise!'

'I'm going to phone Mrs Stebbins in the morning and fix it all up.'

'Do you want me to do it? I will! Honestly! I'll do it first thing!'

'Don't be ridiculous.' Her face softened. 'Look, it won't be too bad. Two days a week will be enough, and you'll be at school most of the time. You'll hardly see her. And Hope will be here in the holidays. She'll help to mop up Tabitha.'

I swallowed. There was no way out. I composed my face into a dignified expression.

'I will be gracious,' I promised.

'Not gracious. That's being proud and grand. You've got to be kind. Friendly.'

'I'll try.'

We sat in silence for a moment.

'Actually,' Faith went on, 'I don't think it was only stress over the house that made Mother ill. She was in a dreadful state of anxiety while you were down with polio. We all were. We thought you might be paralysed for life.'

'Did you? No one ever said!'

'Of course not. We didn't want to worry you. I found Mother crying a few times.'

'Mother crying? Because of me?'

'Oh, Char, just because she doesn't show her feelings, it doesn't mean she doesn't care.'

Things I'd forgotten came floating back to me out of the shadows of those dreadful months of sickness and paralysis. Mother washing me with a flannel, Mother rolling me over to change my sheets, Mother coming up the stairs dozens of times a day when I called out for her, Mother putting flowers from the garden on the windowsill where I could see them, Mother lifting me up to help me drink. And all the time I'd been cross with her, because the flannel was rough, the fresh sheets were cold and the drinks made me feel sick.

Now I was feeling worse than ever. How could I have been so thoughtless? And so mean about Mrs Stebbins when Mother really needed help?

'We can't sit here all night,' said Faith, pushing her cup away and standing up. 'There are the dishes to wash and all that custard to clear up as well.'

I was glad to have something practical to do. I loaded up trays in the dining room and took them into the kitchen while Faith dealt with the sticky tablecloth. Mr Fischer was crossing the hall as I carried the last load out.

'I volunteer myself,' he said cheerfully as he rolled up his sleeves. 'I am an expert in cleaning dishes.'

He wasn't bad, I must admit. Very thorough, but rather slow. Faith stood beside him, tea towel at the ready, watching him rinse the suds off each plate before he handed it to her to dry while I hovered, waiting to put things away in their proper place.

Mother being ill had wiped everything else from my mind, but now I remembered what I'd wanted to ask Faith.

'Did Justin tell you what he and Dad talked about?' I asked her. 'Whatever it was, Dad seemed to be all right about it.'

'I haven't had time to ask him,' she said, waiting while Mr Fischer meticulously cleaned each prong of a fork.

'Only the thing is,' I went on, 'I'm in a muddle now. The Lucasites are supposed to be the elect, aren't we? The Holders of the Truth. That's what they kept telling us in Sunday School. But suddenly it's all right for you to go off with Justin and join the Church of England. Where does that leave the Truth? Don't you *want* to be a Lucasite any more? I mean, think about it. Doesn't it matter? A lot?'

She handed me the dried fork to put away and stood waiting for the next one.

'It's complicated,' she said at last.

'Not so complicated.' Mr Fischer had been quiet up to now. 'In Germany there are no Lucasites. They are not in France, or Holland, or anywhere in Europe. I think your community is only in Britain, and in the United States, perhaps. But does that mean that God has abandoned us? We in our own churches are faithful in our own ways. I think you will find that your papa agrees with me, Fräulein Charity.'

I wasn't sure what Dad thought, and I really wanted to know.

'Well, anyway, I'm a Lucasite and I'm going to stay one,' I said, feeling like the boy on the burning deck when all but he had fled.

The telephone rang. Faith and I rushed into the hall. Faith got to the phone first.

'That was Justin,' she said, replacing the receiver. 'Mother's been admitted and the others are on their way home. Justin asked if he could stay here tonight. We'll make up the bed for him in Hope's room. If we ever get to finish the washing-up, that is.'

The clock was striking eleven when Dad, Justin and Ted came in. They didn't have much to say. Mother had been taken off to the ward, the specialist would see her tomorrow, she was in good hands and visiting hours were from 2 p.m. to 3 p.m. on Wednesdays and Saturdays.

Dad caught sight of Mr Fischer stifling a yawn.

'Bedtime,' he said, shooing us towards the stairs as if we were all still children. 'Good thing it's Sunday tomorrow. We'll have time for prayer, and time to make all the necessary arrangements. Ted, lend Justin some pyjamas. Come here, girls, and kiss your old father goodnight. Up you go, now.'

Everyone wanted the bathroom, of course, and I was nearly the last to get in. I came out licking smears of toothpaste off my teeth to find Justin waiting outside. He looked funny in Ted's old pyjamas. A lot less smooth and handsome with his hair all messed up. There was something I needed to say and this was the moment to say it.

'I wish to thank you, Justin,' I said, pulling the cord of my dressing gown tighter, 'for saving my mother's life. Probably.'

His lips twitched and for a horrible moment I thought he was going to laugh, but he said, 'It was a pleasure and, anyway, she's going to be my mother-in-law, so it was the least I could do.'

I hadn't finished. The next bit needed a deep breath.

'I don't think I've been very — very welcoming to you. Into our family, I mean.'

'It's all right, Charity.' He nodded to show he was taking me seriously. 'Do you know, it's not very easy for me, either. I haven't got any brothers and sisters. I'm not used to them.'

'Believe me,' I said darkly, 'they're not always all they're cracked up to be.'

This time he did laugh, but in a nice way.

'I don't believe you. I honestly think your family is the most wonderful there could possibly be and I can't wait to be a part of it.' He stuck out his hand. 'Friends?'

I took it almost willingly.

'Friends.'

The door to the attic burst open and Ted appeared. 'I've just remembered that there's a gorgeous-looking apple crumble sitting uneaten in the kitchen.'

Dad came out of his bedroom wearing his dressing gown and slippers.

'Did you hear that, Dad?' said Ted. 'We're going to have a pyjama party in the kitchen. Apple crumble and cocoa. Get Faith, Charity, and I'll tell Mr Fischer.'

CHAPTER TWELVE

Guilty feelings swilled around in my dreams that night, but I must have fallen into a deep sleep at last because I didn't wake up until late. Breakfast was nearly over by the time I went downstairs, and from behind the dining room door I could hear that family worship was in progress. Everyone was reciting one of Dad's chosen chapters from the Bible.

'*Repent and be baptised,*' they were chorusing, '*and ye shall receive the gift of the Holy Spirit.*'

I stood stiff with shock, my feet rooted to the red hall carpet.

Repent? I thought. *I do! I do! I've been repenting all night! It's all my fault that Mother's ill. I know it is!*

And at that very moment I knew what I had to do. A decision leaped into my mind, only it felt more like a visitation from the Holy Spirit. I threw open the dining room door and marched in.

'I want to be baptised,' I announced.

Everyone turned and stared, shocked into silence. Then Dad jumped up from his chair.

'Charity! This is marvellous!' he said, giving me a hug. 'Your mother will be delighted!'

I don't remember what happened next because I felt shrouded in a sort of aura of holiness. What I do remember is Dad calling me into his study and being pleased and proud and saying he'd already phoned the Chairman of the Oversight to fix a date and that I should make the weeks until my baptism a time of Dedication and Purification.

'You mean like a squire of old who spends his last night in a vigil before he's made into a knight?' I said.

'Ye-es,' said Dad, looking a little puzzled, but he didn't explain any more, and I decided that what I had to do was behave in the most moral way possible by doing things like tidying my room, writing to Mother in hospital, writing to Hope to reassure her that Mother wasn't going to die and thinking kind thoughts about Tabitha Stebbins, as well as reading the Bible and praying for twice as long as usual, which would be a holy sacrifice because what I really wanted to do was spend every spare moment with Rachel.

I was quite excited about going to the Meeting that morning. Everyone would have heard about Mother being taken to hospital, of course, but they'd know about my baptism too. I was a bit nervous, quite honestly. What if people didn't think I was worthy? After baptism you become a full member of the Lucasites and you can take part in the Breaking of Bread. If you're a boy, you can even get up and pray in public, though girls can't. That's St Paul's fault too.

Baptism means you are a grown-up person, who has put away childish things. No more messing about in the Meeting, doing things like playing noughts and crosses on the floor with a piece of chalk between our toes, as Hope and I secretly tried to do when we were younger. Mother never caught us out, which was strange because you can't easily take off your shoes and socks in the middle of the Meeting. Hope thinks she knew, but let us get away with it. That's not very likely. It doesn't sound like Mother at all.

The walk to the Meeting, which usually seemed to take hours, felt shorter than usual, and we arrived early, which was just as well because everyone was still milling around in the forecourt. Lots of people came up to ask about Mother. In all the fuss, hardly anyone remembered about my baptism. I tried not to mind, but, honestly, I did.

I concentrated *fiercely* during the Meeting. My brain felt super-sensitive and twanged like a guitar string with every hymn and Bible reading. I seemed to find hidden messages, just for me, in every word.

When it was over, and we were all standing around again outside, I saw Tabitha and, filled with good intentions, went over to talk to her.

'Hello, Charity,' she said, with what I can only describe as a smirk on her face. 'You've decided to be baptised too, have you? I suppose you heard that I was going to be and that gave you the idea.'

It was only by snapping my mouth tight shut and pinching my arm till it really hurt that I managed to hold on to my self-control.

'I didn't know about your baptism,' I managed to say. 'The Holy Spirit has clearly moved in both our hearts, Tabitha, His wonders to perform.'

She flushed and walked away.

'There's no need to be sarcastic,' she said over her shoulder.

'Charity,' hissed Faith, coming up behind me. 'Don't be so unkind.'

'I wasn't being unkind!'

'Yes you were. Grand and patronizing. Just think how Tabitha must feel, having her mother come and clean our house. It's humiliating for her.'

So then I felt guilty all over again, as well as being irritated, and I stood there, biting my lip, not knowing what to do.

Mrs Prendergast came up to me.

'How lovely, Charity, that you are to be a candidate for baptism!' she said. 'We need to arrange your interview with Mr Prendergast.'

'Interview?'

'All candidates for baptism are interviewed. Didn't your father tell you?'

'No, he didn't.'

'Wednesday afternoon will suit Mr Prendergast. You can come and see him after school.'

'Oh, but I have my piano lesson on Wednesday.'

She frowned.

'You're learning piano? Who's your teacher? I offered to give you lessons myself, but your mother said you weren't keen.'

'It wasn't that,' I said, blushing. 'It's just that there's a teacher in the house next door to us, and I don't have to walk too far to get there. I get – I still get rather tired.'

Her face softened.

'I see. Perhaps for once you can change your piano lesson. I'll speak to Faith about it. And Mr Prendergast will drive you home afterwards. Do give your mother my love, dear. We were all so sorry to hear . . .'

I stopped listening. I felt even worse now. I hadn't exactly told a lie, but I hadn't been quite honest with Mrs Prendergast, either. And now I was going to have to trudge all the way up to the Prendergasts' house on Wednesday and miss my precious hour next door.

'Will Tabitha be interviewed on Wednesday too?' I asked.

'Dear Tabitha's interview was last week,' Mrs Prendergast said. 'Isn't it lovely that you'll be baptised together? You've always been such great friends.'

Faith was waiting for me a few days later, when I got home from the Prendergasts.

'How was it?' she asked.

'Not bad. He was nice. He told me all about Jeremiah Lucas founding the Lucasites, as if I didn't know.'

'Exactly what he told me when I got baptised,' said Faith. 'Have they still got that poor old dog?'

'Yes. He was coughing and snuffling all the time and Mrs Prendergast kept saying, "Come on, Fairy. Come to Mummy."'

'Anything else?'

I groaned.

'Yes! And it was so embarrassing, because she asked if I'd started my periods yet. She thought she was whispering, but I'm sure Mr Prendergast heard. I must have gone scarlet. Anyway I nodded, and then she said, "Because we have to pick a Sunday when you're not — you know — because you'll be going right under the water, like in a swimming pool, and you can't do that if you're wearing a sanitary towel." I nearly *died*.'

She laughed.

'You stop being embarrassed about that kind of thing when you're a nurse.'

'Then when it was all over Mr Prendergast stood up and said, "Mrs Prendergast and I now consider you to be our friend and sister, Charity," and he shook my hand and went to get his coat and drove me home in his car.'

'That was nice of him. Hadn't you better go and do your homework?'

She had put the interview out of her mind, but I couldn't put it out of mine.

'Why do you want to be baptised?' Mr Prendergast had asked me.

I could hardly tell him that it was all my fault that Mother was ill and I thought God might forgive me and make her better if I was baptised. I'd mumbled something about taking the next step along the Christian path and hoped he'd drop the subject. Which he did.

Supper was weird that evening because Dad and Mr Fischer were out, so it was only Ted, Faith and me sitting at the kitchen table. Faith had tried to make a steak-and-kidney pie, but the pastry was still raw and the meat was tough.

'Poor old Justin,' said Ted, ostentatiously chewing on a tough bit of beef. 'I hope he knows what he's letting himself in for.'

'Don't be *mean*, Ted,' I burst out.

He spread out his hands with a look of injured innocence.

'I'm being honest, that's all. Faith can't cook. So what?'

Faith slammed her fork down on her plate.

'I'll tell you what's what. I'm leaving tomorrow. The hospital called this afternoon, and I've got to go back on duty. Ted, I'm handing the cooking over to you. See how you like planning, shopping and cooking for four people.'

Ted's jaw dropped.

'Hey! No need to be so hasty. Look, it's not that bad. This bit of kidney looks fine. Anyway, you can't just walk out on us.'

'I can. I've got to. Mother's going to be in hospital for several more days. I've made a shepherd's pie for tomorrow, and then it's Friday and you're on your own.'

'I'll do the cooking,' I said. 'I'm sure I can manage.'

Faith stabbed a commanding finger at me.

'You,' she said, 'are going to concentrate on your schoolwork. You've got months to catch up on.' Her finger swivelled round to point to Ted. 'And you're going to pull your weight, for a change.'

'That's not fair!' Ted's face blazed with indignation. 'Who's chopped all the wood for the winter fires? Who fixed the leaking tap in the bathroom? Who—'

'Stop it! Just stop!' I shouted at them. I felt like crying. 'What do you mean, several more days? I thought she was coming back this weekend. She's really ill, isn't she? What if she never—'

Faith leaned across and put her hand on mine.

'She's doing well, Char, honestly. She just needs more time. Justin spoke to the doctors yesterday. There really is no need to worry.'

'All right then, I will,' Ted said suddenly, startling Faith and me.

'Will what?' we said together.

'Do the cooking.' He tilted his chair back and gave us a lordly smile. 'Can't be that difficult. Faith, you can trot along back to your bedpans, and Char can keep on brushing up her algebra or whatever. It's going to be top nosh from now on.'

'Ha!' snorted Faith. 'I'd like to see that.'

'But you won't, will you, dear sister? You'll be too busy canoodling with Justin in the sluice.'

Faith ignored him.

'Charity, clear the plates, will you? I've made a blancmange for pudding. Chocolate. Your favourite.'

'But what about the housework?' I said anxiously. 'I don't think I can—'

'Mrs Stebbins starts tomorrow.' Faith had set the blancmange triumphantly down on the table. 'Set to perfection. See?'

My heart missed a beat at the mention of Mrs Stebbins.

'No need to look so shocked, Charity. Your tantrums didn't work. Mother fixed it all up with her weeks ago. She'd have

175

started work by now, but there was another job she had to finish first.'

I felt indignant.

'Why didn't anyone *tell* me? All this time I've been thinking . . .'

I stopped. I almost felt like crying.

Ted was catching up slowly.

'You don't mean Ma Stebbins?' he said, looking appalled. 'Coming here?'

Faith nodded. 'Thursdays and Mondays. She starts tomorrow. We've got to have everything tidy and ready for her.'

'She's not going into *my* room,' objected Ted.

'She wouldn't touch your stuff with a barge pole,' said Faith coldly. 'You'll both be out while she's here. I've given her a key. But if you should happen to see her, please be nice. Poor woman, she's suffered enough already.'

'Mrs Stebbins? Suffered? How?' I asked. Faith and Ted exchanged looks. 'You mean because Tabitha's father was killed in the war? He was a hero. Tabitha told me. A fighter pilot.'

'Except that he wasn't,' said Ted.

'Shut up, Ted,' said Faith.

'Why not? Char might as well know. She's half grown up now, isn't she?'

'I don't think——' began Faith.

'Know what?' I said. 'What are you talking about?'

'Ma Stebbins had an — exciting experience, you might say,' said Ted. 'In the war. With a Yankee soldier. Tabitha was the result. Lover boy pushed off back to the Wild West or wherever, never to be seen again. Probably never knew what he'd left behind.'

'You mean she wasn't *married* to him?'

I was rigid with shock.

'No,' said Faith, 'but it was wartime, you know? She was on her own. Her parents had been killed in the Blitz. Don't judge her, Charity. You don't know what it was like for her.'

I was still trying to catch up.

'Does Tabitha know?'

'I hope not,' said Faith, 'and it would be cruel and wicked to say anything to her, hint anything, look mysterious – all that kind of thing. Ted should never have told you.'

I kept thinking about Tabitha as I sat through my Biology class the next morning. I'd known her for years and years, but I'd had no idea about the story of her life. I'd never thought before about what it must be like to have no father. I'd been almost jealous of the glamorous hero pilot she'd talked about so often. And Mrs Stebbins! It was hard to imagine that stern, disapproving woman being in love with a dashing American soldier.

It just shows, I told myself, *that you never know what's going on in other people's lives.*

I thought of Mr Fischer. You wouldn't have any idea, if you saw him walking down the street, that his wife and little girl had died in a bombing raid and that he'd been almost starved to death in a prison. And Mrs Stern! How could you guess, if you saw her buying onions in the greengrocer, that her whole family had been wiped out in the Nazi death camps?

I looked round at the other girls in the class. What was it that had turned Monica into such a bully? And Miss Wedderburn, standing there in her drooping mauve cardigan, pointing at the diagram of the human eye she'd drawn on the blackboard. Why did she look unhappy all the time and snap at us for the least little thing?

It was almost as if she'd read my thoughts.

'Charity!' she rapped out suddenly, making me jump. 'Pay attention. Daydreaming wastes your time and mine.'

CHAPTER THIRTEEN

The next night Ted triumphantly dished up fried sausages, eggs and bacon with mounds of baked beans and toast on the side. He wore Mother's pink flowery apron as he went backwards and forwards from the cooker to the table, shovelling eggs from the frying pan on to our plates and making pots of strong tea.

'Your English food, how I shall miss it!' said Mr Fischer. I looked at him suspiciously, but he wasn't being sarcastic at all.

'What's for pudding?' I asked.

Ted's eyes filled with panic, then he noticed the open door of the cupboard behind my head.

'Tinned peaches!' he said triumphantly. 'Fetch them out, Char.'

'We must enjoy them,' said Dad, 'because tonight is a special occasion. A happy one for our dear brother Karl, though not such a happy one for us. Tonight is his last with us. He's leaving tomorrow, to return home to Germany.'

'No!' I cried. 'Oh, please don't go!'

Mr Fischer gave me a slightly wobbly smile and I thought his eyes looked a bit wet.

'Fräulein Charity, I cannot stay here forever. My church has been rebuilt and my congregation waits for me to return.'

'But I'll miss you!' I felt almost tearful myself.

'And I will miss you. You have — you have all . . .' His eyes had spilt over now. 'When I came here I was — you have healed me, with your loving care.'

'With God's help,' Dad put in.

'Of course. And one day perhaps you will visit me in Germany.'

'I will!' I nodded firmly. 'I'm going to learn German, as a matter of fact. And French. And lots of other languages. It's what I'm going to do.'

Prayers after supper that evening were quite long. I tried my best to pray, but I felt too sad. Everyone was leaving Gospel Fields. Until Mother came back, only Dad, Ted and I would be left, and when they were out I'd be alone in this big, shadowy house, which still didn't feel quite like home.

Even though the next morning was Saturday, I got up early to have breakfast with Mr Fischer and Dad and see them off. I stood at the front door waving as the car disappeared down the drive. The house behind me felt like a sad, empty place, the rooms too big, the life in them gone.

Was this how Margery Austen felt, as she stood at this same door, watching Mr Spendlove drive away after he'd done a job for her, wishing she could call him back? The thought made me shiver.

I scrawled a note for Dad.

Gone next door. Back soon. Love C.

Rachel answered my knock.

'Oh good, it's you!' she said, reaching out to drag me inside. She nodded significantly towards the half-open kitchen door. 'Have you come to do homework with me?' She dropped her voice and hissed, 'Say yes!'

'Er – hmm,' I mumbled. I couldn't bring myself to tell an outright lie, not even for Rachel. 'I suppose I could – we're doing *Romeo and Juliet*. I've got to learn a whole lot of speeches.'

'We're doing it too! Come and tell Mutti. She's baking again.'

I'd guessed that already. Delicious smells were wafting through the house.

'Ah, Charity!' said Mrs Stern. She dusted flour off her hands, then to my surprise drew me into a hug. 'Your mother, how is she?'

'Still in hospital,' I said stiffly, addressing the buttons on the front of her blouse.

She let me go.

'That is good! Better she should stay until she is well. This thing – the thyroid – it is not nice, but it is not dangerous.'

Faith, Ted and Justin had told me the same thing over and over again, but somehow it sounded more real coming from Mrs Stern. Something inside me relaxed.

The smell of burning sugar, wafting from the cooker, was becoming more intense.

'Ach! My caramel!' She whipped the smoking pan off the gas ring and poured a thick brown stream over the tart cooling on a rack.

'Charity's come to do homework with me, Mutti,' said Rachel.

'Really?' Mrs Stern tightened her lips. 'You think I don't know what girls are like? You think you can pull the sweater over my eyes?'

'Wool, Mutti. Not sweater.'

'Wool, sweater, it's the same thing. Never mind. You go and pretend to do your homework. Wait! Why the hurry?' She fetched out a plate and piled some biscuits on to it. '*Vanillekipferl*! I made them yesterday. Now go, and not too long, Rachel. On Monday there is your Maths test.'

I followed Rachel up the narrow staircase, eager to see her bedroom. I blinked with surprise as I looked round. I hadn't been expecting a little girl's room, the walls pink, the curtains lacy, and an array of old-fashioned dolls on the shelf.

'I know,' sighed Rachel, watching my face. 'You'd think I was five years old.'

'No – I – it's lovely.'

'It *was* lovely, when I was little.' She picked up the cushion that lay on the bed and turned it over so that the picture of the fairy castle on it was hidden. 'Nearly everything comes from Austria. Mutti had it all when she was a child. My grandmother sent it over with the other stuff, in case

182

Mutti had a little girl of her own one day.'

'Did they know about you? That you'd been born?' I asked.

'No. They were arrested too soon.'

I pointed to a faded photograph in a gilded frame of a little girl cuddling a dog.

'Who's that?'

'Mutti. With the dog.' She jerked her chin towards a painting of a dog over her bed. It had a pink bow tied round its neck and gazed out at the world from big brown eyes, its head tilted appealingly sideways. 'It was called Kathi. My grandparents adored her. They even had her painted.'

'It's sweet.'

'Exactly. Sweet. Sentimental. Kathi wasn't *my* dog. I don't even like dogs that much. Anyway, I don't want to keep being reminded about all that – stuff. The past.' She threw out her arms as if she was sweeping everything away. 'I want to make my own kind of room. I want it to have *style*. But I don't want to hurt Mutti's feelings.'

I suddenly understood why Rachel had been so excited about finding things in our attic for my bedroom.

I'll let her do up my room, I thought. *At least, I'll let her help me.*

Rachel settled herself cross-legged on the bed and patted the other end of it. I sat down too.

'So what's going on?' she said. 'Your sister's looking after everything, I suppose. When's your mother coming out of hospital?'

It was lovely talking to Rachel. She was fascinated by

everything. She listened wide-eyed, her hand over her mouth, when I described Mother's trembling hand as she dropped the jug of custard, and she wriggled with envy when I told her about our late-night party in the kitchen. She burst out laughing when I told her how Faith had made Ted do the cooking, and said she wished now that she'd had a chance to meet Mr Fischer properly before he left because he sounded so nice.

It was more difficult telling her how I'd decided to be baptised. I was afraid she'd think it was weird. To my relief she only nodded.

'It's like a barmitzvah,' she said.

'A what?'

'It's when a boy gets to be a teenager. He has to learn a part of the Bible and sing it in the synagogue. And after that he's sort of a full member of the community. He counts as a man.'

'That's a bit the same as us!' I was astonished. 'Once you're baptised you can take part in the Breaking of Bread, and boys can do readings and pray and things like that in the Meeting.'

'Not girls?'

'No. It says in the Bible that women have to keep silent in church.'

Rachel was shaking her head and frowning and I was afraid she'd say something about it being unfair. And then I'd have to put on my armour and go into battle to defend the Bible as the true Word of God and the Lucasites as Christ's faithful disciples, which was an exhausting thought because actually I thought it was unfair too. So I quickly asked, 'Is the bar thingy only for boys? Isn't there one for girls?'

'No. And even if there was I wouldn't have one. My family don't go in for all that. I told you. We're not religious. Anyway, it would be called a "batmitzvah" if it was for girls.'

Before I could think of an answer, Mrs Stern called up the stairs.

'Homework, girls! Don't forget!'

'I'd better go,' I said. 'Dad'll be home by now.'

'Can I come over tomorrow?' asked Rachel.

Here was another pitfall. I couldn't face explaining to Rachel the specialness of the Lucasite Sunday.

'Sorry. Busy,' I said, 'but I'll see you on Wednesday when I come over for my piano lesson.'

Faith had been right about Mrs Stebbins. I didn't see her at all. I knew when she'd been, though, because the house looked so good. Dust had gone from the corners and the bathroom taps gleamed.

Now that Mr Fischer had gone, it was strange being at home at the weekend with only Dad and Ted for company. I guessed that Ted had reached the limits of his cooking abilities, and anyway I wanted to show them both what a terrifically good cook I could be.

It was nice having breakfast with Dad, the two of us alone together. Sort of peaceful and friendly. I had accidentally burned the toast, but he didn't seem to notice and passed his cup over from time to time for a refill of tea as if I'd been Mother. We didn't talk much. I was leafing through a worn copy of *All the New Zealand Housewife Needs to Know About Cooking*, trying to find recipes I could manage, while he worked through the latest issue of *Gospel Gleams*, the Lucasite quarterly magazine.

Later, Dad shut himself away in his study and I ploughed through my beastly homework in my bedroom. We met in the kitchen at lunchtime.

'Sorry, Dad,' I said. 'I'm going to cook something lovely tonight, but I haven't thought about lunch.'

'Never mind,' Dad said cheerfully, opening one cupboard after another. 'Look what I've found! Fish paste! Pickled beetroot! And what's this? Piccalilli!'

I felt low once Dad had gone off to the hospital. There was no hope of Rachel.

'We're going to a play at the Old Vic on Saturday afternoon,' she'd told me. 'I wish you could come, but I know you can't.'

'That's perfectly all right,' I'd replied, which was a lie, of course.

Does Mother always lie when she says she's all right, I thought afterwards. *She did when she was ill. She must have been feeling terrible. But surely that was a sin? I mean, shouldn't we always be truthful? Only, if we are, and it makes other people feel bad, isn't that wrong too?*

It was the kind of mental tangle I hated. I put it out of my mind.

I couldn't face the thought of planning supper after those fish-paste sandwiches. I decided to do it later. I was on my way upstairs when I heard footsteps on the gravel drive outside.

Rachel didn't go to the theatre, after all! I thought, rushing down to open the door.

'Good heavens, Charity,' said Auntie Vi, sweeping past me into the hall. 'I hardly recognized you. Last time I saw you, you were languishing in your hospital bed. Must be a whole year ago. Here, take this bag. Mind out, the bottom's about to collapse.'

She took off her jaunty black beret, releasing her short dark hair, which was cut in wedges round her face. I was so mesmerized by her crimson lipstick, tight black trousers and the leopard-print jacket that swung out round her when she turned, that for a moment I was quite unable to move. She looked terrifyingly worldly.

And she's my own aunt! I thought.

'Where's the kitchen in this mansion of yours?' she went on. 'I'm gasping for a cup of tea. And where's my little brother? Bug-hunting in the garden, I suppose.'

'He's at the hospital,' I managed to say. 'It's visiting day.'

She followed me into the kitchen.

'Good Lord! What magnificence!' she said, taking in the array of green painted cupboards and the pretty china on the dresser. 'Do you like it, darling? Come on. Kettle on first, and after that you must show me everything. I'd have come months ago, but our play's had such a marvellous run on Broadway we stayed in New York a whole six months longer.'

I remembered my duty.

'Thank you for the book you sent me, Auntie Vi,' I said, keeping my eyes averted from her fascinating face as I filled

187

the kettle. 'It was very — interesting.'

'Glad it got through the Brown censorship system,' she said. 'Your education isn't complete until you've read *Catcher in the Rye*.'

Please, please don't say anything bad about Mother and Dad, I silently begged her, feeling my pulse rate quicken.

She saw the expression on my face and smiled understandingly.

'Dearest Charity, don't panic. You really don't have to go into battle. Never with me. I know exactly how you feel. Believe me, no one knows better. I adore your parents, you know. I practically brought your father up. With a little help from Josephine, of course.'

'But you're only six years older than him.'

'I know. That makes my achievement all the more remarkable.' She paused. 'I may have, let's say, moved on in life, but I still have a great fondness for the Lucasites, dear good souls that they are, though whether they have a fondness for me is another question entirely. Goodness, look at these teacups! Hideously Art Deco, aren't they? Your dear mother can't have known what hit her. Now, I want to hear all about everything — poor Jeanie, Faith, her delicious young doctor, that handsome brother of yours — there's an awful lot of catching up to do.'

The afternoon with Auntie Vi passed in a confusing flash. She was so relaxed, amusing and friendly that I slowly shed my terror of her. The tour of the house didn't take long. I'd expected her to be impressed and astonished, but she only glanced into one room after another then headed back to the kitchen.

'A 1900s period piece,' she said. 'Charming if you like that sort of thing, though a devil to heat in the winter. Dreadfully out of fashion now. Poor Jeanie, an awful chore keeping it all up. As for the garden, it's practically a park. I wouldn't swap all this splendour for my little modern flat. Clean lines, bright colours and efficiency, dear, that's the future.'

Gospel Fields still didn't quite feel like home to me, but I was offended to hear her dismiss its glories so brutally. She caught sight of my face and laughed.

'Don't take any notice of me. Most of my friends think I've got the worst taste imaginable.'

She pulled the corners of her mouth down and rolled her eyes in a comical look of regret and looked suddenly so like Dad that I almost gasped. I'd been wondering how she could possibly be his sister and here was the proof, right in front of me.

I watched, fascinated, as she unpacked the contents of her bags.

'What are those?' I asked. 'Gooseberries?'

'No, dear, olives.'

I'd never heard of olives.

'Try one,' she said, opening the bottle and fishing out a little green ball with a teaspoon. 'There's only one shop where you can buy them in London. A Greek place in Soho. I'll take you there one day. Don't break your teeth on the stone.'

I'd expected something sweet, and the sharp, strong taste made me choke. I had to stop myself from spitting it out.

'You have to persevere,' she said crisply. 'You'll love them in the end. Now, get me an apron. We're going to make a lasagne.'

'A what?'

'It's an Italian thing. I learned to make it in New York. Never heard of it in dear old England, of course. You'll love it, I promise you.'

I found myself talking non-stop to Auntie Vi as she put together the strange ingredients she'd brought with her. I forgot about the lipstick, the tight trousers, the short hair and the English accent. Here was a person who belonged to me, who knew from the inside what it was like to be in the Brown family and grow up in the Lucasites.

But she's fallen away, I told myself. *She's living a sinful life in the world.*

Had the Devil sent Auntie Vi to me? I couldn't believe it. This was Dad's own sister. I watched her as I talked, alert to any sign that she might try to tempt me from the true path. But as I told her my worries about Ted, about not witnessing to the Lord at school, about trying to purify myself for baptism and about how easy it was to talk to Rachel next door, she listened without interrupting, and nodded sympathetically from time to time.

'There is nobody,' she said, cutting into a strange red vegetable, 'who understands all this better than me. You're treading the path I had to tread, and it's been painful sometimes, believe me. But you know, Charity, no one can make your decisions for you. You'll find your own way.'

'That's what Dad says to Ted.'

'Sensible of Iver —' she nodded — 'though I can't imagine that it's easy for any of you. The ideal, I suppose, is to embrace the new while hanging on to your affection and respect for the old. Anyway, I won't encourage you to follow my rather, let's say, more extreme example.' And she wouldn't say anything more.

'Auntie Vi,' I said, after a long pause, 'why haven't you got a Scottish accent any more? You sound like a really — I don't know — posh English person. Dad hasn't lost his accent much at all.'

For the first time she looked a little defensive.

'Ah, well, things move on, you know. One has to fit in.' She paused. 'When you — if you — leave a closed world like the Lucasites, and branch out on your own, it can be difficult. Lonely, even. Now, tell me more about your friend Rachel. She does sound rather wonderful.'

Auntie Vi left as suddenly as she'd come, before Dad had even arrived home from the hospital.

'She was really sorry not to see you,' I told him. 'She had to get back to London before her theatre opened. She made the most amazing thing for our supper. It's got vegetables called red peppers in it. It's in the oven now.'

'Vi came? I thought she was in America.'

'Got back last week. She — oh, Dad, you should have seen what she was wearing!'

He didn't answer. I noticed how tired he was looking and suddenly realized I hadn't asked about Mother.

'How is she, Dad? Is she feeling better?'

He brightened.

'She's making progress. You know your mother. She never complains. But I think she's finding the hospital very trying. Olive Prendergast has sent some beautiful flowers and she's had plenty of cards and letters, which have helped.'

My hand flew to my mouth. I'd made stern resolutions about preparing for baptism, and writing to Mother had been one of them. It was awful to think that I'd never actually got round to it. I left the lasagne to bubble away in the oven, and flew upstairs to write her a letter at once.

CHAPTER FOURTEEN

As it happened, I never had to use *All the New Zealand Housewife Needs to Know About Cooking*, because once the Lucasite women heard that Faith had left us to manage on our own, they sprang into action. Every afternoon, when I got home from school, something was sitting on the doorstep with a note giving instructions. *Heat in the oven 40 minutes*, or *Stir well before serving*. We had Mrs Prendergast's Irish stew one day, Mrs Glass's lamb hotpot the next and Mrs Gill's fish pie with Miss Rhys-Jones's apple turnovers the following night. They kept it up for three whole weeks, and even went on after Mother at last came out of hospital, which was just as well, quite frankly, because for the first few days she couldn't do anything much.

I hadn't known she was coming home. I'd just got back from school and had let myself into the empty house with my key, when a taxi swung round the side of the house. It pulled up by the front door and Mother got out. I rushed back outside to help her with her suitcase. She looked pale and tired, and the faint hospital smell clinging to her made me hang back, but she put out her arms to give me a brief hug.

'Well,' she said, stepping into the house. 'You all seem to have managed very well without me.'

'Are you better, Mother? Really?'

I saw the words *I'm perfectly all right* hovering on her lips, but instead she smiled and said, 'I'm going to be, but apparently I need to take things gently for a week or two.'

'But you'll be all right after that?'

'So they tell me. Goodness me! Who's polished the gong? I had no idea it would come up so nicely.'

'Mrs Stebbins. She comes on Mondays and Thursdays. Faith sorted out her days with her.'

'I know. Your father told me.'

She was looking at me quizzically. I said quickly, 'I haven't seen her at all because I've been at school, but she makes everything so nice. And I'm really sorry, Mother, I should never have . . .'

She was already moving on towards the kitchen. I followed close behind her down the narrow corridor. There was more I needed to say.

'Was it me who made you ill, Mother? It was, wasn't it? The stress of looking after me and then all the fuss I made about Mrs Stebbins.'

She stopped abruptly and I nearly cannoned into her back.

'No, dear! Of course not!' She had turned to face me. 'Whatever put that idea into your head?'

'Faith said . . .'

'Faith is a very good nurse, I'm sure.' Mother's voice was dry. 'But she doesn't know everything yet. You haven't been torturing yourself about it, have you?'

'Well, I . . .'

'Put it right out of your mind, darling. The world doesn't revolve round you, you know.'

It was the kind of remark I usually hated, but this time she said it with a spark of humour in her eyes. She'd said 'darling' too. I felt as if a band had been tied round my chest and that it had suddenly loosened. We went on into the kitchen.

'Where on earth did all these come from?' she asked, eyeing the array of empty bowls and dishes on the dresser.

'This one's Mrs Prendergast's, and this is Miss Rhys-Jones's — I'm not sure about the others.'

She took hold of the back of a chair and slumped down on to it as if her legs could no longer hold her up.

'How kind!' She gave a little laugh. 'I might have known they'd do something like this. And so many letters and cards they sent to me in the hospital! Yours too, dear. Much appreciated.'

'Can I get you a cup of tea?' I said. 'And you needn't worry about supper because I found this cheese-and-onion flan on the doorstep when I got home.'

'One of Phyllis Carter's, I suppose. Well, never mind. It'll have to do for this evening.'

'It's only you and me and Dad, anyway,' I told her. 'Ted's out again tonight and Mr Fischer's gone. I suppose Dad told you. I'll see to it all, Mother. You won't have to do a thing.'

Her bright hazel eyes were full of warmth as she looked at me.

She is better! I thought. *She hasn't looked happy like that for ages.*

'You're a good girl, Charity,' she said. 'Your father's told me how helpful you've been. And I'm so pleased about your baptism. It's what we've always wanted for you, to commit your life to the Lord and declare it in faithful witness.'

I turned my back on her in order to put the kettle on.

That's not why I wanted to do it, I thought. *I wanted to save your life.*

Now it turned out that she hadn't needed saving at all. Had I been a fraud? Would it be dreadfully wicked to get baptised for the wrong reasons? But perhaps, after all, I really *did* want to show everyone that I'd dedicated my life to Jesus?

'Auntie Vi came,' I told her. 'Did Dad tell you?'

'Yes.' She sighed. 'Poor Vi. Life's not easy for her.'

She didn't look like poor Vi *to me*, I thought.

'Mother, do you believe in Hell?' I blurted out.

'Of course, dear. Why do you ask?'

'I mean eternal fire, and the Devil, and everything?'

She was listening now.

'It's there in the Bible, Charity, so it must be true. But we have the wonderful assurance of salvation. Hell isn't something we need to dwell on.'

'Miss Crabtree liked dwelling on Hell in Sunday School,' I told her. 'We had to imagine what it felt like to hold our hands in the fire and keep them there forever. Daphne Miller had nightmares for weeks. Adrian Simmons tried it at home and had to be taken to hospital.'

'Yes, well, Miss Crabtree should never have been put in charge of children. The Oversight had to step in,' Mother said. 'She was asked to sort out the coffee rota instead.'

'But what about people who've never heard the gospel and haven't had the chance to be saved? And what about all the people who lived before Jesus? And babies who died when they were too little to understand? Are they all supposed to go to Hell?'

'It's a great mystery,' said Mother, taking the cup I handed to her. 'But we have to trust in the infinite mercy of God. We can't pretend to know everything.'

She took a sip of tea.

'Anyway, since you're so interested, there's an excellent book by Professor Proudfoot on the theology of Heaven and Hell. I'll look it out for you.'

It was time to change the subject.

'Did Dad tell you that Faith phoned? She's thinks the bridesmaids' dresses should be blue,' I said.

Mother went upstairs to rest after we'd had our tea. The house settled quietly round us. It was getting dark earlier now that October was halfway through, and I'd been nervous at home on my own. Even though she was tucked away in her bedroom, it was a relief to know that someone else was in the house. Once or twice I left my homework and tiptoed along the landing to peep in at her, but she was always lying with her eyes closed as if she was asleep.

Dad rushed straight up to see her as soon as he got home.

'She's doing so well!' he said, running down the stairs again and rubbing his hands with pleasure. 'But I've insisted on her staying in bed this evening. Can you take her supper up on a tray?'

Dad and I sat in cosy warmth in the kitchen that evening, eating our way through the soggy flan, with the red-and-white checked curtains closed against the wind and rain.

'Ted's out again this evening, I presume,' Dad said. 'You're not keeping any back for him?'

'I don't think he'd eat this stuff anyway,' I said. 'And he's almost never home for supper any more. What's he doing all the time, Dad? Aren't you worried about him?'

He looked at me over his glasses.

'Are *you* worried, dear?'

'Of course I am! Can't you stop him doing wrong things, Dad? Forbid him to . . .'

Dad shook his head.

'No one can force a person to be a disciple of Christ. Our task is to uphold him in prayer, and—'

He was trying to fob me off in the usual way as if I was still a child.

'Yes, but if he leaves the Lucasites, won't you mind? And Faith. She's going off to join the Church of England! Don't you care about that, either? And what about Auntie Vi? Is she even a Christian any more?'

Dad pushed the remains of the quiche to the edge of his plate.

'You children all have to find your own path to faith, Charity.

Being a Lucasite is one way. We think it's the best, but—'

'Being a Lucasite is *one way*? Do you mean we don't have to be Lucasites if we don't want to? That's what Auntie Vi said, but I didn't think you'd say it too.'

'Your mother and I can't make you be or do anything, darling. We can lead, but we can't drive.' He hesitated. 'Every community of the faithful has its strengths and weaknesses. I grew up in the Lucasites. Our dear friends in the Meeting are our brothers and sisters. We're a community of love! Think of all the excellent meals they've brought us. They've cared for us throughout this time of trial.'

'I'm glad you think this quiche is excellent,' I said. 'Frankly, I couldn't eat another mouthful.'

He ignored this.

'I think you must feel the same, Charity,' he said with a searching look, 'or you wouldn't have chosen to be baptised.'

This was bad.

'I think I do love the Lucasites,' I said cautiously. 'Some of them, anyway. Because they're like family. I mean, I've grown up with them. They're the only people I know, really, apart from the girls at school, and they think we're just weird. And Rachel, of course. She sort of understands because of being Jewish. But there are so many rules! I mean like keeping my hair long and having to wear a hat in the Meeting, signing a pledge never to wear lipstick, not being allowed to go to the cinema, or – or knit on Sundays.' I was getting steamed up now. 'And people are so nosy! Miss Laws saw me on the bus on the way to school last term, and she phoned Mother up and told her my skirt was too short.'

'And was it?' said Dad.

'A bit maybe, but it wasn't my fault. I'd grown out of it and Mother couldn't afford a new one.'

Dad laughed.

'None of us are perfect. Not even Miss Laws. But, anyway, being baptised isn't about becoming a Lucasite. It's about committing your life to the Lord.'

There was no answer to that, but I still had my killer question. I'd tried it out on Mother, and now it was time to test Dad.

'Do you believe in Hell?' I asked him.

He was starting to look harassed.

'Well now, there's a question.'

'Do you, or don't you? I mean the burning pit? The everlasting fire? The demons?'

'What makes you ask that, Charity?'

'It's important, isn't it? I know we're the saved, but you ought to know what you're being saved from. And, anyway, Tabitha talks about Hell all the time.'

'Ah, poor Tabitha. Life isn't easy for her.'

I didn't want to be sidetracked on to the sad life of Tabitha. I waited, my arms crossed, my eyes on his face.

'The thing is,' Dad said unwillingly at last, 'I've never quite been able to bring myself to believe in Hell. An eternity of cruel suffering. It seems to me that our loving Father—'

'You don't believe in Hell?'

My voice had risen to a squeak. I felt an odd sense of

disappointment. Had I been conned all my life?

But Dad hadn't finished.

'These are great mysteries, Charity. The Bible isn't entirely clear. But it seems to me that a better understanding of Hell is a state of separation from God. From love. That would be a terrible fate indeed.'

'But you can be separated from God and from love without being dead at all.'

'Yes, and for many people Hell is right here on earth.'

My eye fell on Phyllis Carter's rejected quiche. Was she a person living in Hell? I thought of her tight, unhappy face and the way she smelt of old sweat if you got too close. She certainly seemed lost to love. I gathered up our unfinished plates and took them over to the sink.

'This quiche is awful, isn't it, Dad? There's some of Miss Craddock's chocolate mousse left over from yesterday. Why don't we finish it off?'

CHAPTER FIFTEEN

After my first piano lesson, I'd made a solemn vow to myself to do my muscle exercises a million times every day. But when the next lesson came round, I realized with a jolt that I hadn't done any exercises at all. I'd missed so many lessons, what with my baptismal interview at the Prendergasts, and Mrs Stern having a heavy cold, that they had completely slipped my mind.

'Can I have a ball of wool?' I asked Mother urgently as I was about to rush out of the house on Wednesday morning. She was getting better already and was down before me now every morning to put the breakfast on the table.

'Whatever for?'

I nearly lied. It was a dreadful temptation. I wanted to say, *We've got to take some in for Domestic Science*, but I was supposed to be pursuing Purification and Dedication, and lying just wouldn't do.

'Mrs Stern asked me to keep squeezing a ball of wool to strengthen my hand,' I mumbled. 'I – I forgot.'

To my relief, she smiled.

'Hardly surprising, with everything that's been going on. I'll look one out for you. Mrs Stern will understand. Now drink up your tea, Charity. You don't want to miss the bus.'

Later that afternoon, Mrs Stern sat me down in the sagging chair opposite hers and pushed a plate of home-baked hazelnut macaroons towards me.

'Your father met Rachel's papa on the way to the station, yesterday,' she said. 'He told him that your sister had gone back to the hospital and you have been managing on your own. I would have been so happy to cook for you, my dear, if I had known!'

A glow settled on my heart.

'It's been all right, really, Mrs Stern. The Lucasites . . . that is, the – our church, they've brought food every day.'

'Ah. Yes, I see.'

She seemed to draw back a little.

'But thank you very much,' I said quickly. Now seemed the right moment to confess. 'I'm afraid – what with everything, I forgot to do my exercises.'

She gave me a measuring look, then said, 'From today we start again, no? Come. Sit at the piano. With the right hand first we will try a few notes.'

My lesson passed more slowly this time and I felt on shaky ground. I managed with my right hand to make a run of notes, and even enjoyed the sound they made, but when it came to my left hand all my fingers were clumsy and the fourth one didn't seem to work at all. I sat at the piano, feeling frustrated and angry with myself.

'Charity,' said Mrs Stern, after a painful pause, 'why is it you want to play the piano? Your mama wants you to learn? You wish to be like your sister? You love to make music?'

I ought to have said, *No, Mrs Stern. All I want is to come to your house and see Rachel*, but I couldn't say a word.

'Because,' Mrs Stern said, 'it is not something that you can do without work, work, work on the muscles of your hand, and even then you may not succeed. I am not sure that you want it enough, Charity.'

Don't send me away! I pleaded silently. *I'll try again. I will.*

'I think I will visit your mama,' Mrs Stern said, standing up. 'We will talk together about what is best for you.'

She saw me looking up the stairs as we passed through the hall.

'Rachel is not here today. On Wednesdays now she has the rehearsal for the school play.'

I kicked out savagely at the gravel as I walked back up our drive.

For a moment I felt like crying.

Stupid, stupid polio! Why did it have to get me?

There was no point in going down that road. I'd been there often enough and there was no answer, anyway. But then another thought occurred to me. What was the point of having piano lessons if Rachel wasn't going to be there? I'd never actually wanted to play the silly thing, anyway.

I'd nearly cheered up by the time I reached the front door.

My plan worked, though, didn't it? I thought. *Rachel and I are friends now and I'll make sure we see each other as often as we want to. I'm not going to let anything get in our way.*

Mrs Stern took me by surprise, ringing our front door bell on Saturday morning while I was still getting dressed.

'I'll get it!' I shouted, running downstairs and flinging open the door, hoping to see Rachel.

Before I'd had a chance to say anything, Mother came out of the dining room.

'Charity told you, I think, that I wished to speak with you?' Mrs Stern said.

Mother nodded. 'About the piano lessons. Yes, of course. Do come in.'

She stood back to let Mrs Stern into the dining room. They sat down awkwardly at the table, then Mother saw that I was listening and came over to shut the door.

Something I haven't explained about our house is that there's a little sort of window with wooden shutters between the kitchen and the dining room. It had been covered over by a cupboard on the kitchen side, which Mother had got Ted to move so that we'd have a hatch to pass plates and dishes straight through from the kitchen without having to go up and down the corridor.

I quickly searched my memory. No – I couldn't think of a single verse in the Bible that tells you not to eavesdrop. I still hesitated. It didn't seem right somehow, but I was too desperate to hear what they were saying to hold back. I dashed down the kitchen corridor and almost crashed into Dad.

'Good morning, dear,' he said, giving me a hug. 'Sleep well? . . . Now what was it I wanted to say to you?' He scratched his head. 'Wait. Let me think. No – it's gone.'

I was trying not to dance with impatience.

'Sorry, Dad,' I said, squeezing past him. 'Got to get on.'

He nodded, and ambled off.

The kitchen side of the hatch was above the worktop, between the sink and the cooker. There was a pile of dishes stacked up in front of it. It took ages to move them without making a sound.

By the time I'd opened the hatch a fraction and could start listening, Mother and Mrs Stern had moved on from piano lessons. Mother had her back to me, which was just as well, as her sharp eyes would have seen the hatch opening. Mrs Stern was opposite her and I could watch her face.

'She's a bright girl. A lovely girl,' Mrs Stern was saying.

Mother's shoulders were stiff. Compliments made her uncomfortable. In her opinion, they led down the slippery slope to vanity.

'She's missed a great deal of schooling,' she replied. 'She had only just been put in the top group for French, which is her favourite subject. She's dropped down to the middle group now. It's disappointing for her.'

Mrs Stern had seemed to be about to stand up, but she settled back on her chair.

'I wonder – Mrs Brown, an idea occurs to me.'

'What on earth are you doing?'

I'd been listening so hard I hadn't heard Ted come into the kitchen. I spun round.

'Nothing,' I said, trying to look honest. He had explained to me once that a swift counter-attack is the best strategy when you're cornered, so I quickly said, 'Why are you up so early? It's Saturday.'

He yawned, and started to fill the kettle.

'Mind your own business. Do me a favour and make me some toast.'

'Sorry. Busy,' I said. I could hear Mrs Stern and Mother moving around and the dining-room door opening. I hurried out to the hall.

'Here she is!' Mother said. 'Well, Charity, Mrs Stern has explained about your piano lessons. But she's suggested that instead she might tutor you in French.'

My mouth fell open.

'Yes! Yes, please!' I said, trying not to look too enthusiastic.

'Wednesdays as before?' Mother said, turning back to Mrs Stern.

This was dreadful! I had to think quickly.

'Could it be Thursdays, Mrs Stern?' I asked. 'The thing is we have gym on Wednesday afternoons and I get rather – I get . . .'

I'd never usually have admitted it, but this was an emergency. And, in fact, I did always feel wiped out after school on Wednesdays and my leg did ache after trying to keep up with the others.

Mrs Stern patted my arm.

'Thursdays will be fine. Soon you will be reading Molière,

207

Balzac — all the great French writers!'

I shot a quick look at Mother, afraid she'd be alarmed. 'Hmph!' I'd once heard Aunt Josephine say. 'French literature? All sex and revolution,' and Mother had nodded in agreement.

Now, though, she was smiling.

'That's very good of you, Mrs Stern. I'm sure Charity will do her best. Won't you, dear?'

'Oh yes! Yes!'

On the doorstep, Mrs Stern turned.

'And Mrs Brown, let me say again, if you feel unwell please let us know. We will be very happy to help.'

'What an extraordinary woman!' Mother said, shutting the front door behind her.

'She's nice, though, isn't she?' I put in anxiously.

'I suppose so. I hardly know what to make of her. I was surprised when she said she'd help you with French. "Don't you mean German?" I said, and she snapped out quite crossly, "I would not help anyone to learn that language." Understandable, I suppose. I asked her how she'd learned to speak French and she said her mother was French. She lived in Paris till she was ten. French is practically her first language.'

'Oh! I didn't know.'

'How could you? So what do you think, Charity? I hope you don't feel too bad about the piano, dear. I know it's a disappointment. You were so keen. But she did say that if you get the strength back properly in your hand you could try again.'

'No, it's fine, Mother. I've thought about it. It's really Hope's thing, isn't it?'

'You shouldn't let that put you off. But what about French tutoring? I thought you'd be pleased. I know you're worried about slipping behind, in French especially.'

'I am pleased! It . . . it'd be perfect. Mrs Stern is a great teacher. I could tell, just after that first music lesson.'

'That's settled, then. Have you finished your homework? Good. It's a long time since we've baked together. Let's go into the kitchen and make some things for tea tomorrow. Justin and Faith are coming.'

In the kitchen, Ted was making himself some tea.

'I'm going down to Portsmouth today, Ma,' he said, shooting Mother an uneasy look. 'Adam's going to show me round his ship. Maiden voyage next week. Cutting-edge technology in the engine room. Can't wait to see it.'

An anxious frown creased Mother's forehead.

'On your motorbike?'

'Of course.' Ted winked at me. 'I know what you're going to say, Ma, and, yes, I'll be careful.'

'That's just what I *am* going to say. Please, Ted, don't drive after dark.'

'I won't have to,' said Ted, leaping into this opening. 'That's why I'm staying overnight. Adam's putting me up. I'll be home tomorrow evening.'

'But that means you'll be travelling on a Sunday!' I said indignantly.

Ted scowled at me.

'I know, but—'

'It's your brother's decision,' Mother said, but her mouth had settled into a tight, round knot.

'Look, I'll try to be back by six for the evening Meeting,' Ted said roughly.

'Good, dear,' Mother said, turning away to fetch out the baking trays.

CHAPTER SIXTEEN

It had indeed been a long time since I'd baked with Mother. We'd always had our best times together measuring, sifting flour, breaking eggs and stirring delicious mixtures. Now we talked comfortably about the wedding, which was going to be in April, and about the aunts coming for Christmas, and about how much better Mr Fischer had been by the time he'd left. It was lovely just being with her. She'd always been at her happiest when making something or experimenting with new things. Now she was trying out a recipe for little round cakes called ginger gems, which one of her sisters had sent from New Zealand.

We'd just got them out of the oven when the doorbell rang again.

'If that's Rachel, can I invite her in?' I asked Mother.

'Yes, of course, dear,' she said. At least, I think that's what she said, because I was already flying to the front door.

Rachel was on the doorstep.

'French lessons!' she said. 'That's such a good idea.'

'Your mother thought of it.' I was grinning back at her. 'Come up to my room.'

'Mutti was upset, you know,' said Rachel, plumping herself down on my bed. 'Telling you she couldn't teach you to play the piano. Didn't you mind?'

'Not really. I'd worked out that I couldn't do it. I'd much rather learn French anyway. I didn't know your grandmother was French! It sounds so exotic.'

She frowned.

'Not exotic. Normal if you're French. But she was a bit special, actually. She was an opera singer.'

'I hope she didn't tell Mother that.'

'Why not?'

I'd spoken without thinking and now I could see I was on dangerous ground.

'Opera, theatre, cinema – all that kind of thing. We – the Lucasites don't – well – we don't usually go. Except for Shakespeare, if it's for school.'

'You don't go to the theatre? Or the opera?' She looked appalled.

'It's – um . . .'

'My grandmother was one of the most famous singers in Paris,' Rachel said, frowning. 'She sang in the Paris Opera for Puccini!'

I'd never heard of Puccini. It was time to change the subject. Quickly.

'Would you like to help me cheer up my room a bit?' I asked her. 'I thought we could go up to the attic and see if we can find some things.'

She leaped off the bed in a fluid bound.

'I'd love to! Is — what about your brother? Won't he mind if we go up there?'

She was blushing. I pretended not to notice.

'Ted? No, he's gone to Portsmouth. He won't be back till tomorrow.'

I'd thought I'd discovered everything interesting in the attic, but Rachel, burrowing under piles of boxes and diving into chests, found things I'd never seen before. She worked seriously, wiping the dust off glass-fronted pictures, holding up lengths of cloth against the light of the one small window in the gable end, and pouncing on things that I'd thought were too old or odd to bother with.

We staggered downstairs, our arms full, and ran into Mother.

'What *have* you been doing?' she said.

'Finding things!' I told her enthusiastically. 'We're going to decorate my room.'

'I see,' she said mildly. 'Make sure you check that old rug for moths and shake the dust out of those cloths.'

Back in my bedroom, Rachel became silent and intent. She laid our finds out on the bed and studied them, then she looked round the room with a measuring eye.

'We could paint the walls in different colours,' she said at last. 'A deep red on one wall and off-white on the others.'

'I don't think . . .' I began nervously.

She seemed to come back to reality.

'No, perhaps not. But look at this lovely wall hanging!

It's just the red I was thinking of.'

'It looks – I don't know – idolatrous or something.'

She shot me a puzzled look.

'It's Chinese. Those golden dragons on the scarlet background are fabulous. They would look wonderful above your chest of drawers.'

The dragons looked dangerous to me. There was something wild and fierce about them. But I saw what Rachel meant.

'Come on, Charity. Hold this end up. Let's see what it looks like.'

'I don't know how we'd hang it up,' I said.

'We'll think about that later. Now, this blue velvet would make a beautiful cover for your bed.'

'Little bits are coming off the ends,' I objected.

She swept this aside.

'We can easily sew them up. Let's do it now.'

It took a while to find Mother's sewing things, but we were soon at work, sitting on my bed, folding over the ends of the velvet and stitching them into rough hems.

'You know I'm going to be baptised?' I said.

'You told me. When? Can I come?'

I shuddered at the thought of exposing Rachel to the Lucasites.

'No, sorry. Anyway, I'd be too embarrassed. The thing is, when I was praying last night, I had a realization.'

She bent her head over her sewing so that her hair swung down over her face.

'Don't panic. I'm not going to get religious on you. It's just that I suddenly realized that I had a choice. Choices.'

She shook back her hair and looked at me.

'Choices about what?'

'About everything! Being a Lucasite, mainly. I've decided I will stay one, or I wouldn't be going to be baptised. But I don't have to believe things just because the Lucasites tell me to. I checked out a — a particular concept on Mother and Dad, and they gave me completely different answers!'

'What concept?'

I couldn't face talking to Rachel about Hell.

'Just something in the Bible. But what I mean is I can decide about things for myself.'

She looked amused.

'Charity, that's just basic. Of course you can!'

'There's no *of course* about it!' I felt irritated. 'I've always believed what I was taught to believe. I mean I'm not about to throw it all away. I think it's good. It's just that I've realized I'm allowed to decide for myself. I think.'

She broke off another length of thread and squinted up to the light from the window as she threaded it.

'I don't see that it's such a big deal. Of course you can believe whatever you like. This is a free country, isn't it?'

'No, but think about it. You can choose too.'

'I can't choose being Jewish,' said Rachel. 'You are or you aren't. Even if I wanted to — which I don't — I couldn't choose to be anything else.'

'No, but everything that goes with it. The — I don't know — the sorrow.'

That startled her. Her hands froze in mid-air.

'I can't not have the sorrow,' she said furiously. 'How can you even think that? How can I forget my whole family? How could I pretend that all those people were never murdered?'

'I didn't mean it like that.'

'I've lost my grandparents, my uncles and aunts, and my cousins who never even got born! My parents have lost their home, their country, everything they knew and loved! You want me to ignore all that? To *choose* not to have the sorrow?'

I felt dreadful.

'Mutti was right,' she said savagely. 'She told me it was better to stick to my own people.'

'Well, go back to your precious Susi, then!' I flashed at her. 'Anyway, my mother said exactly the same thing to me about you!'

'Yes, and you can go back to your lovely Tabitha Stebbins,' she snapped back.

My anger went as soon as it had come, leaving behind a lump of misery in my chest. I stole a glance at Rachel. She looked miserable too. She threw her sewing down and scrambled off the bed.

'Rachel, please don't go. I didn't think — I didn't understand. I don't know how you can bear it. Just living with it all the time.'

My voice tailed away. She'd gone over to the window and was looking out down the long length of garden where fallen leaves were blowing about in furious gusts. Neither of us said anything for what felt like an endless moment.

At last she turned round.

'You're right about one thing. I *have* got a choice. I don't care about Susi. I'm choosing to be friends with you, because I want to be.' She sounded severe and I could tell she was still angry. Then she let her breath out in a long sigh. 'But you know what? You're right in a way about the other thing. The sorrow. It'll never go away, but I'm not going to let it rule my life.' She came back to the bed and sat down. 'And, come to think of it, I could actually choose to tell Mutti that I don't want a little girl's bedroom any more.'

I nodded, not daring to say anything.

'But if I did,' she went on, 'it would hurt her feelings. And I'd feel disloyal to my grandmother.'

I was on firmer ground again.

'And if I started putting on lipstick and wearing trousers it would upset Mother and Dad, and scandalize everyone at the Meeting.'

'You're not allowed to wear make-up? Or wear trousers?'

'No.'

'Do you want to?'

'Not really, but that's not the point.'

We stared at each other.

'We're stuck,' I said.

Her face screwed up in a grimace.

'Yes, and you know what, I am. Literally. I've got my feet all tangled up in the flex of your new lamp.' She bent down to free herself, then stood up and shook out the velvet cover. 'Let's finish sewing it later. I can't wait to see what it looks like.'

217

I stuck my needle securely into the hem and we spread the lush blue velvet over my bed.

'Fabulous,' I said.

'It is, isn't it?'

The door opened.

'Girls,' said Mother, 'I think it's time to . . . Goodness!'

I watched anxiously as she took in the riot of colours, ornaments and pictures lying all over the room.

'We want to hang this up over the chest of drawers,' I said, showing her the Chinese tapestry.

She felt a corner of the material and rubbed it between her fingers.

'Silk. It's quite fragile. It shouldn't be in direct sunlight where it would fade. And you certainly shouldn't put nails through it. Over there, above the desk, would be better.' She gathered it up, wrinkling her nose at the dust. 'What did I say about shaking things out? Leave this with me. I'll put a backing on to strengthen it, and make some loops to hang it from. Now, Charity, I need some help in the kitchen. Rachel, it's half past five. Perhaps it's time you went home?'

'Sorry,' I said to Rachel, after Mother had gone. 'She's sending you home as if you were five years old.'

'No, it's all right. I can't believe she doesn't mind you doing all this and is actually going to help. So different from Mutti. Honestly, Charity, you've no idea.'

CHAPTER SEVENTEEN

The wind, which had been gusting all afternoon, blew itself up into a proper storm that night. I took a while to get to sleep, and then, in the middle of the night, an explosion of thunder woke me up. I fumbled for the switch on my new bedside lamp and looked at my watch. One o'clock. I could feel the draught as the wind found the gaps in my window frame. Something was pattering against the glass. I ignored it, turned off my lamp and tried to go back to sleep.

A terrific crack jerked me upright. Thunder was rolling angrily round in the sky. There was that rattling sound on the window again! I was properly awake now. I put the light back on, got out of bed and looked out of the window. It was completely dark, but a sudden bolt of lightning lit the garden in vivid, unearthly brilliance. I jumped back in fright. A man was standing under the window, his face turned up to mine. As the light faded away, I recognized Ted. A second later, it was pitch dark again.

I wrestled with the window, but the catch seemed to have stuck. The rattle came again. I could see what was making it now — little stones. Ted was throwing gravel up to my window.

I slipped on my dressing gown, groped for my slippers and ran downstairs. Ted almost fell inside as I opened the front door. I leaped away from him, horrified.

'You're covered in blood! And soaking wet!'

''S nothing. Crashed my bike. *Shh*, Char, don't — mussen wake them up.'

'Are you hurt? You look awful! Where's your bike now?'

'Dunno. Somewhere. Adam brought me home.'

I stepped away from him.

'You smell funny. Disgusting.'

'Had a bit to drink. Stop asking me things. I gotta — gotta . . .'

He stumbled towards the stairs and fell on the bottom step.

I looked up, sure I'd heard a floorboard creak upstairs.

'Shh!' I hissed at Ted.

He sat still, his head in his hands.

'You're a good girl, Char. Favourite sister.'

I looked helplessly at him. Was I being a good girl? Ought I call Dad? Someone pulled the chain in the lavatory at the end of the landing, then I heard footsteps, and Dad and Mother's bedroom door softly opened and closed. There was no more sound. Whoever it was had gone back to bed.

It was awful helping Ted up the stairs. He kept missing the steps and lurching towards me. The noise of the howling gale outside must have covered up for us, though, and we made it to the little door at the bottom of the attic stairs at last. Then I heard voices, and a strip of light appeared under Mother and Dad's bedroom door.

'Quick!' I hissed at Ted, shoving him through the attic door and closing it behind him.

I darted back towards my bedroom and nearly made it before Dad appeared.

'Charity? What's the matter? It's only a storm, dear. Nothing to be frightened of.'

'I'm not frightened, thank you,' I said. If I hadn't been so nervous I'd have been insulted by his babying tone of voice. 'The storm woke me up and I'm going downstairs to get a glass of water.'

And to clear up any mess Ted's left on the stairs, I added silently to myself.

'Oh. Well, goodnight, then.'

He went back to his room. Behind me, I could hear Ted stumbling up the wooden stairs to the attic and a bang as he crashed through his bedroom door.

Ted's lost, I thought miserably as I fetched a torch from the kitchen and cleared the few leaves and twigs that he'd brought inside in his wake. *And I'm being his accomplice.*

Back in bed, I curled up, cold and anxious. I squeezed my eyes tight shut, praying for Ted with all my strength, but the wind seemed to catch my prayers and hurl them angrily back to me.

I was on high alert, listening out for Ted at Sunday breakfast with Dad and Mother the next morning. I felt awful. I'd hardly slept, and I was all torn up inside.

Ted came home drunk in the middle of the night, I nearly blurted out. *I had to let him in. He'd crashed his bike and was bleeding like mad.*

I didn't say anything, although during the recitation of the Bible and Dad's long prayers, worries were hammering at me so insistently I could hardly believe that no one else could hear them.

'You're very quiet, Charity,' said Dad as we set off to walk to the Meeting.

'Storm kept me awake.'

The words were blown away in the wind, which was still gusting strongly and threatening to tear off my hat. Having to wear a hat was always irritating, but this morning it seemed just too much.

'Why do we have to wear these stupid things to the Meeting?' I burst out. 'It's so unfair! Men don't have to.'

'You know why, dear,' Mother said in her reasonable voice. 'It's Biblical.'

'So are a lot of stupid things,' I muttered, jumping away from the edge of the road as a bus rushed past, sending a spray of last night's rainwater across the pavement.

I couldn't concentrate on the Meeting at all. I was too worried about Ted. He couldn't stay in his room forever. What would Mother and Dad say when they saw his bloodied face and found out about his bike?

My stomach was churning as we walked home afterwards. We turned into the drive at last and walked up to the door.

To my surprise, Ted opened it. He looked pale and heavy-eyed. He'd cleaned the blood off his face, but angry red cuts and grazes ran down the side of his face, and one eye was bruising to a dark hollow. He'd roughly bandaged his left hand.

Dad was the first to speak.

'Ted! What's happened? You're hurt!'

'I'm going to tell you,' said Ted. His jaw was tight, as if he was bracing himself. 'Can we go into the study? Mother, you come too. And Charity.'

I was really nervous now. Dad's study was where serious family conferences happened. Ted had actually got things ready, setting out four chairs in a circle. We sat down.

'I've got things to say,' said Ted. His hands were shaking and his voice was unsteady. 'About last night first. I did go to Portsmouth yesterday, but not to see Adam. I went to Danny's birthday party. He's an old naval mate. Adam said I was a fool to go. I knew Danny's friends were a – a rough lot, but I wanted to. There's this girl, Miranda, Danny's sister. I met her once. I wanted to see her again.'

Mother's eyes were fixed on him with painful anxiety. Her mouth was working. Dad was leaning forward in his chair, his hands clasped tightly together. I could hardly breathe.

Ted ran a hand through his hair.

'Adam was right. I shouldn't have gone. It was awful. There were all these stupid drinking games, and Miranda – she was all over this stupid fellow – egging him on. "Go on," she kept saying. "Get Ted another drink. Look at him, all sweet and innocent. Come on, Ted. Let go! Enjoy yourself! Have another!"'

I hate that wicked Miranda! I just want to — to hit *her!* I thought savagely.

He looked round at us defiantly.

'Look, I was an idiot, all right? I shouldn't blame anyone else. It was all such a mess and a muddle and I can't even remember what happened. I know I got out of there at some point and was sick, then I got on my motorbike to go back to Adam's place, and — well, to tell you the truth, I crashed it just before I got there. Came off at a sharp corner. Good thing nothing was coming or I'd have been . . .'

Mother gasped and put her hand up to her mouth. For the first time, Dad looked angry.

'I've *loathed* that thing from the first moment you got it! How could you be so stupid, Ted? To ride it when you'd been drinking? You could have killed someone, or yourself!'

'Don't think I don't realize that.' Ted was trying to look defiant. 'I didn't know what I was doing. I was—'

'Drunk.' Mother's voice was rich with disgust.

'Yes!' Ted flashed back at her. 'I was, and if you want to know what it felt like, I hated it. All the way through National Service I never — I managed not to — and, just this once, I let myself be persuaded and . . . If you must know, I wanted to know what it felt like.'

There was a pause.

'How did you get home?' asked Dad, in a quieter voice.

'I got Adam out of bed. He'd said I could stay with him, but his parents had suddenly turned up. He knew they'd be shocked to see me in the state I was in, so he drove me home in his car.'

He looked over at me.

Don't tell! Don't say I let you in! I silently begged him, giving him a tiny shake of my head.

His eyes sort of flickered. He'd understood.

'He drove you all the way back from Portsmouth? In the middle of the night?' Dad sounded incredulous. 'Four − no, five hours there and back? He must have been driving all night.'

Ted's lips tightened.

'He's a good friend. I'd have done the same for him.'

'So where's the bike now?' demanded Mother.

'At Adam's place.' He swallowed. 'He phoned just now. He says it's a write-off.'

'Good,' said Dad savagely. 'I hope it is. I haven't had a moment's peace since you got your hands on that wretched thing.'

'Never mind the bike,' said Mother. 'Or what you did in Portsmouth. It's deceiving us that hurts, Ted. I didn't think you'd do that.'

Ted had eaten enough humble pie. Now he was exasperated.

'Look, Mother, I'm grown up! Aren't I entitled to a life of my own?'

No one said anything. Then Mother stood up.

'You'd better let me look at your hand. And those cuts on your face. They need disinfecting.'

I jumped up too.

'I'll get the Germolene,' I said, desperate to do something.

'It's in the bathroom cupboard, isn't it?'

'Sit down, Char. Just a minute, Mother,' said Ted. 'There's something else.'

We sank back on to our chairs. Ted took a deep breath.

'I've got a place in a student hostel near the college,' he said, his eyes on the pale green carpet. 'It'll be easier for me to get to lectures. My scholarship will cover it and the zoo says I can work Saturday shifts if I want to. Mucking out the lions will be easy after dealing with Danny and his mates.'

He looked up hopefully, but his joke fell flat. Tears pricked my eyes. Was Ted becoming a lost soul? Perhaps this was a test for me. Maybe it was my task to lead him back to the True Path?

I sat there, my brow furrowed, trying to think of the right words, but Mother got in first. She only said, 'Oh, Ted,' but there was a universe of reproach in her voice.

'Don't look like that, Mother! It's not the end of the world!' Ted sounded harassed. 'I'm not going to the North Pole! I'll be back often.'

'Where is this hostel?' she asked. 'Where will you worship?'

'I'll find out where the nearest Lucasite Meeting is and get in touch with them,' said Dad. 'You'll need an introduction before you're admitted to the Breaking of Bread.'

'No!' Ted almost shouted. 'Leave it, Dad. I'll sort it out for myself.'

'We'll bear you up in our prayers, my dear boy,' Dad said sorrowfully, after another short silence.

'Yes, well, thank you,' said Ted. 'Look, I'm not moving out

till Wednesday. I've got to go back to Portsmouth tomorrow to sort out the bike and apologize to Adam.'

'You're not going to see that Miranda, are you?' I said with loathing in my voice.

Ted shuddered.

'I'm never going near Danny or Miranda or any of that lot ever again.'

CHAPTER EIGHTEEN

Even though Ted hadn't been around much, it took me a while to get used to the fact that he'd finally left home. Dad drove him up to the hostel with some of his things and came back with reassuring news. The place was clean, there were strict rules about drinking, no girls were allowed into the men's rooms and Ted said he'd be working too hard to think about anything else. He'd be able to concentrate better, he'd said, now that he didn't have to travel up and down from London every day.

After that, I tried to put Ted out of my mind.

Autumn was well and truly on us now. When we'd first moved into Gospel Fields, it had been high summer and I'd been drawn into the garden all the time. I'd explored every corner, on my own and with Rachel, and when she wasn't there I'd made myself climb 'our' tree again and again until I could do it confidently. It still wasn't easy, but the reward was to feel that I had made her favourite tree my special place too. Sometimes I'd perch in the branches on my own with an apple and a book, and after a while I'd forget to read but sit and daydream, imagining myself trekking across a desert on the back of a camel, or riding through a jungle on an elephant, like Phileas Fogg in *Around the World in Eighty Days*.

Once or twice, Hope and Faith had played a game of tennis and I'd watched from my hiding place above, half envious, half relishing the fact that they didn't know I was there.

Now, though, my tree had shed its leaves. There were only a few late blooms on the rose arch, and the flowers in the long border running down beside the lawn were mostly dead, their seed heads hanging heavy. Orange beech leaves from the patch of woodland were scattered on the lawn, and the wind had blown drifts of them into corners. Mr Barlow spent hours sweeping them up and putting them in big bins to rot down. He'd never been very friendly to me. Sometimes I'd smell smoke drifting up from a bonfire he'd made, and I'd wanted to go and help him feed it, and maybe roast marshmallows on the embers, but I knew he wouldn't welcome me.

The house felt different too, bigger and gloomier now that the evenings were drawing in. There were cold draughts that I hadn't noticed in the summer. We hardly went into the drawing room any more. It was too difficult to heat, but Mother had started lighting the fire at the end of the dining room, and we sat around it in the evenings, or stayed in the kitchen, which the stove always kept warm.

School was endurable. I kept out of the way of Monica and her gang of friends, but the other girls didn't seem to like me much, either. I knew that I was boasting too much about Gospel Fields, trying to dazzle people with its magnificence. I could see that I was turning the others off, but I didn't know how to stop myself.

Then, suddenly, the day of my baptism was looming. It took me a long time to get to sleep the night before. What with failing to witness to anybody, being (possibly) corrupted by Auntie Vi and her peculiar vegetables, not to mention her lipstick, and failing to keep Ted's errant footsteps on the straight-and-narrow way, I didn't feel that I'd made any progress at all with Purification and Dedication. In fact, I'd been backsliding.

It was too late to do much about it now.

'Please don't be disappointed, Lord,' I prayed. 'I'll keep working at it. I promise.'

The baptism was set for 6.30 p.m. on Sunday evening. Justin and Faith were coming (it would be Justin's first exposure to the Lucasites). I could hardly expect Ted to come, although I'd prayed and prayed for him to be there. I'd had this vision of a pure young girl (me), dedicating her life to the Lord through the waters of baptism, a sight so moving that her beloved brother (Ted), lost in sin, would fall to his knees and plead for forgiveness. There were illustrations of just such events in Aunt Josephine's Victorian novels. I could hardly hope for a shaft of sunlight to fall upon me as I emerged from the water (it was November, after all), but there would be music, if you could call Lucasite singing music, and I was hoping for an atmosphere of rapturous holiness, as long as old Mr Hollins didn't ruin everything by falling asleep and snoring.

Mother came in to wake me on the fateful morning. I rolled

over, groaning, and buried my head in the pillow.

'It's all right, Charity, you don't need to get up,' she said. 'I heard you coughing in the night. You're not ill, are you?'

I blinked at her through bleary eyes.

'I don't think so. I feel all right.'

'You'd better stay at home this morning to be on the safe side. You need to be at your best for this evening.'

It ought to be nice when you've been told you can stay in bed, but I'd had too many months of not being able to get up at all, and it wasn't a treat for me. I rolled over and dozed for a while, trying to go back to sleep, but my nerves were all jangled. Tonight was my baptism! Was I ready? I was sure I wasn't.

The hours stretched ahead till Mother and Dad were due back from the Meeting. As it was Sunday, I was only supposed to read Christian books, stories from the Bible or novels about missionaries, and children's souls being saved. I'd read them again and again when I was younger, but I felt suspicious of them now. They'd taken liberties with my childish heart, wringing tears from me till my hankies were sodden. Was that right? Was that honest? Anyway, they were full of heroic white Englishmen (a few Scots, to be fair, and the occasional woman), but the Africans and Indians they were trying to convert were just supposed to do what they were told and be grateful. They weren't portrayed like real people at all. They weren't even made to seem interesting. Anyway, Dr Sturges had put me off missionaries for life.

Today of all days, I needed to reach for the top. Only

the Bible would do. I got dressed, brushed my teeth, made my bed, hurried down to the kitchen, ate a quick bowl of cornflakes and rushed back upstairs. Then I picked up my Bible, intending to read all four Gospels – Matthew, Mark, Luke and John – with pauses for meditation if so inspired.

To put myself in the right frame of mind, I started by tidying my room. The Chinese wall hanging was in place now. The golden dragons seemed to wink at me, but I turned my face away from them. I mustn't contemplate their exotic splendour today. The blue velvet cover on my bed only needed a few tweaks to smooth it to perfection. I noticed for the first time that Mother had sewn up the ends properly on her sewing machine. She must have done it while I'd been out at school. How typical of her selfless devotion to family! What an ungrateful daughter I had been! I hastily confessed in prayer, and asked for forgiveness.

Dotted among the brass elephants striding along the windowsill, which Rachel had pulled out of an old trunk in the attic, were the few cards I'd received. Aunt Josephine's showed an open window with a white bird flying out of it into a blue sky. *Congratulations on your baptism*, she'd written, then added several cryptic references to Biblical texts, which I hadn't yet looked up.

Sorry I can't make it! Don't drown!! Hope had scrawled inside a card with a picture of roses on the front. She'd added lots of *XX*s.

Justin and I hope to be with you in the flesh, if not we'll be with you in spirit, Faith had written on a card showing the front of her hospital. *P.S. Sorry, haven't had time to get you a proper card. Madly busy here!*

There was even a letter from Mr Fischer. He'd written, *God be with you, Fräulein Charity, and stay true to your brave heart.* At the bottom he'd done a little pencil sketch of a church rising up out of piles of rubble, and printed under it, *We here in Germany are rising from destruction with joy!*

I reread them, set them tidily in a row and settled down in my chair, the Bible open on my knee. Then I heard the letterbox clatter. I raced downstairs and threw open the front door. Rachel stepped back, surprised.

'I thought you'd be out at your church,' she said. 'Isn't it your thing today?'

'Tonight.'

'Oh – well, good luck.' She sensed she might have struck the wrong note and went on, 'I mean, I hope it goes well and everything.'

'Thanks.'

I fought briefly against temptation and lost.

'Do you want to come in? Mother and Dad are at the Meeting.'

She followed me into the kitchen.

'Have you heard from Ted yet?' she said, her cheeks flaming. 'Is he coming to your baptism?'

'No. At least, he hasn't said. He came home yesterday for more of his stuff. His friend Adam helped him.'

She'd followed the saga of Ted's disgrace in Portsmouth

and departure from Gospel Fields with passionate interest. I'd given up trying to tell her the truth about Ted. She was a hopeless case, after all.

'How did he look? Is he getting on all right?'

'He didn't say much.'

I didn't tell her that I'd kept out of their way. I hadn't been able to look Adam in the face since Ted had mentioned my secret armpit hair, right out loud, in front of him.

'Oh, I nearly forgot,' said Rachel. 'I only came round to drop in a note for your mother. It's from Mutti. It's ages away, but she's buying opera tickets for December and she wants to know if she can get one for you. I told her you weren't allowed to go, but she said she couldn't believe it, and anyway it was worth a try.'

An invitation to the opera! On the day of my baptism! My head whirled in panic.

'It's Puccini,' went on Rachel. '*Madame Butterfly*. It's dreadfully sad, but quite moral really.'

I swallowed. Rachel was my best friend! How could she be a servant of the Prince of Darkness? But Mother might think she was. Mother might think that the Sterns were bent on luring me away from the Path. Mother might even stop my French lessons.

'I — I don't know,' I stammered.

'I do hope your mother says yes,' Rachel said cheerfully. 'I'd love it if you could come. Opera's all right, but to be honest it's quite boring sometimes, and Mutti and Papa are so sort of solemn about it.'

Boring? Solemn? About the opera? That didn't sound very sinful.

'Look, I'd better go,' Rachel said, unaware of the turbulence she'd set up in my head. 'People coming to lunch. Panic in the kitchen! You've no idea!'

The clock in the hall struck twelve as I went back upstairs. The morning had gone! Mother and Dad would be home in half an hour and I hadn't read a word of my Bible.

A choking November pea-souper smog had settled over everything by the time we left for the Hall that evening. Thick yellow curls of tarry smoke made me want to cough. There was no question of walking. Dad drove us in the car, leaning forward to peer into the murk, unable to make out anything except for the nearside kerb. All we could see of the approaching cars and buses were pools of light from headlamps that didn't look as if they were attached to anything.

Even inside the Hall there was a faint yellowish mist, but it hadn't put off the Lucasites. The congregation was beginning to trickle in.

Everything gets moved around for a baptism. For the morning Breaking of Bread, there's a table in the middle of the Hall covered with a white cloth, and the chairs are set in rows radiating out from the table.

The table had been cleared away and the chairs now faced the far end of the Hall where the floorboards had been lifted to reveal the baptistry, a wide, waist-deep tank. It was already full of water.

Mother had been kind and tender with me all afternoon.

'It's all right,' she said, seeing me shiver at the sight of so much water. 'Those metal coils are heating it. You won't get cold.'

She hurried me past the baptistry into the back room. Tabitha and Mrs Stebbins were already there, and Mrs Prendergast was laying a couple of long white robes over a chair. Tabitha's face was stiff and set. She was pushing away her mother, who was trying to comb her hair. Mrs Prendergast hurried up to me and folded me in a hug. I had time to notice a faint whiff of lavender, then she pulled away.

I bet she didn't hug you, I thought, trying to read the disapproving expression on Tabitha's face.

Mrs Prendergast seemed to have caught the unfriendly looks we'd exchanged.

'You two girls!' she said brightly. 'The pride and joy of us all.'

It came out awkwardly, but I could see she was being kind, and at that moment I realized that I loved Mrs Prendergast.

You never had children of your own, I thought. *You've only got your wheezy little dog.*

'Now,' Mrs Prendergast said, assuming her usual brisk manner. 'Have you girls got your bathing costumes?'

The colour fled from my cheeks. No one had said anything about a bathing costume. I watched with rising panic as Tabitha triumphantly held up a brand-new pink creation with an inset wired brassiere.

'Here's yours, Charity,' Mother said, pulling my old black

swimsuit out of her bag. I looked at it with horror. It was already too small for me. It would be worse than my worst nightmare to show myself to the entire Lucasite community in such a horrible thing.

'Good,' said Mrs Prendergast. 'Now pop along to the Ladies, girls, and get changed. Don't look like that, Charity! No one will see your costumes. They'll be covered by your baptismal gowns.'

I followed Tabitha out to the Ladies.

'Are you nervous?' I said, trying to be friendly. 'I'm terrified.'

I caught a flash of her hostile face as she went into her cubicle.

'Why should I be? We're doing the Lord's will.'

'Yes, of course, but—'

'I heard all about your bedroom,' she went on, raising her voice so that I could hear her over the cubicle's partition. 'Mum told me you've got a heathen picture on your walls. Dragons and suchlike.'

'It's not heathen! It's Chinese!' I said indignantly.

I could almost see her frown as she tried to work this out.

'What's the difference? It's not Bible-based, anyway.'

I took a deep breath, furious words on my lips, and snapped my mouth shut just in time.

Here comes the Devil again, wanting you to quarrel with Tabitha, right now, on this holy night, I told myself sternly. *Don't. Just don't.*

We came out of our cubicles at the same time and stood facing each other. Her eyes were wide with angry expectation.

'Your costume's really pretty,' I said. 'I think I've grown out of mine.'

That took the wind out of your sails, I thought, turning my back on her.

The women were waiting for us. Mother was holding up one of the long white robes. She pulled it over my head and the skirt fell to the floor with a clunk.

'Weights,' she said. 'To stop it floating up.'

She tied the girdle round my waist while Mrs Stebbins dressed Tabitha.

Robed in white, I was starting to feel unreal. I could hear low voices now as the congregation filled the Meeting Hall beyond the wooden partition. There was a discreet knock on the door. Mrs Prendergast hurried over to answer it.

'Are they ready?' came Dad's voice.

She opened the door to let him in.

'Charity! Such a wonderful moment! So . . .'

His voice shook. He was holding a bag and took a new Bible out of it. It was bound in black leather and the edges of the pages were gilded. A red marker ribbon fluttered from it.

'From your mother and me, on this special day.'

I took it, thrilled. The leather felt soft and lovely in my hands, and when I opened it the thin India-paper pages made a rich rustling sound as I turned them.

Behind him I could see Tabitha's face. Her eyes were bright with tears.

Dad took an identical Bible out of his bag.

'Dear Tabitha,' he said, turning to her and putting it into

her hands. 'For you, from your old friends with our love.'

He put a hand on each of our shoulders. 'We'll say a prayer, shall we, before we go in?'

I felt almost faint as I followed Dad out of the back room and into the main Hall. Rows of familiar faces swam in front of me, but I couldn't take them in.

What would happen when I rose up out of the water? Would I actually see Jesus?

Tabitha and I and our mothers, along with Mrs Prendergast, took our seats in the reserved front row. There were prayers, I think, people sang, someone read things out of the Bible, Dad stood up and preached a little sermon.

Suddenly, Mr Prendergast was standing at the top of the steps leading down into the baptistry. He was wearing chest-high fisherman's waders and a waterproof jacket. I had a wild impulse to laugh as he splashed down the steps into the water, but now he was holding out his hand towards me and the look on his face was too kind and solemn for giggles.

Mother nudged me to my feet. She and Mrs Prendergast took hold of my arms and guided me to the steps. As if in a dream, I walked down into the water.

It wasn't really cold, but the feel of it was still shocking. I was trembling.

Mr Prendergast said something about a special verse that he had chosen for me. Then in a rising voice he proclaimed, 'I baptise you in the name of the Father!' and he grasped me round the waist and plunged me down on my back, till my head was right under the water. I came up spluttering. He took a firmer grip.

'And of the Son!' he cried.

I was ready this time and had taken a deep breath. Down I went again.

'And of the Holy Spirit!' he called out.

He was panting by now with the effort of heaving me upright.

I stood there, up to my chest in the water.

Now He'll come! I thought. *Now He'll show Himself!*

But all I could feel was the heaviness of the wet gown, the straps of my too-small bathing costume biting into my shoulders, and my hair dripping round my face. Then Mr Prendergast's hand was on my back, gently urging me towards the steps and up out of the tank.

Someone started crooning, '*Happy day, happy day, when Jesus washed my sins away.*'

Everyone joined in, but I didn't hear them because two faces had swum sharply out of the crowd. Ted was sitting right at the back, and beside him, her face stripped of lipstick and with a demure, beige, Lucasite-ish hat on her head, was Auntie Vi.

Mother was waiting at the top of the steps with an enormous bath towel. She wrapped me up in it and hurried me out to the back room.

Was that it? I thought. *Where's my divine revelation?*

Mother lifted off the white robe and eased me out of the tight bathing costume. I stood shivering, barely able to move. She dried me with the towel as if I was still a baby, then handed me my clothes and helped me to put them on. Now she was vigorously towelling my hair.

'Ted's here,' I said, through chattering teeth. 'And Auntie Vi.'

She had no time to answer before Tabitha, swathed in more towels, came in with Mrs Stebbins. Mother started combing my hair as the congregation burst into song again, louder this time.

'Joy! Joy! Joy! With joy my heart is ringing!'

Mother and Mrs Stebbins took our white robes away to the kitchen, to drain into the sink.

'What was your special verse?' said Tabitha, as she pulled on her navy-blue skirt.

I gaped at her. I had no idea. But Mother was back already and was urging me out into the Hall.

I subsided into my chair, deeply disappointed. Why hadn't the Lord spoken to me? Had I failed in some way?

The service was soon over. People crowded round to congratulate Tabitha and me, but I pushed past them, desperate to see Ted and Auntie Vi.

Faith was suddenly in front of me. Justin, beside her, was fending off enthusiastic Lucasites who had heard lurid accounts of how he'd saved Mother's life, and were anyway deeply curious about Faith's non-Lucasite young man.

'Where's Ted?' I asked Faith urgently. 'I saw him. With Auntie Vi.'

'Just leaving. You'll catch them if you're quick.'

I pushed my way through the crowd to the main door. Ted

was already almost through it. I caught his arm.

'You came!' I said stupidly.

'Couldn't not,' he muttered, looking embarrassed.

'But why are you rushing off? I might have missed you altogether!'

He exchanged a look with Auntie Vi.

'Black sheep, darling,' she said. 'Spectres at the feast. Had to support you in your big moment, rite of passage and all that, but better not confuse things for poor old Iver and Jeanie. Come here and give your wicked aunt a kiss.'

'Watch out,' said Ted. 'Faith and Justin are coming this way.'

'Oops!' said Auntie Vi. 'Run for it, Ted. Not the right time for a family reunion.' She turned to me. 'You're a wonderful girl, Charity, and I actually rather adore you. Come and see me soon.'

And seconds later the fog had swallowed them up.

I lay awake for a long time that night. For some reason, I cried a bit too. I felt jangled, confused, unreal.

Then, at last, when I was almost asleep, I heard Mr Prendergast's voice again, quoting my special verse.

'The whole law is summed up in one sentence,' he'd said. 'You must love your neighbour as yourself.'

I hadn't got it quite right, but that was more or less what he'd said.

Love! All I had to do was love!

And that doesn't literally mean your neighbour, like Rachel, I reminded myself. *You've got to love everyone.*

And then it happened. A flooding feeling filled my head, a kind of lightness and calm. This was it. This was the moment. I could feel the presence of God right there inside me. There was no need for wordy prayers. No need for anything except this feeling of peace. And love.

Now that I'd finally solved the mystery of life, worked out what lay at the foundation of the universe and actually experienced the presence of God, I'd assumed, as I went to sleep, that my life had changed forever.

But when I woke up, it was Monday morning. A mean, bitter, November rain had swept in, clearing the smog away. Also, I realized that I hadn't done my Maths homework.

So did Love carry me triumphantly through the rest of that day and into the week beyond?

It did not.

'Charity,' said Miss Clement wearily as I tried to make myself small at the back of the Maths class, the first lesson of the day, 'you're going to have do better than this. You've missed a lot. You really must try to catch up. Your homework on my desk first thing tomorrow, please.'

'Sorry, Miss Lemmy,' I said, then bit my lip as everyone around me sniggered. Miss Clement's nickname was Clemmy Lemmy, so you can't blame me for letting it slip out.

It was even worse in French, which I'd been keenly looking forward to. I'd now had three lessons with Mrs Stern and they'd been lovely. No grammar exercises, no boring lists of vocabulary to learn, but really interesting conversations in actual French, when I'd felt for the words I'd wanted and she'd helped me find them.

Now I was dying to show off my progress. It just shows, however, that pride comes before a fall, and a haughty spirit before destruction, because when Mrs Hamilton asked for volunteers to read out the stupid little story in the textbook, I put up my hand and stood up almost before she'd pointed to me. Then I read it triumphantly loudly in my new Mrs Stern-ish French accent.

It occurred to me too late that this was a mistake. Mrs Hamilton's French accent was incredibly awful. She'd admitted herself that she'd never actually been to France in her entire life, but if you ask me that's no excuse.

'Well, well, Charity,' she said as I sat down. 'Been to Paris, have we? There's no need to show off.'

My temper rose. I could feel it.

'My neighbour speaks proper French,' I said hotly. 'She's been giving me lessons.'

Now the colour was rising in Mrs Hamilton's face too.

'Sit *down*, Charity. A fancy accent is one thing, but you would do well to work on your irregular verbs, of which you have an inadequate grasp.'

There was a hiss from behind me.

'*Oo là là*! *Lady* Charity is having private lessons!'

It was Monica, of course. I whipped round to snarl at her, but it was too late. Other girls had heard and they were nudging each other delightedly.

It had been sort of all right at school since the beginning of term, when everyone had wanted to know what having polio was like, but it was clear, when the bell rang for break, that my novelty had run out. Monica was everywhere, dripping poison into people's ears in the clever, funny way she had. 'Holy Charity' had been bad enough, but 'Lady Charity' was worse. I realized once again that I'd bragged too much about the wonders of Gospel Fields. As I stood alone in my old, miserable corner of the playground, watching knots of girls talking and laughing, I could almost smell the miasma of envious disgust billowing around myself that Monica was cleverly creating.

I just had to endure school after that. The lessons were all right, mostly, if I kept my head down, but break-times were miserable. The Lord was definitely looking after me, though, because Mrs Thorpe, the librarian, came into our class and asked for volunteers to help in the library during lunch breaks. I was so desperate to be picked that I practically dislocated my shoulder as I punched my arm up into the air. Then I realized I needn't have tried so hard because no one else was interested.

The library was a haven for me. Mrs Thorpe, who had been our school librarian for years, never raised her voice, but she didn't need to. She only had to lift an eyebrow and the noisiest person subsided like a pricked balloon. Perhaps it was because of the way she looked. Her grey hair was elegantly permed and she wore cream silky blouses and tailored skirts. She was the sort of person everyone tried to impress. Me most of all.

She examined me over her gold-rimmed glasses on my first

day of volunteering, opened her mouth to say something, then changed her mind.

'You like reading, do you, Charity?'

'Yes, Mrs Thorpe. But . . .'

'But what?'

I made a decision to trust her.

'While I was ill . . .'

'Ah yes. The polio. I heard. I hope you're quite better now?'

'Nearly.' I wasn't going to admit to my weak arm and leg. 'Anyway, while I was in bed I read a lot, but Mother had to choose all the books for me in our local library and she always got me the same kinds of things because I'm not supposed to . . .'

'Not supposed to what?'

I took a deep breath.

'Read books that are, well, worldly. Mother always chose Christian books, about missionaries and things.'

'And did you like them?'

'Some of them. She got me to read the classics too. Like *Jane Eyre*. I *loved* that. And Dickens.'

Her eyebrows shot up.

'You've been reading Dickens?'

I nodded.

'I liked *Nicholas Nickleby*, but it's rather long.'

'It is indeed. And perhaps a little old-fashioned. I think we can find things your mother won't mind you reading that are a bit more up to date. Now, you came here to work, and here's what I want you to do.'

I would have spent every lunch hour in the library if I'd been allowed to, but Mrs Thorpe limited me to Mondays and Thursdays. I loved the quiet, steady jobs she gave me to do, but they never took long, and then she'd let me sit in a corner and read something she'd chosen for me. I got so absorbed in *Animal Farm* that I didn't even hear the bell ring and she had to shoo me out of the library.

'Woof, woof! Here comes Thorpie's poodle dog!' Monica crowed as I came late into our classroom, but even as I curled up inside I tried my best to ignore her.

CHAPTER NINETEEN

Life was more interesting at home than at school. To my amazement, Mother and Dad had decided that I could go to the opera, after all.

'I've had a word with Professor Stern,' Dad told me as he gave me the news. 'He understood my concerns – in fact, he expressed his own views on bringing up a teenage daughter!' He waited for me to laugh, but I didn't. 'He assures me,' Dad went on, 'that there's nothing indecent in the production. An educational opportunity for you, in fact. We know we can trust you, Charity, if temptations open up before you, but we can't guard you forever from all that is around us.'

Mother was more practical and surprisingly anxious.

'You'll have to have a new dress,' she said. 'It's not till December, so the weather will be colder. Something warm. It had better be velvet. A golden brown would show up the lights in your hair.'

My mouth fell open. I'd worn Faith's and Hope's cast-offs for so long that a new dress of my own had seemed like an impossible dream. Visions of trying on some of the elegant gowns I'd seen in shop windows swam before my eyes. Could this really be Mother speaking? The woman for whom vanity held one of the top spots in the list of the seven deadly sins? She was actually telling me that there were lights in my hair?

'I won't have the Sterns or anyone else thinking we don't know what's correct,' she added, looking rather sheepish.

'Perhaps Auntie Vi would take me shopping,' I said hopefully. She looked appalled.

'No need for that. I'll make your dress myself. I've looked out a few old patterns. You can choose the one you like best.'

'Oh.'

Just in time, I bit back a furious objection. The main thing was that I was going to the opera with Rachel. If I started making a fuss, permission might be withdrawn.

A few days later, I came home from school to find the dining-room table covered in a length of brown velvet. Mother had pinned the chosen pattern to it and was already cutting out my new dress. By Saturday morning, it was nearly finished, and after breakfast Mother made me try it on so she could adjust the fitting.

I heard voices in the hall. Rachel had come round, and Dad had opened the door for her. She came into the dining room and stared at me, all swathed in brown velvet, and at Mother, kneeling on the floor pinning up the hem.

'I can't believe you're making it yourself, Mrs Brown,' she said admiringly. 'Mutti can't sew at all. She hasn't had any new clothes for years and years, actually. She's still wearing things she had made for her in Paris before the war.'

Mother removed the pins she was holding in her mouth. 'Is she now?'

'They're twenty years old,' Rachel went on blithely, 'but Mutti says that haute couture never dates.'

Mother didn't answer.

'What are you going to wear?' I asked hastily.

She shrugged.

'My blue dress, probably. Mother says that blue looks good in the opera house where everything's dark red and gold.'

Neither Mother nor I could think of anything to say. Rachel noticed our silence.

'Oh, but your dress will look gorgeous, Charity. Anyway, it's dark most of the time, so no one notices what anyone's wearing.'

Mother stood up.

'It's nice to see you, Rachel, but we're rather busy this morning. We have a guest arriving this evening and there's a lot to do.'

'A guest? Who?' I said.

'Kurian Devasy. He's been in hospital with pneumonia, and we're going to have to look after him.'

'Kurian!' I said. 'That Indian boy? I remember him.'

I suppose I must have made a face. I felt like making one, anyway. Then I saw that Mother was frowning at me.

'And no fuss from you, please,' she said.

I could see in her eyes that she was remembering how rude I'd been to Mr Fischer when he'd first arrived. I still felt ashamed when I thought about it.

'India!' Rachel said excitedly. 'I've never met anyone from India.'

'His father's an old friend of Dad's,' I said, trying not to sound gloomy. 'They were students together in Glasgow.'

Mr Devasy had visited us years ago, when he'd come to Britain for a conference. He'd brought Kurian with him and I'd disliked him intensely.

'How long's he going to stay for?' I asked Mother.

'He'll be with us till he's properly better,' she said. 'It's a shame. He only arrived in London a month ago. He won a scholarship to study law here, but he caught a bad cold as soon as he arrived and it turned into pneumonia. The hospital have so many emergency chest cases, thanks to the smog, that they want to discharge him today, but his landlady won't let him go back to his room. She refuses to believe that he hasn't got a tropical disease that's going to infect her.'

'That's mean!' said Rachel.

'It is indeed. Now, Charity, mind the pins when you take your dress off. We've got work to do.'

'Would you like me to stay and help, Mrs Brown?' Rachel said eagerly as I changed back into my skirt and jumper.

'We'll manage, thank you,' Mother said, clearing away her pins and thread. Then she changed her mind. 'Well, if you're sure. Perhaps you two could get the spare room ready. Make the bed and put out towels. Better put a hot-water bottle in the bed, and turn the gas fire on to take the chill off the room. That end of the house always feels cold.'

'Wow!' said Rachel, after Mother had gone. 'Your life is so thrilling, Charity. It's really boring at home. No one ever comes to stay. What do you think Kurian will be like?'

'You don't need to get excited about Kurian,' I said. 'I met him years ago. He and his dad stayed with us once.'

'Why are you making that face?'

'I didn't like him. I must have been about six, and he was twelve or something. All he wanted to do was throw balls around in the garden with Ted. I showed him my precious little china fox and he dropped it and broke it.'

'He probably didn't mean to.'

'No, but he wouldn't talk to me after that. He was too stuck up to bother with a kid like me. Come on. We'd better make that bed.'

Rachel was desperate to stay and meet Kurian, but Dad didn't even set off in the car to pick him up till after lunch.

'You girls did a good job in the spare room,' said Mother as I shut the front door behind Rachel. 'Rachel obviously isn't as impractical as she looks.'

I let this pass. It was a sort of compliment, after all.

The afternoon stretched ahead. I went upstairs, meaning to go into my bedroom, but went on down the corridor and up to the attic. I'd been in Ted's room a few times since he'd been away. It was like being in another world, somewhere far removed from Gospel Fields. Ted's carefully crafted shelves and partitions were still there. His records and record player had gone, along with his books, but the charts and maps were still pinned to the wall.

I liked to sit at his desk and think about things. What was happening to him now that he'd left home? He phoned occasionally, but never said much. Where would I be when I was twenty-one, I wondered. Girls didn't do National Service, so I couldn't be like him and wear a smart white uniform and sail away o'er the ocean wide. I'd always thought I'd be a missionary, but Dr Sturges had knocked that idea on the head.

Whatever happens, I'm going to go off and see the world, I promised myself for the hundredth time.

I realized that I was shivering. Ted's room was bitterly cold and he'd taken his little two-bar electric heater away with him. Reluctantly, I went back down to my bedroom and opened my Biology textbook.

It was six o'clock before Dad came home with Kurian. I'd been in the kitchen helping Mother, who was rushing to make milk jellies, egg custard, lamb broth and lemonade with pearl barley – all the food for sick people she'd fed me when I'd been so ill with polio. I felt quite sorry for Kurian when I realized he'd be expected to eat it all.

I'd talked myself into behaving really well by the time the car pulled up outside the front door. The revelation from my baptism was still fresh in my mind.

I don't have to like *him*, I thought, *but it's my Christian duty to* love *him*.

But what did that mean?

I shall extend to him, I told myself, *the hand of friendship, while*

generously accepting him into my home. Plus I've got to forgive him
for breaking my china fox, which, now I come to think of it, might
have been cracked anyway.

But when the front door opened, and Dad was standing there, propping up a tall, slender figure wrapped in blankets, all that went out of my head. I saw a slim brown hand holding the edges of a shawl under his chin, a pair of laughing dark eyes and a smile that lit his face with an inner beauty, which . . .

But before I could take the thought any further Kurian croaked out, 'Charity! You're all grown up! Have you forgiven me yet?'

Then he started coughing, and swayed as if his legs were giving way. Mother rushed forward to take his other arm, and together she and Dad almost carried him up the stairs.

I stood looking up after them, too stunned to move. Why, oh why, hadn't I changed out of my grubby jumper and old navy skirt? Why hadn't I at least brushed my hair? Kurian was the most beautiful human being that had ever existed (at least, as far as I could tell from the bits of him that were visible). One thing was clear, anyway. Loving Kurian was not going to be difficult at all.

I hung about in the hall and pounced on Mother as she came downstairs.

'Can I go and see him? Can I take up a drink or something? Doesn't his hot-water bottle need to be filled again?'

She shook her head.

'Best leave him for tonight. He's still very ill. He really ought to have stayed in hospital, but they can't cope with all the emergency chest cases. Your father was shocked by how little care he was getting. He's sure we can look after him better at home.'

The ground heaved under my feet. Kurian was desperately ill! Was he going to *die*?

I wanted to stay at home with Kurian the next morning while Mother and Dad went to the Meeting, but Mother wouldn't hear of it.

'Why can't I?' I demanded. 'You haven't even let me see him yet, but I could look after him just as well as you.'

She frowned.

'Think, Charity. What would you do if he took a turn for the worse? If his temperature went up very high, or he choked?'

'I would . . . I could . . .' I began, then I realized that I sounded like a five-year-old, which left me with the problem of how to back down gracefully.

'Tell him that I'm upholding him in prayer,' I said, with as much dignity as I could muster. Then I fetched my hat. 'Come on, Dad, or we'll be late.'

Later, after the three of us had eaten our lunch in the dining room (because it was Sunday), Mother at last sent me upstairs with a jug of fresh barley water. Holding that plain, white jug gave me a funny feeling. It had sat on my beside table all the way through my polio, and Mother had poured glass after glass out of it for me as she urged me to drink. I'd liked it at first, but in the end I was sick of it.

I do know how you feel, Kurian, I thought as I crept along the landing, trying to avoid the creaky floorboard. *I got better from polio (well, nearly), and Mother will get you better too.*

I knocked very gently on the spare-room door. There was no answer. As quietly as I could, I turned the handle and looked in.

Kurian was lying on his back, his hair a splash of almost-black against the white pillow. His eyes were shut, and I was about to close the door and steal away, when his eyelids fluttered open.

'Charity!' he murmured, and there was that smile again. I had time to take it in properly as I crossed to the bed and set down the jug. It set up a peculiar whirring feeling in my insides.

'I've brought you some fresh barley water,' I managed to say. Did I imagine it, or did his eyebrows flicker together in a slight frown? 'It's supposed to be awfully good for you when you're ill. Mother makes everyone drink it, but would you like some water instead?'

He actually tried to laugh, but ended up wheezing.

'Oh, don't!' I said anxiously. 'I didn't mean to start you coughing!'

'No, no, you are very kind, and clever to read my thoughts.' His voice had a sort of musical lilt to it. 'The drink is nice, but some water . . .'

'All right! Just a sec!'

I snatched up the empty glass by his bed and hobbled as fast as I could to the bathroom at the far end of the corridor.

'I think,' Kurian said, when I was standing once more by his bedside, 'that please you will have to hold it for me.'

The thought of being so close to him, practically touching him, was terrifying.

I can't! I thought. *My hands would shake and I'd spill water everywhere!*

Inspiration struck.

'Drinking straws!' I said. 'There are sure to be some in the kitchen. I'll be right back!'

I took the stairs two at a time, leading with my good leg, a technique I had now perfected.

'Straws!' I panted, bursting into the kitchen. 'Where are they?'

Mother looked up, took in what I'd said and jumped up from her chair.

'Why didn't I remember straws? Well done, Charity. Half a box still left, I think. Bottom shelf, behind the cocoa tin.'

'And he said he wanted just plain water. I got him some from the bathroom.'

'Oh.' She looked disappointed. 'Well, it's the fluid he needs, after all. Now don't stay and talk, Charity. He needs to rest.'

Kurian's eyes were closed again when I went back into the spare room. His face had a sort of greyish tinge and there were dark shadows under his eyes.

A strange thing happened to me then. I seemed to step into Faith's black lace-up uniform shoes. I remembered how she'd made me feel so much better when I was ill with polio. She'd rearranged my pillows, smoothed the rumpled sheet and blankets, helped me to drink, opened the window for a minute or two to let in fresh air, then closed it again to keep out the cold. I knew exactly what to do. I wasn't afraid of Kurian any more. I was his nurse.

I knew I'd got it right, because when I'd finished, he gave a contented sigh, closed his eyes and fell deeply asleep.

I tiptoed out of his room and leaned against the wall outside, feeling weak at the knees myself.

What's a best friend for, if you can't tell them everything? I was bursting to talk to Rachel, but I still wasn't sure if Mrs Stern liked me calling round whenever I felt like it, so I had to endure three days of school misery before at last it was Thursday and I could go next door for my French lesson.

Rachel opened the door as soon as I knocked.

'Mutti's sorry,' she said, 'but she's got one of her migraines. Don't go! I haven't seen you for ages. How's your Kurian? Wasn't that his name? Is he still stuck up and horrible?'

I took a deep breath.

'Kurian Devasy,' I said reverently, 'is the most beautiful human being who ever walked this earth, and that is an objective fact.'

She laughed delightedly.

'You've fallen for him! You've got a crush on him!'

I frowned. This was trivial.

'A crush,' I said coldly, following her into the sitting room, 'doesn't begin to describe it.'

Then I collapsed into one of the deep armchairs, buried

my face in the faded velvet cushion and gave myself up to hysterical laughter.

I was desperate to see Kurian again, but I only managed to steal a couple of peeps at him before the weekend came. Mother had forbidden me to go back into the spare room, but I'd disobeyed her twice without feeling in the slightest bit guilty.

Obedience to one's parent might actually be one of the Ten Commandments, I'd told myself, *but love comes first.*

To be on the safe side, I'd waited till Mother was out of the way, and had done no more than open the door and take a long, lingering look inside. Disappointingly, Kurian had been asleep both times, turned on his side away from me, so that all I could see was his beautiful hair.

On Saturday morning, though, Mother put a lunch tray into my hands and told me to take it up to him.

'Boiled fish, mashed potatoes and a nice little rice pudding,' she said. 'Perfectly digestible.'

Kurian was sitting up in bed. The awful grey colour in his cheeks had given way to a sort of glowing brown. I trod across the few yards of carpet as if I was approaching a throne and placed the tray tenderly on his knees.

He raised his eyebrows at the sight of the food, then looked up at me. I'd been gazing at him rather too frankly, I feared, and I blushed.

He poked at the fish with his fork.

'You have some pepper, perhaps? Or – or some spices?'

I took off at once.

'Spices?' said Mother, when I relayed this to her in the kitchen. 'Very bad for invalids. But it's what he's used to, I suppose.' She opened a cupboard and hunted among the dusty jars. 'Here's some ginger, a bit of cinnamon, oh, and dried thyme. Pepper's in the pot beside the salt.'

Kurian sniffed at the thyme before putting it aside, but sprinkled ginger and pepper liberally on his fish. I sat on the chair in the corner to watch him eat. His face was expressionless as he worked through his fish and potatoes.

'You like to cook, Charity?' he said, looking up at last.

I shrugged.

'A bit. I can do—'

'I love to cook,' he interrupted. 'It is not usual for the men of my family, but our old cook, at home, he taught me many things.'

'You have a *cook*? Of your own?'

He waved a graceful hand.

'Of course. He is the oldest of our servants. He has been with my family for many years.'

A thrilling picture formed in my mind of Kurian, seated like a prince in a sort of palace, complete with pillars and domes, while servants flocked round him.

'Indian food,' he went on, stirring cinnamon into his rice pudding, 'is very different from English. It has taste. One day I will cook for you all an Indian meal. You will like it very much.'

I suppressed a frisson of resentment as he pushed Mother's half-eaten rice pudding aside.

'Your brother, Ted,' he went on. 'He likes to play cricket?'

'He did at school,' I said. 'Now he's more interested in football.'

'Cricket is much better than football,' said Kurian positively. 'I am excellent batsman.'

The vision of the prince vanished and in its place was Kurian in white flannel trousers and a dazzling white shirt, striding masterfully on to a pitch, his bat tucked under one arm as he pulled on his gloves.

'I used to play cricket at school, before I—' I began.

'Girls are no good at sport,' said Kurian. 'They are too interested in their clothes.'

Kurian the ace sportsman went the way of the handsome prince. In his place was a grown-up version of the annoying boy who had broken my china fox.

'I'll take your tray away,' I told him. 'You probably need another nap.'

Falling out of love so quickly was a nasty shock. How could I have been such a fool, swept away by a beautiful smile and a head of lovely black hair? I had resented Justin because he was handsome, so why had I fallen for Kurian? Perhaps deep down I was one of those wicked hussies, like in Aunt Josephine's moralistic novels, destined to flit from man to man in a fruitless search for love, only to end up broken and starving in the gutter.

At least no one knows except Rachel, I thought.

'Well,' said Mother tolerantly as she scraped the remains of Kurian's lunch into the bin, 'poor boy. He must be terribly homesick, especially having been so ill.'

'He only likes cricket,' I told her bitterly, shame and anger boiling around inside me. 'And he says that girls are no good at sport because all they care about is clothes.'

There was an unwelcome gleam of understanding in Mother's eye.

'Has he fallen out of favour already? You were only too keen to see him this morning.'

'It's nothing to do with being *in favour*,' I snapped back at her. 'It's just that he's not like I expected. That's all.'

'Give him a chance, Charity. He's only nineteen, away from his family for the first time. He's not used to girls, anyway. He doesn't have any sisters.'

'But he says that English food doesn't have any taste and he thinks he's a brilliant cook and he wants to cook us an Indian meal.'

I'd hoped that Mother would be insulted, but disappointingly she only smiled.

'That'll be interesting. Your grandfather lived in India when he was young, you know. He loved Indian food. I've never had the chance to try it myself.'

CHAPTER TWENTY

One good thing about not being in love is that you can concentrate on other things. I had a lot of schoolwork to catch up on, and that afternoon I ploughed straight through it. I heard the phone ring at some point, and Dad's voice answering it, but I was too immersed in drawing a cross-section of the human heart to take much notice.

I went downstairs at last to find Mother and Dad sitting by the fire at the far end of the dining room.

'You could go by there on Monday afternoon on the way back from Charity's appointment with the specialist,' Mother was saying. 'It's on your way home anyway. The fog should have cleared completely by then. I'd take her myself, but I've got to be at the dentist's.'

My appointment! I'd forgotten about it. It wasn't much fun seeing the specialist. He never seemed to do anything that helped. But at least I'd have an afternoon off school.

'It'll mean taking the car,' said Dad.

'Taking the car where?' I asked, without much interest.

'To Kurian's lodgings,' said Dad. 'A friend of his phoned –

Joseph, a medical student who's kindly been visiting him in hospital. He rents a room in the same house. Apparently, the landlady's acting unreasonably. Joseph says she's re-let Kurian's room and has bundled up his things and put them in her own rooms. Joseph's afraid she's started selling them off.'

'But that's stealing!' I said indignantly.

'No need to jump to conclusions.' Dad stood up. 'There's probably a rational explanation. I'll go up and explain all this to Kurian. Perhaps he'll be well enough to come downstairs this evening. He must be so bored on his own all the time.'

I suppose I ought to have been sympathetic. I'd spent long enough lying ill on my own, after all, but it's hard to be sympathetic once you've been disappointed in love.

There was nothing unusual about the appointment with the specialist. He put me through all the strength tests I'd done a hundred times already. I thought I'd done a bit better than last time, but once I'd finished he sat down behind his desk and started shuffling his papers.

'I don't think I need to see Charity again,' he said to Dad. 'She's made a good recovery. We've gone about as far as we can expect to go.'

He was talking to Dad about me, as usual, as if I wasn't there at all. This made me so cross that for a moment his words didn't sink in.

'But I'm not better yet!' I objected. 'I still can't run properly, or hold things for long in my left hand. Aren't you going to give me more exercises? Or — or injections? Or anything?'

He took off his glasses and polished the lenses with a large white handkerchief.

'You've made a remarkable recovery, young lady. Lots of other children have to wear metal braces on their legs for the rest of their lives. It's true that there are some things you won't be able to do in the future, but—'

'What? Never?' I felt breathless, as if I'd been punched in the chest. 'But if I keep trying, doing exercises, practising running—'

'Probably best not to overdo it.' His voice was horribly soothing. 'The muscle wastage is irreversible, I'm afraid. Concentrate on what you *can* do, not what you can't. There are lots of people who have made a great success of life with handicaps much worse than yours.'

A handicap? I now had a *handicap*? Suddenly my left leg felt weaker than ever, and my left hand impossibly clumsy.

I stumbled down the stairs after Dad and we stood looking at each other in the street. Dad looked upset.

'There are other doctors. We'll go to—'

'There's no point, Dad.' I was trying not to let my voice shake. 'They'll all say the same. I know they will.'

He put his arm round my shoulders.

'We'll cast this burden on the Lord, Charity. He will . . .'

I shook his arm off.

'This *burden*? So now I've got a handicap *and* I'm a burden?'

'You know that isn't what I meant, dear. I just . . . We should take it to the Lord in prayer.'

'Right now, that doesn't help *at all*.'

He tried again. 'Well, but there's almost nothing you won't be able to do . . .'

I stepped away from him. How could he be so *stupid*?

'I'll always be different from other people!' I wailed. 'No one will fall in love with me!'

'That's utter nonsense.' He sounded angry. 'A fine idea you have about the world.'

Blinking away tears, I stumbled beside him to the car.

'You've always said the Lord loves us,' I shot at him as I plumped myself down in the passenger seat. 'But it's not true, is it? If He did, He wouldn't have given me this . . . this *handicap*.'

I hated the word so much I could hardly bring it out.

His hand had reached for the ignition switch, but he dropped it again.

'He has a plan for all of us, darling. For you and me. It's our task to discover what it is.'

The easy words I'd heard so often made me grind my teeth in fury.

'Don't!' I shouted. 'Don't just say things like that. This is about me! My life! Me! And it's so unfair! Why did I have to get ill? Why does anyone? Why did God make polio worse for children than for grown-ups? Why do some people have to suffer and others don't? What about Rachel's family being murdered by the Nazis, and Tabitha having to lie about her father, and Mr Fischer being in prison all those years, and . . . and the earthquake?'

He was looking bewildered now.

'What earthquake?'

'*Your* earthquake. The one where you met Mother.'

'What about it?'

'You've always said that it was the Lord's doing, to bring you two together.' My voice vibrated with scorn.

'Well . . .'

'But did God really have to destroy a whole town, kill lots of people, and horses, and dogs and cats, just so you could meet Mother?'

'That's not what I meant, Charity.'

'What *did* you mean, then?'

I thought for a moment that he was going to quote something else to shut me up, but instead he sighed.

'You're asking one of the great questions about our faith,' he said. 'Don't think I haven't puzzled over it too. The problem of pain, the injustice of suffering!'

'So for once you don't have any answers.'

He flinched from the sharpness in my voice.

'No, Charity, I don't. And nor do the greatest philosophers and theologians. But now . . .' He smiled in his infuriatingly winning way and put his hand on my knee. 'I *am* going to quote the Bible to you.'

I brushed his hand away and hunched my shoulders.

'Huh.'

'Here goes. *For now we see through a glass darkly . . .*'

'*. . . but then face to face*,' I finished for him unwillingly.

'So there's the promise. We do the best we can here on earth, but we won't understand everything until our story ends here below and we meet the Lord in Heaven.'

'In other words,' I snapped back at him, 'you have no idea why some people have to suffer and neither does anyone else.'

I thought he was going to try again, but he changed his mind when he saw the look on my face and gave up.

'Look,' he said, 'do you want us to go straight home? You've had a shock. I can come back for Kurian's things tomorrow.'

So what do you have in mind? I thought. *A cuddle? A sweetie? Some kind of treat, like when I was three years old with a graze on my knee?*

'No, I don't want to go home, thank you very much. You said we were going to get Kurian's stuff, so let's get on with it. It's probably all cricket bats and sporty rubbish, but why should I care?'

'If you're sure,' he said, looking nervously at me as if he was afraid I was about to bite. 'Actually, I do need your help. I can't navigate and drive at the same time.'

He pulled his street atlas out of the glove pocket, opened it and laid it on my lap.

'You'll have to guide me. Can you do that?'

'Of *course* I can. I'm perfectly capable of reading a map, in case you hadn't noticed.'

'It's not far, but there's such a tangle of small streets round there. Hirley Road's the one we want.' He jabbed at the map with his forefinger. 'It's one of those ones, off the main road.'

He reached for the ignition again, and the engine sputtered into life.

*

On any other day, I'd have loved making this expedition with Dad. The suburb where we lived was quite far out of London and the only times I'd been into the centre were with the family to attend big Lucasite gatherings, and once to the British Museum on a school trip. In places, the railway that took us into Victoria station was built up high on embankments and bridges, and as the train rattled past you could look down into the cramped narrow streets with their rows of small brick houses. Chimneys sprouted from every roof, all of them belching out thick, yellow smoke. I'd often wondered what it was like down there.

Today, though, I wouldn't have noticed if we'd ended up at the Taj Mahal.

It was a gloomy December afternoon. A chill wind had blown away the worst of the fog, but enough of it still lingered to make it hard to see very far. I could only just make out the street names and my concentration was nil. I directed Dad down a couple of wrong turnings, which was embarrassing when we had to reverse out of them, because there were hardly any cars around, and people stared at our big Rover.

'This is it!' I said at last. 'Hirley Road. Happy now?'

He was too busy peering at door numbers to answer, and came to a halt at last.

'Number thirty-two. Over there. Other side of the road,' he said.

I felt quite nervous as we got out. The street looked poor and dingy. Net curtains sagged in the windows and the paintwork on the doors was scuffed and chipped. A sign hung in one of the windows. It read, *Rooms to let. No Blacks, No Dogs, No Irish.*

That's disgusting, I thought indignantly. I wanted to say, *Dr Sturges would be happy round here, wouldn't he?* But I was too cross with Dad to talk to him.

A couple of women, talking by the corner, turned to stare. Two boys had been kicking an old tin can around. They ran up to us.

'Give us a shilling,' one said, 'and I'll guard yer car for yer. Keep any little bleeders round here off yer paintwork.'

I stiffened with fright, but Dad only laughed.

'Sixpence,' he said, 'and an extra twopence if you can say the Lord's Prayer.'

'Whatever for?' the boy said.

Before Dad could answer, the other one said, 'Give yer tuppence to Jimmy. I bet he knows it. His nan makes him go to church.'

'Right, Jimmy,' said Dad, 'you teach this boy – what's your name?'

'Kenny,' the second boy said.

'Good. You teach Kenny, and when I've finished my business there'll be twopence for both of you if Kenny can say it all the way through.'

'Sixpence!' said Jimmy.

'Threepence,' said Dad, 'and that's my last offer. Take it or leave it.'

We left them in an urgent huddle, and started across the road.

'Mr Brown!'

We spun round. A tall man was hurrying along the road towards us, an anxious look on his brown face.

Dad held out his hand.

'You must be Joseph! Thank you so much for—'

'Yes, I am Joseph,' the man said. 'Please, I do not wish my landlady, Mrs Cook, to see me talking with you. Do not divulge to her that I am the one who alerted you. This house is very bad, very cold and dirty, but if she expels me it will be hard for me to find alternative accommodation. I have come to understand that Africans are not acceptable in lodging houses in this country.'

'I see.' Dad looked distressed. 'I'm so sorry. I had no idea that Kurian was in such a — such a place.'

'I myself am studying to be a doctor,' Joseph said, 'and I can tell you that it is very bad to stay in a room so damp that water runs down the walls, when like me you have come from Nigeria, which has a warm climate. It is enough to give the strongest person pneumonia.'

'This is really—' began Dad.

'I will go inside now,' said Joseph, looking up at the windows of number 32, clearly anxious in case he was being watched. 'Please allow a few minutes to pass before you knock on the door.'

'Yes, of course,' Dad said hurriedly. 'But, Joseph, you have our telephone number. Please call me if you have any difficulty. I will do what I can for you.'

Joseph's face opened in a delighted smile.

'That is a great kindness, Mr Brown. I will certainly avail

myself of your offer if the situation should arise.'

There goes the second spare room, I thought. *I bet Joseph's a football nutter. More sport-crazy men. That's all I need.* But then I thought, *Actually, I suppose he's got a really nice smile. Maybe I wouldn't mind him coming to stay. And it must be horrible living in a street with nasty signs like No Blacks in the windows.*

The woman who came to the door was wearing a wrap-around apron and her hair was pinned into place with a bristle of hairgrips. She took a step back when she saw us and for a moment I thought she was going to shut the door in our faces. Instead, she crossed her arms and glared at us.

'If you're from the sanitary, you've come to the wrong house. It's them over the road who've got rats. You won't find anything like that in here.'

Dad ignored this.

'I'm Iver Brown,' he said, holding out his hand to shake hers, but her arms remained crossed and after a moment he dropped his hand again. 'I'm a friend of Kurian Devasy. I believe there's been a misunderstanding about his room? You wish to terminate his tenancy?'

Suspicion and anxiety sparked in her eyes.

'Hasn't paid his rent, has he? Not in three weeks. I'm within my rights. You don't pay, you don't stay.'

Dad's smile faded.

'So you evicted this young man while he was in hospital?'

'Not my fault he's got himself sick. It's all the mucky food they eat. Not healthy, is it?'

Dad's lips had tightened and my fists were balled.

'If you would kindly show me to his room, I'll pack up his things and—'

'Show you to his room?' mocked the landlady. 'What do you think this is? The bleedin' Ritz?'

A movement behind her caught my eye. Joseph was standing at the top of the stairs, listening.

'Look,' said Dad, and I could tell by his stiff shoulders that he was trying not to sound angry. 'There's no need for unpleasantness. I've come to fetch Kurian's things. If you could just—'

Her eyes were shifting from side to side.

'What things? He ain't got no things. Few rags, fit for the bin, that's all.'

Dad pulled a piece of paper out of his pocket and adjusted the glasses on his nose.

'*Two suitcases,*' he read out. '*One warm winter coat. One scarf. One fur hat. One suit. Two pairs of shoes. Six shirts—*'

'That's rubbish!' scoffed the landlady. 'He's having you on! He never had no coat, or suit, or—'

'*One cricket bat,*' Dad read out.

Ha! I knew it! I thought.

'*A number of books. Stationery. Documents.*'

'Nothing to do with me!' blustered the landlady. 'He's made all that up! Must have! They're all the same. You don't know the half of it. Lying, thieving—'

Joseph was still watching from the top of the stairs. He was a reassuring presence, someone inside this horrible house who was on our side.

'Charity,' said Dad, turning so suddenly back to me that I started in surprise. 'We passed a police station a few streets back. I think you'd better go and—'

'Here! No need for that!' The landlady sounded panicky. 'All right, so he did have a bit of stuff. But then he went off to the hospital. Ambulance said he weren't going to make it. What did you expect me to do?'

She had uncrossed her arms and was twisting her hands together. Dad took a step forward. She moved back, as if she was expecting a blow.

'I expected you,' Dad said sternly, 'to behave with common humanity and honesty towards a sick person who had been living under your roof.'

She flushed angrily.

Just don't quote the Bible at her, Dad, I pleaded silently. *She'll run rings round you.*

'So if we're not going to call the police, you'd better tell me,' Dad said, consulting his list again, 'what has happened to two suitcases, one overcoat, one suit—'

'Pawned them, didn't I?' she said sulkily.

Someone behind us yelled, 'Got caught out then, 'ave yer, Gladys? Been thievin' again?'

The women who had been talking on the corner had come up behind and us and were watching with delighted smiles on their faces.

'Get inside,' the landlady said, standing back to let us pass. 'I won't 'ave yer telling all them out there my business.'

I followed Dad into the narrow hall and Gladys shut the

door behind us. The smell of coal dust, damp and bad drains made me wrinkle my nose. Joseph had melted away out of sight round the bend in the stairs.

'So, let me get this clear,' Dad said. 'You took possession of Kurian's room without informing him, and proceeded to steal his goods—'

'Steal? I ain't stolen nothing! Told you. I pawned them. Still got the tickets, haven't I?'

'Then I suggest you un-pawn them straight away,' said Dad.

She gave him a savage look, reached past him for the front door handle, wrenched it open and yelled, 'Kenny! Come 'ere!'

Kenny detached himself reluctantly from the knot of boys by the car, which now numbered four. The landlady marched into her kitchen and marched out a moment later with a sheaf of pawn tickets and a few pound notes.

'Get down the pawnshop,' she barked at Kenny. 'Get this stuff out.'

Kenny looked down at the tickets and then up at Dad.

'This the Indian's stuff? You ain't going to take his cricket bat off me, are yer? Cos I'm not giving it up!'

The landlady aimed a blow at Kenny's head. He ducked and dashed off down the road.

'While he's gone,' Dad said, 'I suggest you fetch out anything in your house that you might have forgotten to take to the pawn shop. That black coat, for example, hanging there on the peg.'

It was hard to get anything out of the landlady until Kenny came panting back from the pawn shop, dragging a heavy suitcase. I looked past him out into the street. The boys by our car were frowning with fierce concentration.

'Forgive us our what?' one was saying. 'What's it mean?'

'Don't matter what it *means*,' Jimmy told him scornfully. 'Want yer thrippence, doncher? Come on, from the beginning. *Our Father . . .*'

I turned back into the house. The landlady was arguing with Dad over the winter coat.

'There's a policeman on the corner, Dad,' I said, which could have been true, only I hadn't bothered to look. 'Shall I . . .'

The fight went out of the landlady, and a little while later we were standing over two bulging suitcases.

'That seems to be more or less everything,' Dad said pleasantly, running his finger down his list. 'Wait. There should be six shirts. You've given me four.'

'Must've took 'em with him,' the landlady said.

'No, he didn't,' said Kenny. He was furious at the loss of the cricket bat and had been kicking the rotting skirting board. 'One's on the back of Uncle Vic, and good luck trying to get it off 'im.'

The landlady cuffed him round the head.

'Get out,' she snarled at him. 'I've had enough of you.'

The two boys with Jimmy jumped excitedly round Dad as we carried the suitcase back to the car.

'We know it, mister!' one said. 'Jimmy learned it to us.'

'Let's hear it, then,' said Dad, slamming down the lid of the boot with the suitcases safely stowed inside.

Jimmy raised his arm as if he was about to conduct a choir.

'*Our . . .*' he began.

'*Our Father, whichart in 'eaven,*' chanted the boys.

Dad beamed as they struggled through to the end, but I was watching uneasily as a small crowd was beginning to gather. I pulled at his sleeve.

'Come on, Dad. Let's go,' I whispered urgently.

'What are you doing with our kids?' a man called out angrily, watching as Dad counted pennies out into the boys' hands. 'You a pervert or what?'

Dad smiled round innocently.

'My friends,' he called out, in his ringing preacher's voice. 'You heard yourselves the sacred words from the lips of these children, saying the prayer our Lord Jesus Christ Himself taught us. And I am here to tell you that the love of God—'

'Tsah!' a man scoffed. ''E's cracked.'

''E's just lifted a whole lot of stuff off Gladys,' a woman called out. 'What she nicked from that poor lad who was carted off to the hospital.'

My heart was beginning to beat uncomfortably fast.

'Dad!' I hissed, tugging at his arm. 'Please!'

He shook me off and raised his voice.

'Lift up your eyes! Your Saviour is waiting, His arms open . . .'

But then I couldn't hear him any more because as the crowd around us shifted, I caught sight of a girl in a familiar uniform walking up the street towards us, a schoolbag swinging defiantly from her shoulder, as if she was ready to take on attackers. It was Monica.

I looked round wildly for a place to hide. Too late! Monica had seen me. Her face went scarlet, then she plunged up to me, grabbed my arm in a painful grip and dragged me out of the crowd.

'What do you think you're doing here? How *dare* you come and spy on me?'

'I'm not spying on you!' I managed to shake her off. 'We came to pick Kurian's stuff up.'

'Who's Kurian?'

'He's one of the students who was staying over there, in number 32. What are you doing here, anyway?'

'Oi, Monica!' a young man called out mockingly. 'That one of your posh friends from the grammar? Introduce us, why don't you?'

She whipped round.

'Shut your face, Stevie!' She turned back to me. 'I live here, don't I? So now you know, Miss La-di-da, with your *tennis court* and your *grand piano*, how the plebs have to live.'

She still sounded angry, but there was a sort of desperation in her eyes too.

You're scared! I thought triumphantly. *I've got you now, Monica. That's a big act you put on at school. I can prick your bubble any time I like.*

She read my expression.

'Go on then. Gloat. See if I care.'

Suddenly I didn't feel triumphant any more.

'I won't say anything at school,' I said. 'Why should I care where you live? But you've got to promise me something.'

'What?'

'Two things, actually. Stop all the — you know, Lady this and Holy that.' My face was getting hot and I was dreadfully afraid I would cry. 'Stop trying to turn everyone against me.'

She tossed her head.

'What's the other thing?'

'Don't let on that my dad's preaching in your street to a whole load of people he's never met before.'

She raised her eyebrows in a jeer as she took in the scene for the first time.

'That your dad?'

'Yes, and he's——'

She burst out laughing.

'What, that skinny bloke in the scruffy raincoat with the funny accent?'

'It's not funny. He's Scottish.'

'He must be a nutter.'

'No! He's . . .' Words welled up inside me. *A messenger of the Gospel, a faithful servant of Christ, a bringer of the Word.* I couldn't bring myself to say any of them.

'Got the gift of the gab, anyway,' said Monica, half admiringly. 'Even my auntie Flo's shut up for long enough to listen to him.'

She was right. Most people had wandered off and were watching from a distance, some laughing, some shaking their heads. But half a dozen were standing close to Dad, listening intently with the soft look on their faces that he always seemed able to produce.

Monica turned back to me.

'What was that you said about Gladys Cook's lodger? She said he'd died in the hospital.'

'He didn't die. He might have done if he'd stayed there because the nurses are too busy to look after him properly. Dad went to get him out. My mother's nursing him at home.'

'Why on earth? What's he to you?'

'His dad and my dad are old friends. They were at the same university.'

I could see she'd been about to say, *Oo! University! Posh!* but had thought better of it.

'You know what, Charity,' she said suddenly, 'if you want to be popular, you ought to join in more. Stop hiding in the library and bunking off games.'

'I can't do games,' I said bitterly.

'Why not? You had polio ages ago. You're just feeling sorry for yourself.'

'I'm not. I've got muscle wastage in my arm and leg.'

'So? You have to build them up, that's all.'

'Can't. It's permanent.'

'You don't know that! You ought to—'

'I do know. I found out this afternoon. The specialist's just told me. I'm as better as I'm ever going to get, and I can't do anything about it.'

I couldn't believe I was talking to Monica like this. I'd just given her another weapon to attack me with. *Lame.*

Handicapped. I could hear her spiteful voice now.

But she was looking uncertain.

'Oh. Right,' she said.

Behind me, Dad was winding things up.

'And so, my dear friends, let us pray . . .'

'How on earth did he do that?' breathed Monica, as his listeners bent their heads. 'Your dad's a magician.'

I ought to have said, *There's no such thing as magic — it's the working of the Holy Spirit.* Instead, I smiled weakly.

Dad and I didn't talk much on the way home. I suddenly felt too exhausted even to think. The smog was thickening again, slowing the traffic to a crawl. I must have fallen asleep because when I woke up we were nearly back at Gospel Fields.

CHAPTER TWENTY-ONE

I woke early the next morning and lay still, listening to the house. No one was up yet. It should have been getting light, but the smog had returned. Thick, yellow curls of it were rubbing up against the window above my bed. Some of it had got into the house, coiling down the chimneys, seeping under the doors and sliding through the cracks where the windows didn't quite fit.

Living at Gospel Fields has changed everything, I thought. *If we hadn't moved here, I'd never have met Rachel. Monica wouldn't have been so jealous. Perhaps Mother wouldn't have got so ill. Dad wouldn't have decided after all to take the money Great-grandfather Moses left us, and we'd still be struggling to make ends meet. There wasn't any room in our old house for the weary, so I'd never have met Mr Fischer, or Kurian, or even that horrible Dr Sturges. I'd be stuck with Robert-next-door, and I'd still be trying to persuade him to give his heart to Jesus.*

For some reason, a picture of the toy cupboard in the old bedroom I'd shared with Hope bounced into my head. It brought with it a sort of regret. Sternly, I moved on.

You were still only a child in Old Manor Road, I told myself. *You're almost absolutely mature now, so it's hardly surprising that the Lord is setting new tests for you all the time.*

A small voice inside said, *Why would the Lord bother to set tests for you? Hasn't He got enough to do?*

Obviously that was the Devil talking, so I banished him at once. Or tried to.

The trouble is, though, that once you've had a thought like that, it's difficult to get past it. And that brought up another question, which needed prayer.

'Am I still a good and faithful Lucasite, Lord?' I said out loud.

Silence.

'Am I? I really need to know.'

Nothing.

'Well, I probably am,' I explained cautiously, 'but the question is, does it matter? After all, You told me Yourself that all I've got to do is love.'

It's annoying the way your mind drifts away when you're trying to grapple with the great questions of life. I bet it happens to everyone, the saints included, even the Virgin Mary, who, let's face it, must have wondered what was going on when the Angel Gabriel appeared. She probably got tired of trying to work it out after a while and went back to chopping up onions or whatever she was doing at the time.

My mind wandered back to the day before and I squirmed all over again with mortal embarrassment at the memory of Dad with his arms stretched out, telling all those people that

Jesus loved them, while most of them smirked and sniggered.

Monica, though, had neither smirked nor sniggered. She'd actually been impressed.

'Your dad's a magician,' she'd said. 'How on earth did he do that?'

He does it because he loves everyone, I thought. *He sort of brims over with it. And that's what's so annoying. Why can't he be like ordinary fathers and just love his own family? His actual children? Exclusively?*

I remembered the look on Tabitha's face when Dad had given her a Bible that was exactly the same as mine. I hadn't admitted to myself at the time that I'd minded, but I had. Quite a lot, actually. It had made my gift less special.

My bedroom door suddenly opened, making me jump.

'The fog's worse than ever,' said Mother. 'No school for you today.'

For once the prospect of not going to school was disappointing. I'd actually been looking forward to seeing Monica.

'I can get to school perfectly well, you know, fog or no fog!' I said.

'Then you'll have to walk four miles there and four miles back,' she said briskly, 'because the buses won't be running. And even if you get there without losing your way in the fog you'll probably find that the school's closed.'

There was no answer to that, so I hunched my shoulders away from her, turned over in bed and pretended to go back to sleep.

*

I found to my surprise, when at last I went downstairs, that Kurian was up and dressed and had found his way groggily to the kitchen.

Mother was trying to chivvy him back to bed.

'It's too soon, Kurian,' she was saying. 'You need to rest. Get your strength up.'

'No, no, Mrs Brown.' Kurian's smile, seen sideways on, didn't have the same impact as the full-on version. Even so, a faint pulse of love knocked against my heart. I resisted it.

'Now I have been reunited with my clothes, I must proceed to wear them. Only there are some strange discoveries to be made in my suitcase. These socks, for example –' he put out a foot for us to see – 'I have never seen them before and they are full of holes.'

'That woman!' I snorted. 'She's such a thief!'

'You were with Mr Brown, isn't it?' said Kurian, turning to me. 'You met my landlady! She is a dragon. No, a tigress!'

'Well,' said Mother, putting a glass of warm milk into his hands. 'It's all over now. Give me those socks and I'll darn them for you.'

'And my cricket bat!' complained Kurian. 'So many dents and scratches!'

'Kenny probably used it to bat tin cans around,' I told him.

I didn't quite manage to sound sympathetic.

'That boy, Kenny!' Kurian's voice was full of loathing. 'He is . . .' But then his voice cracked and he started coughing.

'What did I say?' said Mother. 'Too soon. Go back to bed, Kurian. Have a good rest this morning, and if you're feeling up to it you can come down this afternoon.'

She's treating him just like Ted, I thought, a little resentfully. *Not like a guest at all.*

I made an effort to be magnanimous.

'I'll bring you something to read, if you like,' I said.

'I don't read girls' books,' he replied grandly, draining his milk and making for the door.

'See what I mean?' I said to Mother, once he was out of earshot. 'Stuck up!'

She raised her eyebrows.

'Didn't you see the naughty look in his eyes, Charity? He was teasing you. You ought to know by now what young men are like. You've lived with Ted for long enough.'

I didn't want to believe her.

'Since you can't go to school,' she went on, 'you might as well make yourself useful. The silver needs polishing. I've lit the fire in the dining room. It'll have warmed up nicely by now. You can listen to the radio. *Desert Island Discs* will be on in a minute.'

'I thought you did the silver a couple of weeks ago,' I said, although actually I quite enjoyed polishing Margery Spendlove's beautiful forks and spoons. Every time I did it, they felt a bit more like ours.

'We need to get ahead,' said Mother, putting a can of Silvo and a chamois leather into my hands. 'For when Justin's parents come to dinner.'

286

'But that's weeks away!'

'Only two weeks, and there's a lot to do before then.'

Kurian looked almost jaunty when he came downstairs after lunch. He found Mother and me in the dining room, putting the sparkling forks and spoons back into their felt-lined drawer.

'You were very right, Mrs B,' he said. 'Now I will always listen to your advice. This morning I was tired indeed, but then I slept again so well! And now I am fit enough to bat for India.'

He pretended to hold a cricket bat, twisting round as if he was watching a bowler ready to throw.

'Hm,' said Mother. 'Perhaps a quieter game would be better. I found our old Monopoly board this morning.' She pulled it out of a drawer in the sideboard and put it on the dining-room table. 'Charity, why don't you—'

She was interrupted by the doorbell. I rushed to answer it.

'Rachel! Thank goodness!' I reached forward to drag her inside. 'Come and help me. I've got to play Monopoly with Kurian.'

She dropped the scarf that had been protecting her nose and mouth from the smog and raised her eyebrows in surprise.

'Wouldn't you rather have him to yourself? I mean—'

'Shh! He's in there!' I hissed, pointing at the dining-room door.

She stared at me, puzzled. I shrugged and turned down the corners of my mouth.

'Really?' she whispered. 'But I thought you were . . .'

I shook my head.

'*Thinks he's the cat's pyjamas*,' I mouthed.

'What?'

'You know, full of himself. The bee's knees,' I whispered.

'Oh.'

'He's just as bad as Ted.'

Her eyes sparked at the mention of Ted. Now she looked intrigued.

'Anyway,' I said loudly, opening the dining room door. 'Come in and meet Kurian.'

Kurian was lounging in Dad's chair at the end of the table, staring down curiously at the Monopoly board. He lifted his huge brown eyes as we went in and Rachel received the full onslaught of his smile.

'This is my friend Rachel,' I said.

'H-hello,' said Rachel, blushing.

'Rachel,' said Kurian, holding out a slim hand for her to shake. 'You are the wife of Isaac!'

Rachel stepped back, shocked.

'I'm fourteen!' she said. 'I'm not married to anybody. Oh . . . !' She laughed. 'You mean Rachel in the Bible? You know the Bible? Aren't Indians Hindus? I mean . . .'

She stopped, flushed with embarrassment.

'I am a Kerala man,' said Kurian, leafing through the sets of Monopoly money. 'We are Christians since nearly two thousand years.'

'It's true.' I nodded to Rachel. 'Dad told me. There was one of Jesus's disciples, called Doubting Thomas—'

'But now you will tell me about Monopoly,' said Kurian, bored by Doubting Thomas. 'I like to play games. We Indians are the best at games. We invented chess, you know.'

I hadn't expected that playing Monopoly with Kurian would be so much fun. He was completely ruthless, laughing delightedly when either of us had to hand over our money, and pulling tragic faces when it was his turn to pay up.

'You British! You are a nothing but wicked imperialists!' he groaned. 'See how you have sent this poor Indian to jail! You are exploiting me for your colonialist ambition. Look at you, so proud of your map all painted pink!'

'You're the one who's proud,' I said. 'Just because you're a boy, you think girls are no good at sport!'

His eyes gleamed mischievously.

'I am a tease!' he crowed. 'You see, Rachel, how Charity has fallen into my trap!'

I had to laugh.

'Well, anyway, India's not painted pink any longer. You're independent now.'

'Yes! We have shaken off the shackles of British oppression! At least, until this afternoon, when Charity has made me land on Park Lane and taken away all my money.'

'It's no more than you deserve,' I said severely. 'You wouldn't look at all my lovely books.'

'Now, now, you two. Stop squabbling,' said Rachel, whose head had been swivelling from Kurian to me like the umpire at a tennis match. 'You sound like a couple of children.'

'Rachel doesn't have any brothers and sisters,' I explained to Kurian. 'She's not used to teasing.'

He laughed delightedly.

'Now I know what I have been missing, because I never had any sisters either and my brother is only eleven. Perhaps I am glad. No, I am sorry. Rachel and Charity, you are my long-lost sisters. Now we can quarrel as much as we like.'

A few days later, Hope came home. There were still two weeks to go before the Christmas holidays, but one of the girls at her school had gone down with polio and Aunt Josephine had closed the school and sent all the girls home.

At least if Hope catches it she'll know what I've had to go through, was my first thought. But then I realized how selfish I was being. I wouldn't mind too much if Hope was just a bit ill, in bed with a temperature for a while, but what if she was paralysed even worse than I'd been, and never got better but had to spend the rest of her life inside a machine, unable to move at all and breathing through an iron lung?

It was a relief when she arrived to see her looking her usual healthy self. As usual, she was full of school-chatter for the first day or two. She could talk about nothing but Annabel's pony and how Miss Frobisher's poodle had bitten the caretaker. She only focused on me when I told her about going to the opera.

'It's so unfair!' she said with a thunderous frown. '*Madame Butterfly!* Who's singing?'

'I've no idea.'

She was marching up and down the dining room, which we were supposed to be tidying up.

'It'll be completely wasted on you. The Sterns ought to take me instead. I'll go and ask—'

'Hope! You wouldn't! You—'

'Only joking. I suppose. When is it?'

'Saturday.'

She heaved a sigh and shook her head. Then her generous nature kicked in. She stopped marching and looked at me critically.

'What are you going to wear?'

'Come upstairs. I'll show you. Mother's made me a dress.'

She followed me up to my room and watched as I took Mother's velvet creation out of my wardrobe and held it against myself.

'Could work,' she said, her head on one side, 'but you need a bracelet. I suppose I'll have to lend you mine. What about shoes?'

I was suddenly anxious.

'I've only got my school ones.'

She tutted with exasperation.

'You can't wear those clodhoppers to the *opera*. How are you going to get there?'

'In the Sterns's car.'

'So you won't have to walk far. I'd better lend you my court shoes, but you must promise not to scratch them. On pain of death.'

*

By Saturday afternoon I was in such a state of nervous excitement that I couldn't keep still. Hope had taken it upon herself to get me ready, and Mother had left us to it, disappearing into the kitchen and closing the door with a snap.

'What's the matter with her?' I asked Hope, as we went upstairs to my bedroom. 'She's been really odd today.'

'Not surprising,' Hope said shrewdly. 'Think about it, Charity. She grew up in a small town in New Zealand. She's never been anywhere as grand as the Opera House in her whole life. She's torn. On the one hand she wants you to look smart so that no one will think the Browns don't know how to do things properly, but at the same time she's worried in case you fall into the snare of vanity. And anyway, you know, it's the *opera*.'

I laughed.

'That's so clever! How did you work it out?'

'Oh,' said Hope, picking a piece of fluff off the dress, which was laid out on my bed. 'When you're away from home all the time, you get a sort of perspective on things.'

I bristled. Was she patronizing me? But as she turned away I thought she might have looked sad.

I bent down to put on my best white socks.

'Socks with court shoes? You can't be serious!' she said. 'You'll have to wear my nylons. I'll lend you a pair, but don't go and ladder them. And I suppose that means you'll have to have my suspender belt as well.'

The stockings felt weird, as if my legs were bare but dressed at the same time, and the suspenders clipping them to the belt dug into my skin. I slipped on the dress, and Hope zipped it up the back.

'I hope you realize,' she said, clasping the bracelet round my wrist, 'that I'm being extraordinarily nice to you when inside I'm a seething mass of jealousy.'

Mother walked me round to the Sterns's house five minutes too early. As we stood outside the front door, waiting for it to open, I had to suppress an urge to grab her arm.

Professor Stern opened the door. He was wearing an elegant evening suit and a black bow tie.

'Is that Charity already?' Mrs Stern called down from upstairs.

'It certainly is,' the professor said, smiling warmly at me. Then he shouted up the stairs, 'Hurry up, Frieda! You're going to make us late!'

Rachel came out of the sitting room. The shimmering blue silk of her dress was almost entirely hidden by a black velvet cloak with a stand-up collar that swathed her from neck to knee. Her shiny black shoes had slightly high heels. My toes curled inside Hope's court shoes and I was agonizingly conscious of the shabbiness of my old Sunday coat.

I look stupid, I thought. *She'll be ashamed to be seen with me.*

But Rachel bounced up to me with a delighted smile.

'You've put your hair up!' she said. 'It looks lovely.'

'Hope did it.'

She pulled me away from Mother and the professor, who were talking by the front door.

'I can't tell you how glad I am that you're coming. Mutti's being impossible. She's always like this before the opera. Papa says it's because it reminds her of going to concerts and operas in Paris and Vienna when she was a child. It makes her sad.'

'Why does she want to go, then?'

Rachel opened her eyes wide.

'Music's the most important thing in the world to Mutti. She couldn't stay away.'

As a good Lucasite, I'd been brought up to believe that theatres were dens of sin and vice, but when we emerged from the side street where Professor Stern had parked the car, and I stood gazing up at the gleaming white front of the opera house, I thought it looked more like a wedding cake than a haunt of Satan. Groups of people were clustered on the pavement by the entrance in a muddle of fur coats and black bow ties with the occasional flash of jewels. I looked to see if there were any other people of my age, but everyone looked old.

We pushed our way inside.

'Give Papa your coat,' said Rachel, carelessly tugging at the strings of her satin-lined cloak. 'He'll take everything to the cloakroom.'

'Frieda! Leo!' someone shouted, waving over heads.

'Here we go,' groaned Rachel. 'There'll be nothing but talk, talk, talk till it starts.' She touched her father's arm. 'Can you give me our tickets, Papa? I'll show Charity round and join you in our seats.'

Oh, how can I describe the glory of the next half hour? I

followed Rachel, hobbling as fast as I could, in a mad surge up gilded staircases, down scarlet-carpeted corridors, peeping into elegant curtained boxes, leaning perilously over the edge of the mile-high gallery, squirming through knots of startled people, begging glasses of water off starchy bartenders in the bar, almost knocking a pile of programmes out of the arms of a programme seller and ending up in the Ladies, where we sank against the wall and tried to suppress our hysterical laughter, watched with disapproval by a queue of frowning women.

'I've – wanted to – do that – for years!' gasped Rachel, wiping her eyes.

'It – was the best – fun ever!' I panted.

Overhead, a bell rang loudly.

'Are you two actually intending to see the opera?' an acid voice said behind us. 'Because you'd better calm down and get to your seats or they'll shut the doors on you.'

We came to earth with a bump.

'Your hair's coming down,' Rachel said. 'I'll pin it back up.'

When she'd finished, I bent over, trying to see if I'd laddered Hope's stockings. Everything seemed all right.

'There you are!' said Mrs Stern as we dropped into the empty seats beside her. 'Where on earth have you been?'

I couldn't make head or tail of the opera. For a start, it was all in Italian. The characters didn't seem real at all. Half the time they just stood and looked at the audience and sang while everyone else on the stage kept still. The music was nice. There were some lovely tunes. But after a while, whenever the main man began to sing, I became aware of Mrs Stern, who was sitting between Rachel and the professor, moving around restlessly in her seat. She'd sigh loudly, drop her head in her hands, shake it violently and shift from side to side.

'He can't sing!' I heard her mutter. 'That tenor can't *sing*!'

People in front were turning round and glaring.

'Stop it, Mutti!' hissed Rachel.

'Frieda,' the professor said in a quiet, warning voice.

Mrs Stern tossed her head angrily.

'It's a scandal!' she said loudly. 'In Vienna they would have booed him off the stage!'

Someone behind us tapped her on the shoulder.

'Shh! Be quiet, or go out!'

I looked sideways at Rachel. She was hunched over in her seat, screwed up with embarrassment and biting her bottom lip.

Suddenly, the music stopped, and the vast red curtain fell. All around us people were clapping ecstatically.

'Is it the end?' I whispered to Rachel.

'No. Just the interval.' She scowled past me towards her mother. 'I'm so sorry.'

'Why? What for?'

'Mutti. She just kills me! Making all that fuss because she didn't like the tenor.'

'Oh. He sounded all right to me.'

Professor and Mrs Stern were already making their way towards the exit.

'Where are they going?'

'To the bar. Papa's ordered drinks. Come on, we'd better go too.'

'Well, Charity,' said Professor Stern, handing me a glass of orange juice. 'Are you enjoying your first opera?'

We'd moved back from the crowded bar and were standing beside one of the long windows.

'Yes, thank you,' I said politely. Then honesty overcame me. 'But I don't really understand what's going on.'

'Leo, look who's here!' said Mrs Stern, pulling him away. 'The Morleys!'

'Rachel,' said the professor over his shoulder, 'tell Charity the story. She can't possibly enjoy it if she doesn't know what's happening.'

'Sorry,' Rachel said as her parents moved away. 'I should have explained before. There's this woman, Madame Butterfly—'

'The one in the long dress with the sash?'

'Yes. It's a kimono. She's Japanese. She had an American lover, called Pinkerton, and then he left Japan and went back to America, leaving her with no money and a baby on the way.'

'She had a baby without being *married*?'

I was scandalized. Mother had been right, after all. This story was full of sin! Sex! Depravity!

'It wasn't her fault,' said Rachel. 'Her family sold her to Pinkerton when she was only fifteen. She thinks she's properly married.'

Things were getting worse and worse.

'They *sold* her? But she was a *child*!'

'Yes. Horrible, I know. So, in the first part, Butterfly is desperately hoping for Pinkerton to come back to Japan so she won't be poor any more and they can live happily ever after with their little boy.'

I was gripped now.

'And does he?'

'Yes. Well, he comes back, anyway. But he doesn't care about Butterfly any more. He didn't even know about the baby. He's got married to an American woman instead, and they both come, and Butterfly's heart is broken, but what's worse is that when his wife sees the little boy she wants to take him back to America.'

I stamped my foot.

'They must be *wicked*.'

'They're rich and white and powerful, and they sort of automatically assume they can do what they like. They don't even think about it.'

'And Butterfly's poor and not-white and powerless, I suppose,' I said savagely. 'So what happens? Do they take the child away?'

'She has to make a dreadful decision. Does she try to keep her son, who'll grow up poor and have a miserable future, or does she let them take him to America, where he'll be rich and get a good education?'

I was hanging on her words.

'So what does she do?'

'You'll see. I don't want to spoil the ending for you. But, I'm warning you, it's awfully sad.'

'You've seen it before?'

'Yes. Last year. But you know what, Charity, I've never really thought about it the way you do. Like a sort of moral story, you know. Now I come to think of it, you're right. It's horrifying! It's—'

The bell rang shrilly. It was time to go back for the second half.

I waited with a thrill of anticipation for the lights to go down and the curtain to rise. It was different now. Everything made sense to me. I could hear the characters' feelings in the music too. Butterfly's tunes were sad and despairing. When Pinkerton swaggered in, so handsome and confident, the music was cheerful and sort of careless.

And I *hated* him! Yes, and his beautiful, blonde American wife, who was pretending to be nice and sympathetic just so she could steal Madame Butterfly's little boy. And then, oh, then, when she carried him off at last, and Butterfly fell weeping to the ground, and picked up her father's sword and plunged it into her heart with a terrible cry of despair, I gave out a cry of anguish too, and began to actually sob. I was being too noisy, but it didn't matter because it was all over and everyone was clapping like crazy. I was desperate to clap too, but I was struggling to get out the hanky that Mother had tucked into the pocket of my dress, so that I could wipe my dripping nose. But after that I clapped as hard as I could, till my right hand was stinging.

I felt empty and pure as we left the opera house. And

world-weary, and wise. And angry and sad, and determined to do something noble and magnificent with my life. I would have liked to wrap myself in a kind of holy silence as Professor Stern drove across Trafalgar Square and down the unlit Mall towards Buckingham Palace, but Mrs Stern, sitting in the front of the car beside him, turned and said, 'So, Charity, were you still confused? Did you at least like the music?'

'I wasn't confused *at all*,' I declared. 'It was so sad, and beautiful, and that man, Pinkerton. I wanted to – to hit him!'

She laughed.

'So did I, *Liebling*, but only because he had gravel in his throat. If this had been Paris, or Vienna—'

'Yes, but, Mutti, you shouldn't go on like that,' Rachel said crossly. 'Everyone gets annoyed. It's terribly embarrassing. I just wanted to die.'

But I hadn't finished. There were things I wanted to get off my chest.

'I feel so, so indignant!' I burst out. 'My life plan has completely changed! I still want to learn lots of languages and travel round the world, but what I'm going to actually do is fight injustice! Free the oppressed from tyranny! Right the wrongs done to Madame Butterfly!'

I didn't mean to sound funny, but maybe I did. Anyway, they all laughed.

'*Mein Gott*,' said Mrs Stern, 'if this is how she feels after *Madame Butterfly*, what on earth will *Tosca* do to her?'

CHAPTER TWENTY-TWO

It was terribly late when I got home to Gospel Fields, but Hope had waited up for me. She pounced on me almost before I got in through the door. Mother appeared at the top of the stairs, called out a soft goodnight and went back to bed. I knew she'd been lying awake to make sure I was home safely.

'How was it?' urged Hope.

'It was absolutely incredibly completely amazing,' I told her. 'And, by the way, Mrs Stern asked if you'd like to go next door and sing with her tomorrow afternoon.'

Hope's face lit up, then she frowned and bit her lip.

'But tomorrow's Sunday.'

'I know.' I yawned. 'You'll have to go over and explain.'

'It's so irritating, this Sunday thing,' said Hope. 'Everyone thinks we're nuts.'

A few months ago, I'd have been shocked at this evidence that Hope, too, was falling away from the Lucasite path. Now I found myself nodding.

She followed me into my bedroom, bombarding me with questions that I couldn't answer as I climbed into my pyjamas.

At last she left me alone. I lay in bed with my eyes open, staring through the dark at the ceiling. I knew I ought to be saying my prayers, but instead I was imagining myself at the head of a great column of people, marching out of the dawn, my chest thrust out. I was holding a huge banner that floated out behind me.

'Justice!' I was shouting. 'Freedom! Save Madame Butterfly and her child from . . .'

But I couldn't find the exact words to save her with and, the next thing I knew, I was waking up on Sunday morning. The banners and the marching revolutionaries had faded away and I was plain old Charity Brown again.

By the time I stepped off the bus outside school on Monday morning, the glory of the opera had disappeared. A few weeks ago, I'd have spent the journey rehearsing show-off lines in my head.

Have you been to Madame Butterfly *at Covent Garden?* I'd be planning to say casually to whoever would listen. *Marvellous soprano, but the tenor's got gravel in his throat.*

But Monica had taught me a lesson.

'Miss La-di-da,' she'd said. 'With your *tennis court* and your *grand piano.*'

I blushed to think of how awful I'd been and what I'd made her feel.

My heart was beating fast as I pushed open the door of our classroom. Monica was there already, perched in her usual position on the radiator under the window, elevated above her group of friends. They all turned to look at me, then swivelled their heads round again to watch Monica, waiting eagerly for one of her withering put-downs.

I braced myself. I'd made a plan and I was determined to carry it out.

'Hello, Monica,' I said, coughing to disguise the quaver in my voice. 'I've got something to show you.'

I dumped my bag on my desk and took out a piece of paper. I'd spent the whole of Sunday afternoon poring over an enormous stack of old *Punch* magazines that I'd found in the attic, hunting for one that would do. It wasn't brilliant, but I'd cut it out anyway and stuck it on a piece of paper.

I pushed through the clump of girls and handed it to Monica.

The cartoon showed a bus full of people watching a vicar getting on. The caption read, *Oh no! Here comes the preacher again! Watch out, everyone. He sat next to me last week and didn't stop talking for five whole hours!*

It wasn't very funny, and I waited breathlessly, scanning her blank face, while my heart sank further and further into my boots. What could I have been thinking? How could I have taken such a risk?

But then a slow grin spread over Monica's face. She looked across at me and in her eyes I read something that might have been respect. Then she threw back her head and laughed.

'What is it? What's so funny?'

Her hangers-on were crowding round to look.

Monica held the paper up high and handed it to me over their heads.

'In-joke,' she said to the others. 'You wouldn't understand.'

As I retreated to my desk, Sandra, Monica's most spiteful friend, put out her foot to trip me up. I staggered, and the joke fluttered out of my hand.

'Butterfingers,' sniggered Sandra.

Monica turned on her furiously.

'Shut up, Sandra.'

She slid off the radiator, picked the paper up and gave it back to me.

'Loved it, Charity,' she said. 'Where did you find it?'

Once I might have said, *We've got this enormous attic full of priceless treasures. I dug it out from under what is possibly a Stradivarius violin.*

Instead, I said, 'In a funny old magazine.'

The bell rang. Everyone drifted to their desks. I folded the joke up and stuffed it in my bag. My heart had stopped fluttering and had settled into a strong, triumphant rhythm.

As our form teacher took the register, the girl behind me tapped me on the shoulder. I turned round warily, braced for the usual mockery.

'Charity,' she whispered. 'I haven't done my French homework. Can you help me with it at break? I can't face another detention.'

I searched her face. There was no wicked gleam in her eye, just a sort of pale anxiety.

'Glad to,' I said.

So that day Mrs Thorpe and the library had to do without me.

'Where's Mother?' I asked Hope, who was crossing the hall when I let myself into the house after school.

'In the kitchen. Making lists with Kurian.'

'What do you mean, lists? What for?'

'Where have you been, Charity? Kurian's been going on non-stop about the Indian meal he wants to cook ever since I got home. He's going to do it on Saturday. Faith and Justin are coming. And Ted wants to ask Auntie Vi.'

'*Haldi*,' Kurian was saying as I went into the kitchen. He and Mother were sitting at the table, and Mother's pencil was hovering uncertainly over a sheet of paper.

'What's that again?' asked Mother.

'Turmeric in English,' Kurian said impatiently, 'but Ted must say it in Hindi or the man will not understand him.'

'Who won't understand?' I asked Mother. 'What are you two doing?' I said, adding silently in my head, *And why haven't you even noticed that I'm here?*

'Indian spices,' Mother said happily, looking up at me at last. 'Ted's going over to Stepney to buy them, and he'll bring them down on Thursday.'

'Hurrah for Ted,' I said drily, but neither of them heard me.

I pushed past them to make myself a cup of tea. Usually, I had tea with Mother when I got home, and she'd have a plate of home-baked biscuits ready on the table.

'You are making some tea?' Kurian said. 'Please make enough for your brother.'

I nearly said, *What? Is Ted here?* but then I realized he was talking about himself.

I made the tea, and handed him a mug. He stirred in two heaped teaspoons of sugar and stood up.

'I think we have finished, Mother,' he said. 'I will go and rest for a while.'

'Mother? He called you *Mother*?' I said as he closed the kitchen door behind him.

'I know. He's such a boy!'

Her smile was too fond for my liking. I swallowed hard.

'How long's he going to stay?' I asked. 'Only he seems quite better now.'

'Till after Christmas. Ted's managed to get him a room in his student hostel. What an answer to prayer! See what the Lord has done!'

Yes, well, it's what Ted has done, I thought rebelliously. Aloud I said, 'Why are you so keen on this Indian cooking idea, Mother? Don't you mind him taking over your kitchen?'

She sighed in a way that was almost sentimental.

'Your grandfather often talked about the curries he'd eaten in Bangalore. He missed them when he left India and settled in New Zealand. You couldn't get the spices there, of course. I've always wanted to try Indian food out for myself. Anyway, it's good for Kurian to have something to do. He's getting his confidence back. He looked like a lost puppy when he came here.'

I couldn't believe my ears.

'Kurian? A lost puppy? You've got to be joking! He's the most arrogant, spoilt . . .'

306

Mother frowned.

'That's not very kind, Charity. You're forgetting that man looketh on the outward appearance, but the Lord looketh on the heart.'

I was silenced, as usual, by the Bible.

'Anyway,' she went on, 'you like him. I know you do.'

I thought about this.

'Ye-es, I suppose so. He's infuriating, but he's sort of fun too. Only I was a bit afraid he was going to live here forever.'

Mother stood up, fetched down the biscuit tin and put it on the table.

'That would never do. We just need to help him get better and send him on his way rejoicing. Don't tell me you won't miss him?'

'No, I won't!'

I took a biscuit. Mother's own ginger snaps. She knew they were my favourite, and I knew she made them specially for me. My world had wobbled for a moment, as if Kurian had somehow threatened to displace me in the family. Now things felt steady again.

'Actually, yes,' I said. 'I will miss him. It'll be boring without him here.'

I got home from school on Thursday to find the kitchen table strewn with strange-looking vegetables, packets of rice, lentils, odd-coloured flour and little boxes printed all over with letters I'd never seen before. I picked one of these up and sniffed at it, then jumped back as if I'd been stung. My eyes watered and a tremendous sneeze gathered in my nose.

'Mother, have you smelt this stuff? It's disgusting!' I managed to say at last as I mopped my streaming eyes.

She laughed.

'It'll taste different when it's cooked. It's time for your French lesson, Charity. Don't keep Mrs Stern waiting.'

My hour next door sped past as usual. I was beginning to talk easily in French now, enjoying the feeling of it on my tongue. When I needed a word, Mrs Stern quietly gave it to me. When I stumbled over a phrase, she corrected me. Sometimes we read a poem or a little story, and she helped me to understand it. Today we talked about *Madame Butterfly*, and by the end of the hour my head was spinning with the French words for cruelty and oppression, racism and injustice, which sounded wonderfully like the words in English.

As usual, Rachel bounced down the stairs when my lesson had ended. I grabbed her arm almost before she'd landed at the bottom.

'Please, please say you'll come,' I said. 'On Saturday. Kurian's going to cook an Indian dinner. Justin and Faith and Ted and Auntie Vi are coming. I sort of feel I might need moral support.'

Her eyes had sparked at the mention of Ted.

'Of *course*,' she breathed. 'I can't wait.'

'Indian food is very strong, *Liebling*,' Mrs Stern said doubtfully. 'I don't think you'll like it.'

Rachel waved this aside.

'She won't have to actually *eat* it,' I said. 'If it's too awful, we can sneak off to the kitchen and make sandwiches or something.'

I woke up on Saturday morning with a strangely quivering feeling inside, as if every nerve ending was alive. Gospel Fields seemed to have come alive too. Ted, Justin and Faith had arrived late the night before. I'd heard their quiet voices on the stairs as I was dropping off to sleep. Now, footsteps were passing along the corridor outside my bedroom, making the floorboards creak. I could hear Faith calling to Mother, and somewhere Hope was singing.

Ted thundered down the attic stairs.

'Come on, Kurian!' I heard him call out as he thumped on the spare room door. 'Breakfast's ready!'

I jumped out of bed, threw on my clothes and tugged my hair into untidy plaits. Dad was crossing the hall as I reached the bottom of the stairs.

'Good morning, Charity,' he said, dropping a kiss on the top of my head. 'Sleep well?'

He ambled on towards the kitchen before I had time to answer.

He'd left the study door open. Low December sunshine streamed all the way across the hall from the side window beyond his desk, making the oak-panelled walls glow. I followed the sunbeams into the study and found myself looking up at the portrait of Margery Austen. Her plain, childish face stared down at me solemnly. She looked wistful. I thought of the tailor's dummy in the attic, with the grown-up Mrs

Spendlove's severe, tweedy skirt and jacket and the funny old hat with its feather.

'You must have been awfully bored being a child in this great big house without any brothers and sisters,' I said out loud. 'And how could you bear it when you were grown up, living here on your own all those years, until Mr Spendlove came along and rescued you?'

'What, dear?' said Dad, who had come in silently behind me. 'Did you say something?'

I laughed, feeling a bit embarrassed.

'I was talking to Margery. Mrs Spendlove. What do you think, Dad? Would she have minded us filling up Gospel Fields, being noisy, using all her stuff and leaving marks on the furniture?'

He put an arm round my shoulders and studied her portrait too.

'I'm sure she'd have loved it. Reg Spendlove certainly would. I think that's why he left the house to us. He wanted it to come alive.' I thought he was about to say something from the Bible, but instead he said, 'Perhaps it's time to put this old picture away in the attic. We could hang up photos of our family instead.'

I shook my head.

'Don't let's, Dad. She belongs there. Don't you see? She's let us in, now. She wants to be part of us, and Gospel Fields does too.'

There were too many of us to fit round the kitchen table, so we had to have breakfast in the dining room.

'Please, Dad,' said Kurian, after the plates had been cleared away and Dad was opening his Bible, 'do not pray for very long today. I must start as soon as possible to make my curries.'

Dad's eyebrows had shot up with surprise at being called 'Dad', and they nearly reached his hairline at this request. Ted stifled a shout of laughter. I caught Hope's eye and quickly looked away in case we both went down with the giggles. Faith was suppressing a smile and squeezing Justin's hand under the table.

Dad recovered. He leaned over and patted Kurian on the shoulder.

'Well, my son,' he said. 'Your enthusiasm to start work does you credit, but our day of fellowship and feasting will be sadly lacking if we don't offer it to the Lord in humble prayer and thanksgiving.'

Kurian, receiving the full blast of Dad's gently reproachful eyes, blushed.

'Yes, I am sorry,' he said. 'I—'

'But the Lord sees into all our hearts,' interrupted Dad. 'He understands our love and gratitude. So we will recite only one psalm this morning and say the Lord's Prayer together before we go joyfully on with the day.'

'Kurian, you are wonderful!' breathed Hope as, ten minutes later, we finally got up from the table.

'No, I am a very bad person,' said Kurian, shaking his head. 'But I do not have time to think about my crimes. Now you, my sisters, Hope and Charity, will clear up the breakfast things, wash the dishes and then please leave the kitchen and do not return. I cannot be interrupted today.'

I looked at him curiously. Young men always fell in love with Hope (which, quite frankly, was incredibly irritating), but Kurian seemed strangely unimpressed by her.

By the middle of the morning, every room in the house was occupied. Dad was in his study, Hope was practising the piano in the drawing room, Mother and Faith were in the dining room discussing the menu for next Saturday's dinner for Justin's parents, while Justin himself had followed Ted into the garden to saw up wood for the house fires. Alarming smells were coming out of the kitchen. They made me wrinkle my nose and worry. Rachel might take one sniff and flee.

There are sterner things in life than Indian dinners, I told myself firmly. *Science homework, for example.*

So I went upstairs and got on with it.

CHAPTER TWENTY-THREE

The trembly feeling I'd had inside that morning was still there after lunch. The weather was turning. The sun had gone behind heavy clouds and it was steadily getting colder. Dad lit the fires in the hall, dining room and drawing room, and by mid-afternoon, when it was already getting dark, their flames were casting warm flickers on the walls.

A sort of cheerful chaos had taken over Gospel Fields. Kurian, who was beginning to panic, had summoned Mother to help in the kitchen. Ted had spread newspapers all over the hall floor and had laid out bits of the Rover's engine on them. He was sitting on the floor, wiping things with a greasy rag.

'Sorry about the mess,' he said as Dad nearly tripped over a chunk of metal. 'I'm trying to fix that clunking sound in the gearbox. It's too cold to work in the garage.'

In the dining room, Faith and Hope had spread patterns and samples of material for the bridesmaids' dresses across the table.

'Not that one,' I heard Faith say. 'It's too low cut. It'd scandalize the Lucasites. And it wouldn't do for Charity.

Her chest hasn't developed much. Yet.'

I put my hands over my ears and fled.

I'd only just got to my room when Dad called up the stairs, 'Charity? Rachel's here!'

I rushed down to the hall.

'Where shall I put this?' said Rachel, shrugging off her coat.

'Oh, anywhere. On that chair, under the gong.'

I headed towards the stairs, but Rachel was mesmerized by the sight of Ted. She went across to the fire and stood warming her hands.

'What are you doing, Ted?' she asked, a blush spreading up her cheeks.

'Not worth explaining,' he said, without looking up. 'Too many long words for little girls. Sprocket. Carburettor. Spark plug. See?'

'Ted!' I exploded, unable to resist taking the bait. '*Tu es un très impoli garcon.* Bet that was too much French for you too.'

He looked up and grinned.

'Fair point. Now make yourself useful and pass me that nut.'

Rachel darted in first.

'This one?' she asked breathlessly.

He took it without looking at her.

'Come on, Rachel,' I said, tugging her sleeve. 'Let's go to my room.'

She shook me off, her eyes still on Ted.

'Couldn't we just – you know – sit on the stairs or something? It's nice and warm down here.'

I made a face, but what could I do? She was lost to reason.

314

Actually, it was fun, perching on the stairs. Even though it was a sort of public space, it felt strangely private when we put our heads together and whispered.

'I've been thinking about changing my name,' I told Rachel.

She swivelled her head round to stare at me.

'What? Why?'

'Charity feels so old-fashioned and Lucasite-ish, and – and I think I'm becoming someone else.'

'What do you want to be called, then?'

'I'm not sure. Something strong. Beautiful. Heroic. Amaryllis?'

'Too complicated. You'd have to keep explaining it to people.'

'I quite like Ariadne, but I looked it up and it means *very holy*, which I'm not.'

'I can't see what's wrong with Charity,' she said with a frown. 'It's a lovely name. It's just – you.'

I ignored this.

'In my heart of hearts,' I confessed, 'I think I might possibly be a Lulu.'

She burst out laughing.

'You can't be serious! There's nothing Lulu-ish about you at all!' She paused. 'I couldn't ever change my name even if I wanted to. I'm called after Mutti's mother.'

For a moment, the weight of history seemed to settle on her. There didn't seem to be anything more to say.

All this time, people kept coming and going in front of us. Dad would cross the hall to the kitchen, then Faith would come out of the dining room, bundles of material samples in her hands. Justin wandered in and out, pausing to watch what Ted was doing, and all the time the smells from the kitchen grew stronger and more eye-watering.

'What do you think it'll actually taste like?' Rachel asked.

'I dread to think,' I said, shuddering artistically, although actually I was dying to find out.

'There's so much happening in your house,' Rachel said after a while. 'It's like being at the theatre.'

'I wouldn't know,' I said, 'but aren't plays more interesting than this? You know. Dramatic?'

It was as if I'd lit the blue touch paper and set off a rocket. At that moment, Kurian ran out from the kitchen, shouting, 'It's ruined! My dal is burned!'

Mother was behind him.

'Calm down, Kurian,' she said in the voice she used for us. 'Your dal is perfectly all right.'

Hope, coming out of the dining room to see what was going on, reared back from Kurian's flailing arms and dropped the little box she was carrying. Pins scattered all over the floor. She went down on all fours and began scrabbling round to pick them up.

The doorbell rang.

'That'll be Vi,' said Ted, jumping up, an oily rag in his hand.

I don't know what got into me then. I suppose I was thrilled with the idea of seeing Auntie Vi. Anyway, I leaped to my feet, shouting, 'Roses are red, violets are blue, sugar is sweet, and so are –' I shoved Ted aside, threw open the front door and shouted triumphantly – 'you!'

But Auntie Vi wasn't there. Instead, there was a tall man with a bristly moustache and a woman muffled in hats and scarves.

Ted was right behind me.

'Who on earth are you?' he demanded.

'Fraser,' barked the man, thrusting out his hand then dropping it again as he took in the sight of Ted's oily fingers.

Faith let out a moan. Mother gasped. Justin, who had been kneeling on the floor to help Ted, lurched to his feet.

'Father? Mother? What are you doing here?'

'I had the impression,' General Fraser said stiffly, 'that we had been invited to dinner.'

'Next week!' said Justin. 'Not till next Saturday!'

'I think not.' The general was glaring at him. 'You specifically mentioned this date. I wrote it down straight away.'

For a moment, everyone froze. Then Dad, who had come out of the study, gently closed the front door behind the Frasers and helped Mrs Fraser off with her coat.

'You're very welcome!' he said. 'It's such a pleasure to meet you. And you've come on the perfect day because our young friend Kurian is cooking us all a splendid Indian dinner. My wife assures me that there's enough to feed an . . .'

I could see that he was about to say *army*, but was thinking better of it.

'A regiment?' Mrs Fraser suggested quietly, her lips twitching.

I had to stuff my fist into my mouth to hold in hysterical bursts of laughter.

Mother, who had been making mewing noises, tugged off her apron and thrust it at Hope.

'How – how delightful,' she managed to say. 'As you can see, Justin's already a member of our family. Iver, why don't you – why don't you – take General and Mrs Fraser into the study? I – I'm sure they'd like a hot drink after their cold journey.'

Dad was already holding open the study door.

As soon as it had closed behind them, Mother beckoned us all into the dining room. She was back in command, out-generalling the general.

'Mrs Brown, I'm so sorry!' began Justin. 'I—'

'Never mind that now, Justin,' said Mother. 'We'll get through all right. Faith, make up a tray of tea. Best china. Take it into the study. Ted, clear up all this mess and check on the fires. Hope, get rid of these pins. And Charity and Rachel, set the table. When you've done that, go upstairs, girls, and change into your Sunday dresses.' Kurian was tugging at her sleeve. 'No more fussing, Kurian. Your dinner's going to be fine. Just keep it all warm, then go and smarten yourself up. Ted, there are smudges all over your face. Build up the drawing-room fire first. I'll take them in there before dinner.'

'Do you think I ought to go home?' Rachel whispered to me.

'No!' I grabbed her arm. 'You heard Mother. You've got to help me set the table. You can't abandon me. Not now!'

*

After a few minutes, I left Rachel to do the table on her own and hurried upstairs to get changed. I came downstairs again in my brown velvet dress, with my plaits retied, to find that Auntie Vi had arrived. She was in the hall, now cleared of engine parts, and was patting a tearful Faith on the shoulder.

'Chin up, darling! The show must go on. I'll go and give Iver a hand. He must be running out of steam by now, poor boy.'

But, before she could move, the study door opened and Mrs Fraser came out.

'I couldn't bear it any longer,' she said. 'The Barker's started telling Mr Brown all about his experiences in the Burma campaign. He'll go on forever. I'm sure you're having more fun out here. Is there anything I can do to help?'

'The Barker?' said Auntie Vi, her forehead wrinkled.

'It's what Justin calls his father, though actually they're the best of friends.' She noticed Faith's tear-stained face. 'Faith, you mustn't take any notice of him! His bark's much worse than his bite. He's terribly sentimental underneath it all. Absolutely adores Justin, and I know he's going to adore you.'

Faith took a deep breath and tried to smile, but before she could say anything, Mother came downstairs. She was in her best dress with her only piece of jewellery, a necklace of crystal beads, round her neck. She ushered Mrs Fraser into the drawing room and I took the opportunity to sidle off to the dining room.

Rachel was standing back, looking at the table with a critical eye. I gasped.

'Rachel! It's incredible! Where did you find those candlesticks?'

'In the china cabinet. Hadn't you noticed them?'

'Not really. I actually thought they were weird vases for tiny flowers.'

'And the candles were tucked in behind them. Do you like the way that I've folded the napkins? Mutti taught me how to do it. They're supposed to look like waterlilies.'

A despairing shout came from the kitchen.

'It's Kurian,' said Rachel. 'He's been going crazy.'

'Do you think we'd better go in and help him?'

'I wouldn't. Ted and Justin are there. Justin put his head through the hatch a few minutes ago and said that it was all nearly ready. By the way, I hope you don't mind, but I opened the front door to your Auntie Vi, and she said, "Who are you?" and I said, "I'm Charity's best friend from next door."'

'Of *course* I don't mind,' I said, beaming at her.

'And Justin said not to take any notice of his father. He's all right underneath the snarling.'

'Mrs Fraser said something like that. She's nice.'

'Justin said to knock on the hatch when everyone's in the dining room,' said Rachel, 'so Kurian can start dishing it all up. It smells so amazing, Charity, but I'm not sure if I can actually eat it.'

'I'm not sure if I can, either,' I said. 'I'll try, though.'

'Me too,' said Rachel bravely.

*

Mother had taken Mrs Fraser into the drawing room. As I went in, I heard her say, 'Faith tells me you're expert at embroidery, Mrs Fraser?'

'I'm not sure where she got that idea from,' said Mrs Fraser. 'My real interest is gardening.'

The desperate look faded from Mother's eyes. She leaned forward in her chair.

'Really? So is mine! I'm looking forward to showing you our garden here. I hope Faith has explained to you that we only moved here recently? Being a New Zealander, I'm unfamiliar with many British plants, and I never expected to have such an enormous place to look after. Perhaps you'll be able to advise me.'

'Justin says that dinner's ready. He thinks so, anyway,' I announced.

'You haven't met Charity, Faith's youngest sister?' said Mother to Mrs Fraser.

At the awful memory of me throwing open the front door and going on about roses and violets, I could feel myself blush to my hairline. Then I had a strange urge to curtsey, but got the better of it.

'Hello,' I said. 'I hope you like Indian food, Mrs Fraser. Personally, I've never tried it, but I'm going to have a go.'

'Thank you, Charity, that will do,' said Mother. 'Go and call your father and the general.'

They both stood up, and as they went out through the drawing-room door Mother whispered, 'Have you remembered to put out the salt and pepper? And serving spoons?'

'Of course we have,' I said, trying not to sound scornful.

Rachel was standing at the dining room's open door when I went past on my way to the study. She'd lit the candles. The room looked more beautiful than ever before. Flickering light from the candles danced on the walls and set the glasses sparkling against the white tablecloth. I paused to watch Mother's face as she took it in. After the first start of pleasant surprise, her forehead puckered.

She thinks we're trying to look too grand, I thought. *Pretending to be something we're not.*

Fortunately, Hope was right behind her.

'Oh, you've made it so pretty!' she said. 'Well done, Rachel. Weird candlesticks. Where did you find them?'

This gave Mother her cue.

'As you see,' she explained to Mrs Fraser, 'we still haven't discovered everything in this house. It's a great deal more — opulent than what we're used to. We've always had a much simpler way of life.'

'Justin told us all about it.' Mrs Fraser nodded. 'What an incredible piece of luck, inheriting all this out of the blue.'

Mother's frown deepened.

'Gospel Fields has given us a wonderful opportunity to do the Lord's work,' she said. 'His will has been marvellously revealed.'

'Ah yes, of course,' said Mrs Fraser politely.

I hadn't needed to call Dad and the general. Auntie Vi had taken control and was ushering them into the dining room. The general was rubbing his hands and sniffing the air appreciatively.

'Curry! Splendid!' he said. 'I haven't had a decent mouth-burner since we left India.'

Everyone sat down. At a nod from Rachel, I knocked on the hatch into the kitchen. A few minutes later, a procession entered the dining room. Ted came first, carrying a huge platter of rice. Behind him was Justin, who threw a sideways look at his father before placing a brimming bowl of coloured mush on the table. Last came Kurian, who was tenderly bearing a tray covered with steaming dishes.

'You're the cook, eh?' the general said genially. 'Learned your trade in the Gurkhas?'

Kurian put the tray down and turned a withering look on him.

'I am a Kerala man, General Fraser, and not a Gurkha. It is very unusual, in fact unheard of, for a Kerala man to cook, unless he is a servant, but I am an exceptional person and I have always taken an interest in the culinary arts.'

He paused while he moved the dishes off the tray on to the table. General Fraser, looking slightly stunned, seemed about to say something, but Kurian went on stiffly, 'And, anyway, I would like to inform you that I am a student of law at the University of London, and my life will be devoted to righting the wrongs done to my country suffering under the yoke of—'

'Yes,' broke in Ted quickly, 'but you're also a terrific cook. That chicken thing. I've never tasted anything like it.'

Kurian's rigid manner deserted him and he shook his head doubtfully.

'The spices are not perfectly balanced,' he said. 'There

should be more chilli, but I have adapted my cuisine to the immature British palate.'

'The law, eh?' said the general, trying to keep up. 'Good for you.'

Dad, seated at the head of the table, beamed round at everyone.

'Before we eat this wonderful feast, let us give thanks to God for the multiple blessings he has showered upon us.'

He caught Faith's agonized eyes and nodded.

'A short blessing,' he assured her.

To do him justice, his prayer lasted less than five minutes.

Rachel and I took nervous dabs from each dish as they were passed round.

'We can fill up on the rice, anyway,' I whispered to her.

She bravely tried a mouthful of the orange mush.

'It's really nice!' she said, surprised. 'Go on, try it. What's it called, anyway?'

'I think it's the dal thing Kurian was going on about,' I said, poking my helping doubtfully with my fork.

Snatches of conversation swirled round us, fading in and out.

'The fish curry is my masterpiece,' Kurian was explaining to Hope. 'You see I have no false modesty. But the chicken biryani is not . . .'

Auntie Vi was getting on surprisingly well with the general.

'Haven't had much time for the theatre,' he was saying, 'but now I've retired—'

'Oh, do come to my *Romeo and Juliet*,' interrupted Auntie Vi.

'We're opening next week. I'll send you tickets.'

'Love to,' said the general, 'though when it comes to Shakespeare his sonnets are more up my street. *Shall I compare thee to a summer's day? Thou art more lovely and more temperate . . .*'

He was looking at Faith as he spoke, and I was sure I saw the glint of a tear in his eye.

Rachel and I exchanged astonished looks.

'He's quoting poetry!' she breathed.

'And he looks as if he's going to cry!'

Then we both had the same thought at the same time.

'Your Auntie Vi's doing *Romeo and Juliet*!' said Rachel.

'I'll ask Mother,' I told her. 'I bet she'd let us go. It's Shakespeare, after all.'

At the other end of the table, Mrs Fraser was gazing sympathetically at Dad.

'So you never knew your mother?' She glanced down the table at Auntie Vi. 'And it was your sisters who brought you up? How remarkable!'

'Darling, stop worrying!' Justin murmured to Faith. 'Look at my old man. He's gone all soft and soupy. And my mother clearly thinks your father's the best . . .'

I tried the fish curry. It was delicious. Rachel was eyeing one of the vegetable dishes. Ted moved it away.

'I wouldn't,' he whispered in her ear. 'Those little red chillies would blow your head off.'

Rachel went scarlet, too overwhelmed to answer.

General Fraser beckoned to Justin, who obediently stood

up and went round the table to him.

'By the front door. My briefcase. Bring it, would you?'

Justin came back a moment later, but instead of handing the briefcase over, he held it angrily away from his father. Something clinked inside it.

'Barker, I *told* you. This isn't appropriate. You can't—'

'Nonsense, boy. Hand it over.'

Everyone had stopped talking and was watching them.

'Justin has explained that you are, generally speaking, not in favour of drinking wine,' the general said, looking at Dad.

'That's not what I said *at all*!' protested Justin. 'There was no *generally speaking* about it!'

His father silenced him with an uplifted hand.

'But tonight is a celebration of such importance, the engagement of Justin and Faith, that I believe we should toast it in the traditional way.'

Taking Justin by surprise, he snatched the briefcase from him, opened it and set two bottles of champagne down on the table.

There was a moment of absolute silence.

'Oh!' said Mother faintly.

Ted smothered a burst of laughter with a cough.

Dad's smile wavered.

Auntie Vi's eyes swivelled from Dad at one end of the table to Mother at the other.

Dad recovered himself.

'It is indeed a special celebration,' he said. 'It's true that, generally speaking, we don't partake of alcohol. But on this unique occasion, a small quantity of champagne – after all, St Paul himself in his letter to Timothy advised him to take a little wine for his stomach's sake.'

I felt a kick of shock in my heart. Had it come to this? Had the Browns fallen from the true path after one nudge from a bossy stranger?

Everyone relaxed. Auntie Vi caught Dad's eye and mouthed, '*Well done, Iver.*'

'I don't believe we have any champagne glasses,' said Mother, with a fixed smile.

'Yes, we have,' said Hope. 'I'll get them.'

'How do you even know what champagne glasses look like?' demanded Mother.

'Oh, you know,' Hope said airily. 'One picks these things up.'

She went out of the room.

Justin, flushed with embarrassment, went back to his seat beside Faith.

'I'm so sorry, darling,' I heard him whisper. 'Whatever must your parents think of us?'

At that moment, a great revelation came to me.

'You know what,' I said to Rachel, 'I've just understood one of life's eternal truths. Everyone, absolutely everyone in the whole world, is embarrassed by their parents. I mean, look at Justin! He's normally so sort of smooth, but right now he's so ashamed of his dad he wants the floor to swallow him up.'

She laughed.

'You're right. Like how I nearly died at the opera when

Mutti made all that fuss about the tenor.'

'That was nothing compared to Dad preaching to total strangers right out in the street.'

We nodded to each other, feeling wise.

Hope came back with a tray of tall, thin glasses.

'Those aren't for champagne, are they?' I whispered to Rachel. 'They look as if they're for medicine.'

The general eased off the corks with a practised hand and poured the foaming, golden liquid into the glasses. He stared commandingly at Justin, who stared back, without moving. Ted jumped up, took the tray and handed round the champagne. We sat, the brimming glasses in our hands, not knowing what to do.

The general stood up. We all obediently copied him, though Justin took as much time about it as he could. The general held his glass stiffly out in front of him. We held ours out too.

'The happy couple,' he barked. Then his eyes went moist again. 'Oh, Faith,' he said, looking across the table at her. 'We're so delighted for you both, dear girl.'

Then everyone murmured, 'The happy couple,' and took a mouthful of champagne.

There's a moment just before you do something that you've always been told is incredibly wicked when your skin prickles, your heart pounds and your hands go clammy. I glanced sideways at Rachel. Champagne seemed to hold no terrors for her. She took a sip, swallowed and smiled at me. I looked at Mother. She had taken a mouthful too, and her face had puckered in distaste. Dad had drunk a bit as well, and was dabbing his mouth with his napkin.

A huge question blazed in my head. Was being polite sometimes more important than sticking to your principles? Did that mean that rules weren't really rules at all? If I was the only person who refused to drink the champagne, would that make me noble, or just rude? But Dad had quoted the Bible! The Apostle Paul himself had told someone to drink wine! Why hadn't Dad ever told us about *that* text before? Did that mean that there were all kinds of other things in the Bible that were all right, only I didn't know about them?

People were starting to sit down again. It was now or never. I lifted the glass, meaning only to wet my lips, but the bubbles confused me and I accidently swigged a whole mouthful.

I nearly choked! The sparkle and the coldness and the sharpness and the sweetness and something else that sent a kind of fire through my veins made me almost dizzy. I sank down into my chair.

But Mrs Fraser was now on her feet.

'I do think,' she said, smiling graciously at Kurian, 'that we ought to toast – Kurian, isn't it? – who created this wonderful meal.'

Kurian lifted his chin and smiled delightedly.

Everyone stood, and drank again. I was more careful this time, but the tiny sip made me even more light-headed.

Before we could sit down, Kurian said, 'And I want to toast Dad and Mother, Mr and Mrs Brown, who rescued me from death. When I am a famous high-court judge, they will become famous too for their part in preserving my life.'

'Kurian, you're outrageous!' Ted laughed.

'I know,' said Kurian, looking pleased. 'It is my trademark.'

Everyone was laughing now. I felt wildly happy. Reckless. Heady with inspiration. I stood up awkwardly, almost knocking over my champagne glass.

'I want to make a speech!' I burst out. 'I've understood something. The meaning of life! Stop laughing, Ted.'

Auntie Vi leaned an elbow on the table and cupped her chin in her hand.

'Go on. I want to hear this.'

'It's a bit from my baptism, and Gospel Fields being about helping the weary, and how I feel about all of you, and . . . and I thought I wanted to change my name to Lulu, but now . . .'

'*Lulu?*' Ted, Faith and Hope shouted with laughter.

'What *is* the child talking about?' muttered the general.

'Go on, dear,' said Dad, smiling with encouragement.

'Only I'm going to stay being Charity, because . . . because . . .'

I suddenly felt the most dreadful fool.

'Spit it out, Char,' cackled Ted.

I took a deep breath.

'Because Charity means love! And the meaning of life is love! And – and being kind. And I'm sorry, Dad and Mother, but that's more important than rules like not cutting your hair and not reading *Jane Eyre* on Sundays or even being a Lucasite!'

The bubbles in my head had burst. I wanted to run away and hide. I wanted never to have existed at all. I sank down on to my chair.

'Good for you, Charity,' Hope said loyally.

'Marvellous, darling!' That was Auntie Vi, clapping her hands in the air.

'Yes, dear,' said Mother, 'but at the same time—'

'Stating the obvious, though, isn't it?' said Faith, looking fondly at Justin. 'I mean about love.'

I didn't dare look at Rachel. I was afraid she might be scornful. But she tapped my arm and said, 'You're so brave, Charity! I'd never have dared stand up like that in front of everyone. And maybe you're right about love, but there are limits. I mean, I could never love a Nazi.'

What had seemed blindingly simple a moment ago was suddenly tangled up.

'Oh,' I said. 'No, I suppose you couldn't.'

Other, bigger ideas were pushing up into my head, only I couldn't get at them.

'The thing is,' Rachel went on consolingly, 'most people never bother to think about the meaning of life. It's what makes you so extraordinary.'

I didn't need champagne bubbles in my head any more, and I didn't even care that I'd made a fool of myself.

My best friend understood me. For now, at least, that was all that mattered.

General and Mrs Fraser were pushing back their chairs.

'We really must be going,' Mrs Fraser said. 'It's been the most – memorable – evening.'

Everyone followed them out into the hall.

'I'd better go too,' said Rachel regretfully, 'before

Papa comes to drag me home.'

'Can we give you a lift, Miss Brown?' Mrs Fraser asked Auntie Vi.

'Thanks, but I think I'll stay the night,' replied Auntie Vi, raising questioning eyebrows to Mother, who smiled and nodded back.

Ted came out from the cloakroom at the end of the kitchen corridor with a pile of coats in his arms. He handed two to the Frasers, and held a third out to Rachel.

'Is this yours?' he asked.

I snatched it from him.

'Of course it isn't! Hers is much nicer. This is my old school mac.'

Rachel picked her coat up from the chair where she'd left it hours earlier and put it on. Dad opened the front door.

'It's snowing!' I gasped.

'Just started,' said the general. 'We'd better get going before the roads clog up.'

Rachel followed them out of the front door. I didn't want to let her go. I didn't want the evening to end.

'Wait,' I said, pulling on my mac.

We stood together outside, letting icy snowflakes ping against our cheeks, then Rachel took off across the gravel, her arms whirling, and ran down the lawn where the snow was already settling on the grass. I hurried after her.

'I had to do that,' she panted, when I caught her up. 'It's been so – I don't know – so *intense*!'

Everyone had come outside to see the Frasers off. They

moved like dark shadows against the light streaming from the windows and the open front door. Their voices floated down to us through the cold air – pointless grown-up goodbyes and thank-yous and promises to meet again soon.

Why don't people say what they really mean? I thought.

I turned to Rachel. Sharp white flecks of snow dotted her dark hair.

'You told Auntie Vi you were my best friend,' I blurted out. 'Well, you're mine. You're always going to be, actually.'

It sounded silly. Saying what you really meant was harder than I'd thought.

'I know,' Rachel said lightly. 'Me too.' She was hugging herself against the cold. 'Look, we've got snow all over us. We'll turn into snowmen if we stay out here much longer.'

The tail lights of the Frasers' car disappeared down the drive.

'Got to go,' said Rachel, starting to run away up the lawn. She called out over her shoulder, 'You simply must come round tomorrow. I want to talk about *everything*!'

Mother was still waiting at the open front door.

'Come inside, Charity,' she called out, 'before you catch your death.'

I walked back to the house. The shadows of the garden were being transformed around me, lightening and brightening under the snow.

'Hurry up!' Mother called out again. 'There's washing-up to be done!'

Everything changes, I told myself as I hurried towards her, my feet making fresh tracks across the new snow. *This time last year I was stuck in that awful hospital, afraid I was going to die. I was stuck inside my head too, worrying all the time in case I wasn't being faithful enough to the Lord. But now I'm on the move! I'm Charity Brown of Gospel Fields and I've discovered the meaning of life!*

'At last,' said Mother, drawing me into the warmth and light of the house, and closing the front door behind me.

AUTHOR'S NOTE

Charity Brown is me, and she isn't me. I did have an older brother and two older sisters, but they're not Ted, Faith and Hope. And my parents were quite different from Charity's mother and father.

But some things are true. I did have a long illness in my childhood, only it was rheumatic fever, not polio. I did have a great-great-grandfather called Moses who was a whisky distiller, and my family did at last accept the money he'd left us after refusing to touch it for years. We did move into a big house on top of a hill with a huge, magical garden when I was about twelve years old, only there was no surprise legacy. Our new home was bought with old Moses's money. My mother was a New Zealander, and my father did meet her after the Napier earthquake in which he helped to look after the injured (he was a doctor, not an entomologist). All four of us children were born in New Zealand, and we left it reluctantly at the end of World War Two when I was two years old. We were met at Southampton by my Scottish aunt, Mona, who was indeed the headmistress of a school. Auntie Mona had a bit of Aunt Josephine in her — but there was some of Auntie Vi in her too, and I loved her dearly.

The important things in the novel are true in a different way. I invented the Lucasites. No such movement exists, but they're very like the group we belonged to. We believed that the Bible — all of it – was the inspired Word of God. We were encouraged to keep ourselves apart from 'worldly' things, such as going to the cinema or theatre, wearing make-up or drinking alcohol. Our family also kept to the strict Scottish tradition of making Sunday 'special'. Our homework and all other chores had to be finished by Saturday evening, and we were only allowed to read 'Christian' books.

It was all rather confusing. We were supposed to keep ourselves apart from people who didn't share our faith, while at the same time it was our duty to try to bring them into the fold. Missionaries were our great heroes, in fact my father was the director of a large international Bible reading and missionary organization. A deeply compassionate man, he was also one of the founders of Tear Fund.

Just like Charity's parents in the book, my parents opened our house to anyone who needed help. Dad sometimes brought home people stranded at the station late at night when all the buses had gone. People recovering from mental illness stayed for weeks. International students far from home came for Christmas or weekends throughout the year. There was a constant flow of people who worked for my father's organization. Some cooked their national dishes for us, others played musical instruments we'd never seen before. I learned a Malay candle dance, heard Indian ragas and watched the effects of shell shock on a German survivor of World War Two. A colonel from Ghana called my parents Mama and Papa.

As I grew up, my horizons broadened. I loved the rich warmth of our home life, but I questioned the narrowness of my religious upbringing and I slowly arrived at a more open view of the world and the mysteries that all religions struggle to solve.

In my first week at university, I met Ros, who was to become my great friend. Her background was very different from mine. Both her parents came from Jewish families, although neither were observant. Her father was a British diplomat, while her Austrian mother, Hedi, had grown up in a world of art and culture. Brahms had been a friend of her grandmother. Mahler was a visitor to the family home. Hedi spoke several languages fluently, she seemed to have read every great work of literature, she knew about music, art and theatre.

Hedi had been acting in a theatre in Berlin until the Nazis came to power, and she fled to Switzerland to avoid arrest. She met Ros's father, then a young British diplomat, in Geneva. It was a lightning romance, and they were soon married. Her mother in Vienna packed up some family treasures and sent them off to Hedi in London, then, realizing that the Nazis were soon to take over Austria, she and her son fled to Buenos Aires. Others in the family didn't heed the warnings, and two of Ros's aunts were murdered in concentration camps.

Ros and her mother were inspirations to me.

'What do you mean, you haven't read *War and Peace*?' Hedi would ask me, and I would feel compelled to get a copy immediately. 'You've never listened to Beethoven's late quartets? But, Liz, you must!'

Rachel and Mutti are not Ros and her mother, but they were in my mind all the time as I wrote Charity's story. I feel sad that they won't be able to read this book. After her father died, Ros went with Hedi on a short holiday to Turkey. The plane crashed on the return journey and they were both killed. Ros had been married only three months earlier. Her adult life had just begun. I have never stopped grieving for her, and I keep her photo on my desk.

ACKNOWLEDGEMENTS

When you write a story that is in some ways based on your own life, where do you start and where do you stop with your thanks? None of the characters in *The Misunderstandings of Charity Brown* are true to life, but they all have elements of the most important people in my childhood: my parents, my brother Graham, my sisters Margaret and Janet, my great friend Ros and her mother Hedi. I'd thank them if I could, and apologize for taking such liberties and turning them into very different people, and I'm very sad that only Margaret and Janet remain alive to read about the doings of Charity Brown. I hope they'll laugh at the memories of all those things we did in our big old house on the top of the hill when we were girls so many years ago, and that like me they'll marvel at how different our lives and our values were way back in the 1950s. Thank you to both of them for being so generous and letting me make such a story out of our young days.

Many others have toiled with me to bring Charity Brown to life. Lucy Pearse inspired me with the idea of making a fiction of my childhood. This novel would never have happened without her. My agent Hilary Delamere championed the idea from the start. My editor Venetia Gosling brought an expert eye to the text and gently helped me to grasp how the attitudes and customs of the 1950s may seem distant and strange to young readers today. She's been patient and forgiving when I've been slow to understand. The wider team at Macmillan too – Sam Smith, Cate Augustin and Alyx Price – have worked with her to make the book the best it can be. I want to thank them all. My last and greatest thanks go to Jane Fior, who has been with me and Charity every step of the way. I couldn't do this work without her.

GLOSSARY

ART DECO was an artistic style popular during the 1920s and 30s. Art Deco designers used bright colours and sharp angles, with triangles, squares and zigzags. By the 1950s, Art Deco style was out of fashion and most people thought it was ugly. Only a few people who knew about art and design appreciated it. Now, collectors pay a lot of money for Art Deco objects.

ART NOUVEAU is French for 'new art'. It was fashionable from about 1890 to 1910. It seemed very new at the time because it was so different from the solid, classical designs of the nineteenth century. Art Nouveau designs have curvy shapes and patterns based on plants and flowers, and are often in soft colours like green, yellow and pale orange. Most people in the 1950s disliked Art Nouveau even more than Art Deco.

BARLEY WATER – a traditional health drink made from water and barley flavoured with sugar and lemons. You can still buy Robinson's barley water today.

BARMITZVAH – a religious ritual in a synagogue to celebrate the coming of age of a Jewish boy. In the 1950s, there was no ceremony for girls, but this has changed and a Jewish girl's coming of age can now be celebrated in a 'batmitzvah'.

BEDPAN – a container shaped to fit under someone who is very ill or who can't move easily. They can go to the toilet in the bedpan without getting out of bed.

CANOODLING – kissing and cuddling.

DOUBTING THOMAS – St Thomas was one of Jesus's disciples. He refused to believe that Jesus had risen from the dead until he could actually see Jesus and touch the wounds on His hands and feet. A person who won't believe something without proof is sometimes called a 'doubting Thomas'.

GERMOLENE – a thick, pink antiseptic cream. The Germolene cream you can buy today isn't such a bright pink and smells nicer!

GESTAPO – the official secret police of Nazi Germany.

HANDICAP – this word comes from horse racing. In some races, like the Grand National, the fastest horses are made to carry weights to slow them down so that the slower horses have a chance of winning. The word 'handicapped' came to mean anything that makes progress or success difficult, and it started to be used to describe people with disabilities who were seen to be disadvantaged by society. It was still commonly used in the 1950s, but is now outdated and has been replaced by the term 'disabled', which is the preferred term to describe a person with disabilities.

HAUTE COUTURE is the French term for 'high fashion'. Leading designers create artistic and very expensive clothes, which are displayed by models in fashion shows. Only rich people can afford to buy haute couture, but the designs are quickly copied by makers of cheaper clothes.

HYPERTHYROIDISM is an illness caused by an overactive thyroid gland. A person with hyperthyroidism produces too much of the hormone thyroxine. Their heart starts to beat too fast, and they lose weight very quickly. Hyperthyroidism can be life-threatening if it's not treated.

IRON LUNG – an iron lung was a machine invented in America to treat patients with polio. Some polio patients were so paralysed that they couldn't even breathe without the help of a machine. They were put into a sealed metal tube, with only their head and neck sticking out, while electrical bellows pumped air in and out. Being in an iron lung was frightening and very boring, especially for small children. Many patients were able to start breathing on their own after a few weeks and could come out of the iron lung, but some had to stay in one for years. Nowadays ventilators are used in hospitals to help people breathe.

LIEBLING is the German word for 'darling' or 'dear'.

LIGHT THE BLUE TOUCHPAPER – firework rockets have

a little strip of blue paper sticking out of the bottom. After you've lit the touchpaper with a match, you have to stand well back as the fire burns up into the rocket and makes it shoot into the sky and explode. 'To light the blue touchpaper' can also mean starting a series of dramatic events, or making other people angry.

MEIN GOTT is German for 'my God' – an exclamation of surprise or shock.

MISSIONARIES are members of religious groups who travel abroad to promote their faith, encouraging people to join their religion. Missionaries have founded many schools and hospitals around the world.

NATIONAL SERVICE – from 1949 to 1963, all the men in the UK between the ages of eighteen and thirty had to spend two years in the Army, Navy or Air Force. This was called 'National Service'. Women didn't have to do National Service.

'NO BLACKS, NO DOGS, NO IRISH' – these shocking and deeply offensive racist signs, put up in the windows of B&Bs and lodgings, were common in the 1950s. It wasn't until 1968 that a law was passed that made it illegal to refuse housing or a job to someone because of their colour, ethnicity or national origin.

PAWN SHOP – people can borrow money from a pawn shop for a limited time on condition that they hand over something of value. Borrowers get their property back if they repay the loan before the time limit. If the loan isn't repaid, the pawn shop sells the property.

PEA-SOUPER SMOG — the word 'smog' is a combination of 'smoke' and 'fog'. Smog was a disgusting yellow-green fog the colour of pea soup. It happened in the winter, when natural fog mixed with smoke from all the coal fires heating people's houses. During a really bad smog you couldn't see more than a metre or two in front of you. Smog was very bad for people with heart or lung problems. In 1952 the Great Smog in London lasted from 5th to 9th December and more than 4,000 people died because of it. A law to clean up the air was passed in 1956, and after that people started heating their homes with oil or gas instead of burning coal.

POLIO — (short for poliomyelitis) is caused by an infectious virus that sometimes damages a person's spinal cord. Thanks to a vaccine invented in the USA, polio is now almost eradicated throughout the whole world. There was a serious epidemic of polio in the 1950s, and people were very frightened of catching it. Children were more badly affected than adults, and some were left with lifelong disabilities, including muscle weakness and twisted feet or legs.

SHELL SHOCK — during the First World War, some soldiers were unable to go on fighting. They became confused, sometimes lost their hearing or their sight, shook uncontrollably and suffered terrible nightmares. Doctors called this condition 'shell shock'. Now people understand more about the depression and anxiety that soldiers can suffer for many years after their wartime experiences. They call this 'combat stress' or 'post-traumatic stress disorder' (PTSD). There are many organizations that can help soldiers recover.

SHILLING – money in the UK was very complicated in the 1950s. The smallest unit was the penny. Twelve pennies made a shilling, and twenty shillings made a pound. Shillings were silver coloured and were about the size of a two-pence piece. When British money was decimalized in 1971, shillings were worth about five pence.

TELEGRAM – the telegram, invented in the late 1800s, was a way of sending a message fast around the world through telegraph wires. Sending a telegram was expensive, and because every word cost money, the sender used as few words as possible. The message would travel along the wires to a telegraph office in the town it was sent to. Then it was printed out and a 'telegraph boy' would deliver it to the person it was intended for, usually on his bicycle. Even though telegrams were expensive, they were still cheaper than calling long distances on a telephone, and, anyway, many people didn't have a phone in their house.

THE SANITARY – Sanitary inspectors were in charge of public health matters, such as infestations of vermin (rats and mice), control of infections such as tuberculosis, the spread of epidemics and the condition of sewers. During the 1950s, their name was changed to 'public health inspectors'. They are now known as 'environmental health officers' and their job includes checking our water, food and air to make sure they're free of pollutants and keeping us safe from other hazards in our environment.

YANKEE – an informal term for an American. It's sometimes shortened to 'yank'.

ABOUT THE AUTHOR

Elizabeth Laird is the author of dozens of much-loved children's books, including *The Garbage King*, *The Fastest Boy in the World*, *Oranges in No Man's Land* and the UKLA award-winning *Welcome to Nowhere*. She is a winner of the Children's Book Award and has been shortlisted six times for the prestigious CILIP Carnegie Medal.

Many of Elizabeth's books reflect her years living and working in the Middle East and Africa, but others, including *Red Sky in the Morning*, *Jake's Tower* and *Song of the Dolphin Boy*, are set in Britain. She now divides her time between London and Edinburgh, but still loves to travel.

www.elizabethlaird.co.uk